If the
Coffin Fits

Also by Lillian Bell

The Funeral Parlor Mysteries
A Grave Issue

If the Coffin Fits

A FUNERAL PARLOR MYSTERY

Lillian Bell

CROOKED LANE

NEW YORK

Published in the United States by Crooked Lane Books, an imprint of The Quick Brown Fox & Company LLC.

Crooked Lane Books and its logo are trademarks of The Quick Brown Fox & Company LLC.

Library of Congress Catalog-in-Publication data available upon request.

ISBN (hardcover): 978-1-68331-711-1
ISBN (ePub): 978-1-68331-712-8
ISBN (ePDF): 978-1-68331-713-5

Cover illustration by Ben Perini
Book design by Jennifer Canzone

Printed in the United States.

www.crookedlanebooks.com

Crooked Lane Books
34 West 27th St., 10th Floor
New York, NY 10001

First Edition: September 2018

10 9 8 7 6 5 4 3 2 1

Chapter One

The Verbena Free Press
October 4
By Desiree Turner

Dangers of Drowsy Driving

On October 2, Verbena resident Violet Daugherty died in what police think was a drowsy driving accident. Ms. Daugherty lost control of her vehicle on County Road 202 at approximately 7:30 PM and collided with an embankment. Despite heroic efforts, doctors at the hospital were unable to bring her back to consciousness.

It's difficult to establish exact numbers when it comes to how many accidents might be caused by people falling asleep at the wheel. There's no test to be done like the ones that determine whether or not a driver has been driving under the influence. Still, estimates as to how many accidents are caused by drowsy driving go as high as 100,000 per year. Officer Carlotta Haynes of the Verbena Police

Department said, "We don't know what caused Ms. Daugherty to lose control of her car, but the lack of skid marks and the fact that no other cars were involved point to a case of drowsy driving."

We should all take steps to make sure accidents like this don't happen. If you find yourself blinking excessively, or don't remember driving the last few miles, or drift from your lane, pull over. Take a nap. Get some coffee. Walk around a bit. Nothing's important enough to risk your life and the lives of others on the road.

* * *

Generally, funeral directors don't see the best version of families. Sometimes we do. Sometimes there are sisters holding each other up, or a son quietly supporting a father. Sometimes hands are held and hugs are given. The burden of sorrow and the good memories of the deceased are shared. More often than not, however, there's squabbling.

Either there's been some terrible illness that has eaten away at the family's emotional, physical, spiritual, and financial resources—possibly for months or even years—or something cataclysmic has happened. A car accident. A tragic fall. An aneurysm no one knew about bursting like a malevolent Fourth of July firework in someone's brain.

People are exhausted or in shock. Neither of those states brings out the best behaviors. Daisy and Iris Fiore, however, were one of those supportive exceptions when they came in to make arrangements for their father's funeral. Daisy was the eldest by about two years. She was a little shorter and plumper with layered shoulder-length blonde hair and some well-applied makeup. Iris was one of those rail-thin women who started to look a little stringy after forty. She would be very low on the list of people to eat if our plane crashed in the Andes. Her dark hair with its gray streaks was cut in one of those sensible cuts. Sort of a reverse mullet with long bangs and short back. Neat, presentable, easy to take care of. If she was wearing makeup, it certainly didn't show. They looked so different, but their care and respect for each other was the same. Iris pulled a tissue out of her purse and handed it to Daisy when Daisy's eyes started to mist over while choosing music for the service. Daisy slipped Iris a cough drop and asked if Iris could have a glass of water when Iris got choked up picking which readings they'd like to have. They touched hands and held to each other. Which is why I was a little surprised when I heard Daisy hiss at Iris as I came back with the requested glass of water.

"What did you do?" she asked.

"Why do you always think I did something wrong?" Iris stage-whispered back.

I stopped on the other side of the door to the Lilac Room, not wanting to interrupt them. It was good to give people a little space.

"Well, did you do something wrong?" Daisy followed up. There was a tapping noise as if she was rapping something softly on the table.

There was a pause, then Iris said, "Define wrong."

Daisy made a noise of disgust. "We'll talk about this at home."

Iris replied, "There's nothing to talk about. What's done is done."

The room went silent, and I pushed through the door with the glasses of water I'd been getting from the kitchen. "Here you go," I said, acting as if I hadn't heard anything. I certainly wouldn't have even known anything could be wrong if I hadn't overheard them. They sat side by side on the plump coach, the coffee table with various brochures and forms and the ever-present box of tissues in front of them. It was a room designed to foment serenity. No bright colors. No hard edges. No bright lights.

Iris and Daisy resumed their supportive-sister act as if nothing had been said, although now it seemed kind of phony. Was this a performance they were putting on for people who were watching? Or had that moment of instant antagonism been the anomaly? I went along with the good-sister act, but I was uneasy. My role as assistant funeral director at Turner Family Funeral Home was not to stir up trouble. It was to make sure there was as little trouble as possible. My job was a lot easier if people weren't squabbling. Daisy and Iris weren't fighting, but if something was bubbling beneath the surface that could erupt at an inopportune time, I wanted to be aware of it. We went through the stack of paperwork required by law and made the other general arrangements. Nothing else tripped my sense of something being wrong.

"I doubt we'll have a very big turnout at the funeral," Daisy said, emitting a waft of honey and lemon. "Dad was sick for so long. People have forgotten they even knew him."

"I barely remember what he was like when he was well." Iris's chin trembled.

"It takes time," I said. Families often got so caught up in the care of their ill loved one that they forgot who the person was in the first place. It was part of the function of the funeral. It was a moment to go back and reflect. People dug out old photos and home movies and rediscovered who the person was, what they'd been like when they'd been healthy and whole. People shared stories that revealed who that person was and what they meant to everyone.

"You never know about attendance," I said. "If you'll fill out this form, I can get your father's obituary and an announcement of the service into the paper right away." I gestured toward that day's copy of the *Verbena Free Press* that sat on the low coffee table next to the couch. "Your father was well-known. I'm sure people will come once they know when it is."

"They sure didn't visit him in the past few years," Iris said with a sniff.

I winced. "People don't always know what to say or do. They get worried about doing the wrong thing so they don't do anything." It was a lame explanation, but it was true. People don't know how to act around death. We always want to shove it under the carpet or into a dark closet so we don't have to look at it. Then it feels unfamiliar and scary when it inevitably makes its presence known in our lives. And its presence is indeed inevitable. I grew up with death all around me. I'd thought that was normal for a very long time. It still sometimes surprised me that it isn't.

"I suppose," Iris said on a sigh. "Do we have to have the funeral right away? Could we wait a little while? So people could make arrangements to get here?"

"Of course." Since they'd already chosen to have their father embalmed, we could wait a week at least before the services.

We finished up the arrangements. As they were leaving, with Iris promising to bring by whatever clothing they wanted their father buried in and some photos for Donna to use to make the memorial video, Uncle Joey knocked on the door. Uncle Joey is my father's younger brother. He and my dad ran Turner Family Funeral Home together since before I can remember. They were always together. Best friends. Brothers. Coworkers. They took over from their father who took over from his father before him. I think everyone assumed that my sister Donna and I would take over from them some day. They were half-right for a while and now were completely right, at least for the time being. Donna did all the classes and training—she needed to do both what Uncle Joey did down in the basement and what Dad did upstairs—and took her place in the family business. I took off for Southern California when I turned eighteen without glancing in my rearview mirror, and I'd still be gone if I hadn't managed to torpedo my own career as an on-air reporter with a hot mic incident that went viral. Instead, I was back in Verbena, working at the funeral home and wondering what was next in my life.

After extending his condolences to Iris and Daisy, Uncle Joey asked, "Are you available to help me with a pick up today?"

"Sure. We're just finishing up here." I turned away from my Iris and Daisy and mouthed "who?" at Uncle Joey.

He nodded to the newspaper on the coffee table. It took me a second to get it. Violet Daugherty whose single-car accident I'd written about for the *Verbena Free Press*. I turned back toward Iris and Daisy who were exchanging their own glances between each other and also surreptitiously trying to check the time on their phones. It only took a few more minutes to finish everything up and they looked relieved to be done.

I watched them go, arm in arm, Daisy's hand tucked through Iris's elbow. When we'd had to plan the memorial service for our father, Donna and I had spent a lot of time like that. Shoulders pressed against each other as we sat on the couch. A hand placed gently on the other's hand or arm. You'd think we would have had it easier than most people. We knew the business. We knew what Dad would have wanted. We'd had months to get used to the idea that he was gone. It was entirely different when it was your own family.

Getting used to the idea that he might not actually be gone was taking even more getting used to.

I sat looking at the paperwork in front of me. Mr. Fiore had been on hospice care. His death had been expected, even, perhaps, welcomed as it released him from pain. What was it that Iris could have possibly done that would have made her sister that angry? That might or might not be wrong? And why wait until they were here at the funeral home to ask about it?

I headed downstairs to Uncle Joey's office in the basement. Mr. Fiore was already there. Uncle Joey had picked him up that morning.

"Everything okay, Desiree?" he asked as I came down the steps.

"I think so." I put the paper work I'd filled out with the sisters down on his desk. "There wasn't anything weird about Mr. Fiore, was there?"

He put his reading glasses on and started going over the paperwork. He was a big man. He filled his desk chair and then some. All bulk when my dad—his brother—had been long and lean. Uncle Joey had gone gray young, which had always made him seem older than he was, but his hair was still thick. If I met him on the street, I might not be able to guess his age. "What kind of weird do you mean?"

I pulled up a chair to his desk. "I don't know. Something out of the ordinary, something not right."

He set the papers down and peered over the top of his glasses at me. "Why do you think there might be something wrong?"

I explained about what I'd overheard. "It sounded like Daisy was accusing Iris of something. Something bad. And Iris didn't exactly deny it."

"Did they say it had to do with their father?" Joey asked.

I thought. "No, but what else would they have been talking about? They were here making arrangements for their father who just died."

"After a long and painful illness," Joey pointed out. "His passing wasn't unexpected."

"I know." I kicked at the floor with my toe. "It felt wrong, though. Maybe not wrong. Just weird. They were all sweet and supportive with each other until I left the room. Then they had this whisper-fight that made it sound like Daisy always thought Iris did things that were wrong. Then they both acted like nothing had happened the second I walked in. Like they were covering something up."

"Or maybe it was something they didn't want to talk to someone outside of the family about." Joey turned back to the paperwork. "You did a good job with these. Very thorough."

"Thanks." I gave him a half smile. Doing good work at a job I didn't want was a step up from failing at a job that I didn't want, but only one step. "When do you want to do the pick up?"

Joey tapped all the papers into place and set them in a file folder, which he then stashed in his desk. He took off the reading glasses and set them on a little tray. He was a very precise man. "Now if you have the time."

We didn't drive the hearse to the hospital. It was a little too conspicuous. We kept that for actual drives to the cemeteries. The van was set up a lot like an ambulance. The back was largely open, but with places where we could secure a gurney so it didn't bounce around in the back as we drove.

We pulled out of the long driveway that led to Turner Family Funeral Home and headed west toward town. Taylor's Pumpkin Patch was open for business. It wasn't crowded on a weekday, but the dirt parking lot would be full come the weekend. People came from all over for Taylor's Pumpkin Patch and the Verbena Corn Maze. They stayed for the Haunted House and the Ghost Tour.

The Ghost Tour had always been a sore spot with Dad. He'd absolutely refused to be part of it despite being begged to be a stop on the tour. He'd said most spirit sightings were the products of grief. People didn't want to believe someone they loved was dead so they found a way to keep part of them alive. He'd felt his job was to help people deal with grief and let go. The whole idea of manufacturing something that would keep someone from processing through their sorrow had been an anathema to him. One year, Tamera Utley, who ran the tour, had brought a group to the foot of our driveway. It was probably the only time that I'd ever heard my father raise his voice in public, with the exception of my volleyball games in high school. Tamera had stood her ground at first, pointing out that she wasn't on Turner property and she could stand wherever she wanted with a group to talk about ghosts. Eventually she'd given up, though. She'd said Dad was putting out negative vibes that were scaring the ghosts away.

Gray clouds gathered west of us in the sky and there was a slight scent of damp in the air. "Do you think it'll rain?" I asked Uncle Joey as he drove at exactly the speed limit through town, hands on the wheel at ten and two.

"I hope not. The corn maze always smells funny if it gets rained on." He wrinkled his nose at the thought. The maze had just gone up. Right now, it gave off a smell an awful lot like freshly mown grass. That could turn fast with much more than a light sprinkle. It was close enough to Turner's to have the smell waft over us if the wind was right.

We pulled into the alley at the back of the hospital. Uncle Joey parked and we slid the gurney out of the back, up the wheelchair ramp, and through the double doors into the back entrance of the hospital to go to the morgue. The squeak in the wheel I'd already greased echoed in the tiled hallway, only partially masked by the buzz of the fluorescent lights overhead. We traveled the short distance to the morgue.

"We're here to pick up Violet Daugherty." I handed the clipboard to the woman behind the desk. Violet had been the office manager at the insurance office where my brother-in-law, Greg, worked and I'd written about her accident for the *Verbena Free Press*. Otherwise, I didn't really know her. She must have moved to Verbena after I left and before I moved back.

The woman looked at the paperwork, nodded, and handed the clipboard back. Then she consulted her computer. "Come on in." She got up from her desk and motioned to us to follow. She found the appropriate drawer for Violet Daugherty and pulled it out. Uncle Joey and I positioned our gurney next to it and made sure the black body bag was in the right spot.

Uncle Joey and I took our places at either end of Ms. Daugherty and shifted her onto our gurney on the count of three. We weren't exactly the most evenly matched transfer team around. Uncle Joey was several inches over six foot. I was quite a few more inches beneath it. We made it work, though. Practice and perfection and all that.

Uncle Joey frowned at Ms. Daugherty's paperwork. "Who's her next of kin that's making the arrangements?"

"A cousin back in Maine," the woman said. "We had a heck of time tracking down who her next of kin was. I guess Ms. Daugherty was kind of on her own. I'm not sure the cousin ever even met her."

"Really?" I couldn't quite imagine that. Then again, my family was kind of tightly wound.

11

"Yeah. You'll have to call her to make arrangements. Oh, yeah. Dr. Nate Johar will be by tomorrow to sign off on the death certificate," she said. "Wasn't he just at your place last week?"

Uncle Joey made a noise in his throat. "Seems like he's always at Turner's these days."

The woman scratched at her head with her pen. "What's up with that?"

Uncle Joey opened his mouth, but I rammed him with the gurney. "I have a service to prepare for back home. We should get moving," I reminded him.

He shot me a look, but he started walking.

The truth was that the ME had been spending a lot of time at Turner Family Funeral Home for the last few months and I was pretty sure it wasn't because we had the best lighting or the newest facilities. I was pretty sure it was because of me. Maybe I'd ask him a favor when he stopped by. Maybe Iris had hurried her father along to his inevitable and imminent demise. I'm sure she wouldn't be the first person to feel it was a mercy to put someone out of their misery, especially if it eased their own suffering as well. Maybe Nate could take a quick look at Mr. Fiore and see if anything looked hinky because something certainly felt hinky.

* * *

Back at Turner, I opened the packet of Ms. Daugherty's paperwork, found the cousin's phone number, and dialed. "May I speak to Lizette Pinkston?"

"This is—" Before the person on the other end could

finish her sentence, I heard the voice of a child chanting, "Mom mom mom mom mom mom."

"In a minute, Clayton. Mommy's on the phone." There was some rustling. "Hi, sorry. This is Lizette. Who is this?"

"Hi, Lizette. My name is Desiree Turner. I'm with Turner Family Funeral Home. I'm calling to make arrangements for your cousin, Violet Daugherty." I straightened the forms in front of me, ready to fill them out.

"Oh, that." She sighed. "Uh, sure. What do I need to do?"

"I can walk you through it step-by-step." That was kind of my job after all.

"Great. Oh. Wait a second. Clayton, get down from there this minute. Clayton, I'm counting to three." A dog barked in the background.

"Is this a bad time?" I asked. "I can call back later."

A heavy sigh traveled down the line. "There is no good time."

"Have you thought about what you want to do with her remains?" I asked. "Any idea what she would have wanted?"

"I didn't even know her. I think I met her once at somebody's wedding." Pause. "How much does it cost to cremate someone?"

We went over pricing. Lizette decided to cremate Violet and we would store the cremains until arrangements could be made. It wasn't the most personal of arrangements to be made. In fact, it wasn't personal at all. I felt more like I was taking an order at a drive-thru window than deciding how to handle someone's earthly remains. Still, the cousin didn't really know her and it really sounded like the woman had her hands full. Sometimes I have to remind myself that these situations weren't mine to judge. Okay. A lot of times I have to remind myself that these situations weren't mine to judge.

"Okay, then. We'll be in touch," I said.

"Thank you. You've been so nice." Her relief was almost palpable.

I smiled. It felt good to help people. That was the part of the job that I liked the most. "No problem."

"Could I ask another favor?" Her voice had gone up close to an octave. It had taken on a wheedling tone.

"Sure." It didn't hurt to ask, although something about that tone made me uneasy.

"She has like a house, right? Do you have the keys or anything like that?"

I was pretty certain she did have a house. I picked up her purse that they'd given us along with her personal effects. There was a key ring with one of those little Italian horns on it. "Yes."

"Would you maybe go by it and see what I need to do about that? I'll pay you." The words came out in a rush.

"Oh." That wasn't exactly in our usual set of services, but this seemed like an extenuating circumstance. Besides, what would it hurt to drive by a place and take a look?

"Please. I don't know when I'll make it out there and I don't know anything about this woman or what she has or, well, anything." The barking got louder. "Clayton, let go of the dog!"

"Sure. I'll check it out."

"Do you know any realtors in the area?" she asked. "Clayton!"

I did. "Yes."

"Maybe you could have one of them contact me?"

"Sure."

"Thanks. Gotta go." And she did. Like right then. No good-bye or anything.

I actually did one of those old-fashioned double takes and stared at the phone receiver for a moment before I hung it up. I glanced up at the clock. I didn't have time to mull over what had just happened. I poked my head into the living room where Donna was working while keeping her feet up on the couch. "I'm going downstairs to let Nate in. He's signing off on Violet Daugherty's death certificate."

Donna snorted. "So that's what the kids are calling it these days."

"Don't work blue," I said. "It's beneath you."

She patted her stomach where my niece or nephew was gestating. "You don't get this kind of belly from not working blue."

She had a point.

I skipped down the steps into the basement. Nate Johar had been my high school boyfriend. We'd broken up before we'd figured out how to work the coin-up laundry machines at the two different colleges we'd attended, but now we were both home. While I wouldn't say we'd picked up where we'd left off, there was definitely something going on. Something good. Maybe. I hoped.

Nate arrived at the back entrance about five minutes

later. "Hey," he said, his voice husky. His hair was a little too long, but it looked good that way. He was tall, a little lanky, and had big brown eyes that looked like melted chocolate.

I reached up to brush the hair off his forehead. "Hey back." I grinned, then backed away. Getting to see each other during the course of our work was good, but making out in the embalming area of a funeral home was a bit too morbid for me. "I'll go get Ms. Daugherty for you."

"Thanks. I'll set up." He disappeared into the embalming room while I retrieved Ms. Daugherty from our refrigerated area. "I'll be right out here if you need anything."

"Should I whistle?" he asked.

I blew him a kiss and left him to do his work. He came out a little more than an hour later, a funny look on his face.

"All done?" I asked.

He nodded his head as if it might fall off if he went too fast. "I think so."

"What took so long?" I pushed back from the desk and turned in my chair. Generally signing off on a death certificate was a formality, especially when the cause of death was so obvious.

He sighed. "Something's not right."

"I thought it was a car accident," I said. Car accidents were pretty straightforward. They were accidental deaths and had to be investigated, but it was generally clear what had gone wrong.

"It was. It was definitely injuries from the accident that killed her." He nodded emphatically this time, less like his head might fall off and go rolling under a desk.

I wasn't following. "So what's wrong?"

He pulled a chair out from the desk and sat down. "She didn't have any bruises on her palms."

I still wasn't following. "So?"

"So most of the time when people lose control of their vehicles, they grip that steering wheel really tightly. They're trying to wrestle the car back under control." He mimed gripping onto a steering wheel with his hands at ten and two. "It's a reflex. The insides of their hands get bruised. It shows up postmortem all the time."

"Carlotta thought she must have fallen asleep," I pointed out. "Sleep is pretty much the same as unconscious, right?"

"I know. Usually, though, the people wake up at the last second. The motion of the car swerving wakes them up. Then they grab wheel." He rubbed his chin.

"Maybe she didn't bruise easily." Not everyone did. If you poked Donna she'd turn black and blue. You had to hit me with a baseball bat to raise a mark.

He looked up. "That's the thing. There were bruises on her hands. Just not on the palms. The bruises were on the backs of her hands."

"What would that mean?"

"If she was unconscious, her hands would have dropped and then bounced up and hit the bottom of the steering wheel as she crashed." He mimed hands jerking up quickly.

"Maybe her hands fell in a different way. Down by her side or something," I suggested.

"Maybe. It still doesn't feel right. I feel like I'm missing something." He rubbed at his jaw. "It just seems more like she was unconscious than asleep or possibly even having a seizure and I can't find any reason for her to be unconscious or have a seizure."

I was starting to get it. "Drunk?"

"Nope. No drugs either." He rubbed the back of his neck. "No underlying health problems that I could find. She didn't have a heart attack or a stroke."

"Could she have tried to dodge something in the road and then overcorrected and, I don't know, hit her head on the window and lost consciousness?" There were a lot of ways to have a car accident.

He shook his head again. "None of the witnesses saw anything like that and there were a handful of them."

"Wouldn't the car have slowed down if she lost consciousness?" The body relaxed when the mind went down. "If the car was going slowly, her injuries wouldn't have been so bad."

"Maybe. Unless she passed out and then had a seizure. Then it's quite likely that her foot would have rammed down on the gas pedal."

"So you think she passed out and then seized." I drummed my fingers on the desk. "What would have caused that?"

"I'm not sure. I'm not seeing anything obvious, though." He ran his hands through his hair, shoving it back off his forehead.

"I'll have Uncle Joey keep an eye out for anything that seems wrong as he works on her. I'm going over to her house tomorrow. I'll see if there's anything there that could explain it." Uncle Joey wouldn't need to do much, but he had an eye for things and who knows what I'd find at Violet's.

"Thanks. I feel like I've missed something. I'm just not sure what." He frowned.

I knew exactly how he felt. "How about a return favor?" I still felt uneasy about what I'd overheard passing between the Fiore sisters. This might be my best opportunity to put all that unease to rest. "Did you sign off on Frank Fiore's death certificate?"

He gave me a quizzical look. "Who?"

"Frank Fiore. Older gentleman. Died at home," I prompted making a rolling gesture with my hands as if that would get him up to speed faster.

He frowned for a moment and then his eyebrows went up. "Oh. Yeah. Frank Fiore. Yeah. Why?"

"Was there anything funny about his death?" I asked.

"Not that I remember, no," Nate said. "He'd been sick for a long time. Wasn't he on hospice care?"

I nodded. "So you, like, didn't do an autopsy or anything, right?"

"There really wasn't a need to. His doctor signed off on everything. Why?" he asked as if he wasn't certain he wanted to hear the answer.

I jiggled my foot. "Just something I overheard his daughters saying when they thought I was out of the room. It struck me wrong. How about you take a look at Mr. Fiore and see if anyone missed anything on him?" I smiled. "Then we'll all be even."

He smiled at me. "Sure. You show me your corpse and I'll show you mine."

I went to the refrigeration unit and pulled Mr. Fiore out. I wheeled him into the embalming room and gestured for Nate to come over. "This is Mr. Fiore. Is there . . . anything strange here?"

19

Nate snapped on some plastic gloves. "Let me take a look."
I left him to it.

After what seemed like forever but was actually only about twenty minutes, Nate came out. "There's nothing mysterious about this man's death. Nothing. He was on hospice. He had congestive heart failure, diabetes, and kidney disease. You understand what that means, right?"

I did. Our bodies aren't meant to go on forever. After a certain amount of time, stuff wears out. "Could someone have hurried him along?" I asked.

Nate sat down in the chair across from me. "How do you think they did it?"

I shook my head. "No idea. Pillow over the face?"

He shook his head. "There'd be petechial hemorrhaging if someone had done that."

"Strangulation?"

"He'd have a broken hyoid."

"Drug overdose?"

He made a face. "That's a little trickier. He had an awful lot of drugs on board. Hospice is pretty careful monitoring morphine, though. They'd have noted it if there was too much missing."

I was out of ideas on how to murder an old man without leaving some kind of mark.

"Why did you think they did it?" He cocked his head to one side. "What exactly did you hear them say?"

"I heard Daisy ask Iris what she had done and it didn't sound like it was anything good, more like she was shocked. Then Iris asked why Daisy always thought the worst of her."

It sounded a little thin as a reason to think someone was murdered now that I was explaining it.

"That's it?" he asked.

"Yep."

He shook his head. "They could have been talking about anything. Clothes. Food. Relationships. Whatever."

"Why would you be talking about that at the funeral home?" I asked.

He shrugged. "Maybe they were tired of talking about death and dying. Frank was sick a really long time. They'd probably discussed everything there was to discuss about his passing." He hesitated. "Do you think there are other reasons that you might be focused on Frank Fiore and his daughters?"

"What do you mean?" I didn't like where this was going.

"Well, they had a good long time with their father and you didn't." He didn't look at me as he spoke. "They got to say good-bye and have everything settled. No unfinished business. No loose ends."

I definitely didn't like where this was going. "So?"

He shrugged. "You didn't. You didn't get to have any of those things. Your dad was here one day and gone the next."

I didn't say anything.

"Do you think you might be, uh, projecting a little?" He lifted his head and looked me in the eye.

I stiffened. "Projecting what? On whom?"

He reached for my hands. "Maybe they're accepting their father's death too easily while you're still having trouble accepting yours?"

I pushed my chair back so hard that I bounced off the desk behind me like a bumper car. "He's not dead."

He held up his hand like a traffic cop to stop me. "Forget I said anything. Let's talk about something else. Why is it that you're going to be at Violet Daugherty's tomorrow?"

I was fine with a change in topic. I didn't feel like fighting. "It's a long story. Her next of kin is in Maine and can't get here and I told her I'd check what needed to be done."

He glanced at his watch. "I've got to go."

We walked up the stairs to the ground floor. The bell rang at the front door as we walked up. I opened it to find Iris Fiore.

"I brought some clothes for Dad like you asked. And some photos." She pushed a garment bag and a box at me.

"Thanks." I stepped aside so Nate could go out.

He stopped for a second and put his hand on Iris's arm. "I'm so sorry for your loss, Iris. Your father certainly suffered a lot these past few years. I'm not sure when I've seen someone with more possible causes of death." He walked down the porch steps to where his car sat in the driveway.

Iris watched him go and then turned to me, her forehead creased. "How did he know what Dad had suffered?"

"What?" I asked, watching Nate walk away.

"Nate Johar," Iris said. "How did he know how much my father had suffered? That there were multiple reasons he might have died when he did."

I straightened up. "Well, he's the medical examiner for the county. It's kind of his job to know about how people die."

Iris's eyes narrowed. "My father died on hospice under

22

the care of a physician. There's no need for the medical examiner to get involved."

"Oh, we're just being thorough." I heard the nerves in my voice.

"Thorough about what?" Iris took another step toward me.

"You know, just being sure that everything's on the up and up." When had my voice gotten that high?

"Why wouldn't everything be on the up and up?" Her eyes narrowed.

"He just took a look since he was here anyway." My mouth was suddenly quite dry.

"At whose request?" Iris squared her shoulders.

"Ummm . . . I guess mine." Might as well own it, I guessed.

"Under what authority did you have the medical examiner investigate my father's death?" Her hand went to her hips.

"Well, no authority, I guess. Like I said, I just wanted to be thorough." My head bowed a little.

"Thorough about what?" she asked.

"About your father's cause of death."

"Isn't my father's cause of death obvious?" Iris took two noisy breaths through her nostrils. "Unless you're implying something. Are you? Are you implying that my father's death was not from natural causes? That he was killed somehow?"

Crud. She was on to me. Although when she put it like that, it did sound absurd. "No! Of course not!"

"Good." Now her lip began to tremble. "My dad was sick for a long time. A very long time. I have spent the past seven years dedicated to his care. I've fed him and bathed him and, yes, changed his diapers, and I did it for longer than I had to do it for my daughter. His death is a release for him and for me. I'm already heartbroken that the picture in my head right now is of a broken old man rather than the strong vital Dad of my youth. Don't make my heart break any more by dragging his funeral out with crazy allegations."

"Of course not. I'm so sorry."

She stared for a moment and then seemed to make a decision. "Fine then. Here are Dad's things." She handed me the garment bag and the box and then turned to leave. At the door she stopped and turned. "Didn't you meddle in Alan Brewer's death, too?"

I spread my hands. "I wouldn't call it meddling. That was a murder and someone had been unjustly accused."

"Well, this isn't a murder so there's no need to accuse anyone of anything." She glared at me.

"I know," I said. "I'm sorry."

She left and I fell against the door. That had been a disaster. I felt terrible. But did it seem as if maybe Iris protested too much? Plus, I'd never actually said I thought her father had been murdered, and yet that was where her thoughts had gone instantly. I wasn't sure what else I should do, though. Nate said Frank Fiore had died of natural causes, and I had nothing more to arouse my suspicion than a snippet of an overheard conversation. Still, something didn't feel right there. I couldn't quite put my finger on it. Yet.

Chapter Two

The Verbena Free Press
October 5
By Desiree Turner

Shocking News

On October 3, Katherine Apodaca was found on the floor of her kitchen with burn marks on her hands and a burned bagel in a toaster on the counter. A singed knife was found nearby. It is likely that Ms. Apodaca electrocuted herself by accident trying to remove the burnt remnants of her breakfast out of her toaster.

The Verbena Fire Department would like to remind everyone that just because electricity is invisible doesn't mean it's not dangerous. You should never touch electrical appliances with wet hands, climb trees near overhead power lines, chew on power cords, poke your fingers or other objects into outlets or sockets, climb utility poles, or stick metal objects into electrical appliances.

Services for Ms. Apodaca will be held today at two PM at Turner Family Funeral Home.

* * *

Death is not rational in its timing. It comes when it's good and ready. It's arbitrary, but in the end, it is inevitable. I have a distinct memory of asking Dad why everybody had to die. Why couldn't we all stay here together? He'd given me a hug and told me that people have to move out of the way so new people can be born, that it's all a big circle like in *The Lion King*. I'd informed him that *The Lion King* was a cartoon. It wasn't real life. It had many breaks in reality. For instance, lions couldn't talk.

He'd told me that the concept was still sound even if it was wrapped up in fantasy and that it wasn't good to be too literal. He'd said that there was a right time to say good-bye, to check out. We might not know it. It might not be our plan, but when it was time that was it. I wondered if he'd thought about telling me that as he'd let us all think he was dead for nearly two years now. If I ever found him, it would be one of the first things I'd ask.

I was thinking about that idea as I set up for Katherine Apodaca's funeral. Her death definitely seemed arbitrary. Who'd have thought a toaster could actually kill a person? It was a little unclear what had happened since Katherine had been alone at the time of the incident, but all bets were on her trying to pry a stuck bagel out of her toaster using a knife without unplugging the toaster. Toasters were supposed to come with an auto shutoff feature to avoid exactly this kind of thing, but apparently that malfunctions a lot. A surprising number of people are electrocuted by their toasters every year. Katherine Apodaca was going to be part of that statistic.

Henrietta Lambert turned to Grace Cohen and said, "I don't even like my bagel toasted. I like them soft. They're easier to eat."

"Apparently Katherine did not agree with you," Grace replied.

"And look where that got her!" Henrietta said, as if the evils of toasting were now self-evident.

Henrietta Lambert, Grace Cohen, and Olive Wheeler attended nearly every funeral at the Turner Family Funeral Home and had for years. I thought it started when they reached the age when their friends started to die off. Then I think they continued coming because they liked my Dad. Now I was pretty sure it was for the postservice cookies and snacks people generally provided afterwards.

When they'd first started coming to services, they'd been easy to tell apart. Over the years, however, they'd started to look more and more like each other. Henrietta's dark skin had faded to more of a khaki tone that matched Grace's. Olive's hair had gone gray and she'd started wearing it cut short with bangs like Grace's. At any rate, they looked up at me like three wizened peas in a somewhat morbid pod.

They knew pretty much everything about everybody. People tend to not notice little old ladies. It's like they're semi-invisible to a good portion of the population. It might have been why they liked my father so much. He had never looked past them, never ignored them, nor acted like they didn't matter.

"Did any of you know Frank Fiore?" I asked.

"Who didn't know Frank?" Henrietta said. "Why?"

"Just curious. We're having his funeral here next week. I met his daughters for the first time. I don't think I knew them before I left here." *Just wondering if maybe his daughters might be the kind to kill him in his sleep.*

"You wouldn't have," Olive said. "They're enough older than you that you wouldn't really have crossed paths. They had both probably moved out of town before you were out of diapers."

"When did Iris move back?" I asked.

"Oh, let's see." Henrietta squinched up her face as she thought, which was impressive since it was kind of permanently squinched. "It was after Mable Stone died, but before Santiago Mills did."

"Are you sure?" Grace asked. "I thought Mable died before Case Davis did, and Iris was definitely here then. I remember Iris bringing her father to the service. She had that sweet daughter of hers with her, too."

"Oh, the daughter," Olive said. "She's a lovely thing."

"Smart, too," Grace chimed in. "Or so I've heard. Went all the way to Regionals with her science project."

"Why did Iris move back?" I asked.

Henrietta leaned in as if she was going to tell me a secret. "I heard that husband of hers was no good. Gambled away all their money and had some chippie on the side."

"A chippie?" I echoed. I didn't think I'd heard that word used in conversation ever.

Henrietta nodded. "Anyway, Frank had his first stroke about the time she found all that out. She moved back home to help him and just stayed."

"It's a good town to raise a child in," Grace said.

"It is." I'd grown up here, been nurtured here, and been educated here. I'd wanted to leave as soon as I graduated from high school, but in retrospect, it was a pretty all right place. So many of us had moved back after living away for a few years that Tappiano's, our local wine bar, had started a special Hometown Happy Hour. I hadn't moved back to raise kids or take care of a parent the way most of my class-mates had. I'd come back because I'd humiliated myself on live television and hadn't had much choice.

I could probably have survived my personal hot mic gaffe if I'd sworn a little or even thrown a minor temper tantrum. I'd been sent on that particular assignment as punishment for uncovering some unsavory practices at a local nursing home. Unfortunately, our station manager was related by marriage to the owner of that nursing home. I had been demoted from doing actual investigative work to standing in the rain to show it was raining, and hanging out on cliffs when it was windy so people could see exactly how windy it was.

Unfortunately, I didn't swear and I didn't throw a tem-per tantrum. Instead, I did an imitation of our station man-ager talking about how he didn't care about old people and how he thought old people smelled funny.

It went out live.

The tape went viral and I was let go after everyone from local senior citizens' groups to nursing associations com-plained. I hadn't known what else to do, so at the urging of family and friends, I'd come home.

It hadn't been too bad so far, though. In fact, I was get-ting to like it.

"So Iris likes it here?" I asked.

Henrietta snorted. "Hard to know. She always looks like she's just bitten into a lemon."

"You think she might want to leave?" I asked, wondering if being tethered to a dying parent in a town she didn't like could have finally become too much for her. That would give her reason to hurry her father off this mortal coil.

"Not until that daughter of hers graduates from high school," Grace said. "I heard she's on track to be valedictorian."

"She wouldn't do anything to get in the way of that girl," Henrietta agreed. "She's devoted to her. That's all she does. Takes care of her father and takes care of her daughter."

Maybe Iris wanted her daughter to go to a more prestigious high school. Maybe that would be why she would want to get away. I was getting ahead of myself, though. I was looking for reasons for a murder I wasn't even sure had taken place yet.

"Is that Katherine's sister over there?" Olive pointed one slightly crooked finger.

I looked where she was pointing at a small woman with glossy black hair and really artful eyeliner. "Yes. Her name is Ellie. Did you want to send your condolences?"

"Doesn't look anything like Katherine." She sniffed. Katherine had had lighter hair with a lot of curl in it and had been quite a bit taller, too.

"I don't look like Donna," I pointed out. I didn't either. Donna took after Dad's Nordic side of the family. I, on the other hand, barely made it to five feet four when I pulled myself up as tall as I could, and I had our mother's dark hair, dark eyes, and olive skin.

"You sure you're sisters?" Olive cackled.

"Behave." Henrietta rapped her knee with a rolled up funeral program. "Your coloring is different than Donna's, but you both have the same shaped eyes and there's something about your ears, too, something that reminds me of your father."

I patted her shoulder and went over to check on Katherine's family to see if they needed anything. The last thing I wanted to discuss with Olive, Henrietta, and Grace was my dad.

Nineteen months ago, my father had vanished. It sounded melodramatic, but it was pretty much what happened. We all thought he'd gone surfing, but he hadn't come home. We'd found his car, with his clothes folded neatly inside, parked near one of his favorite spots. We just hadn't found him. We'd searched for months, checking out John Does that had been found up and down the coast.

Then a few months ago, funny things started to happen. Someone was leaving little gifts for Donna and me in strange places. It was almost like we'd gotten a Boo Radley. I'd set up a camera in one of the spots where those gifts had been left and we'd seen exactly who it was. Both Donna and I had looked at the tape and said "Dad" when we saw who it was.

It's possible that I might have made a bit of a fuss. I might have stormed the police station and ranted at Luke Butler—my nemesis since grade school who was now a police officer—who had investigated my Dad's disappearance and turned up a big nothing burger. I might have run some ads in local newspapers asking if anyone had seen my Dad. I might have tried to get a social media campaign going. It's harder to go viral when you're trying to, rather than when you just don't notice that your mic is hot. That had spread across the Internet before I'd even made it back to the television station. I'd been fired before I'd set foot inside. The social media campaign about Dad, however, went pretty much nowhere.

Actually, none of it had gone anywhere. None of it had turned up anything and now the gifts had stopped. Not everyone who looked at the tape saw what I saw. Even Uncle Joey, my dad's own brother, was skeptical, and the weight of everyone else's doubt was making Donna waver.

"Why would your father disappear?" Uncle Joey had asked.

It was a good question. Why would a grown man with a successful business and two grown daughters suddenly vanish? It wasn't as if he owed money to the Mafia or had seen some crime go down and had to go into Witness Protection. At the time he disappeared, Donna could have taken over for him if he had wanted to stop being a funeral director and try doing something else. I had been out on my own. There had been nothing tying him down. He could have just left.

Since then, things have taken a bit of a turn for the worse. My sister'd lost her first pregnancy. I'd imploded at my job and had to resign, but back before he disappeared we'd all been flying high.

I was pretty convinced that my father loved my sister and me. A lot. We'd always been a team, especially after Mom died. It had been us three against the world. Athos, Porthos, and Aramis. Why would he have left us? And if he had left us, why would he suddenly start coming back, leaving little gifts and a note stuck to our back door that simply said "Sorry" in Dad's way too distinctive handwriting?

None of it made sense. Yet. I was pretty sure that at some point, I'd be able to piece it all together. I wouldn't stop digging until I did. Dad must have known that was how I'd react, which meant, in my opinion, that he wanted me to find him. He wanted me to know. Otherwise, he would have stayed vanished.

* * *

By the time I had the Apodacas taken care of, the day was nearly gone. I decided I'd put off checking out Violet's house until the next morning. It's not like there was a rush. I was pretty sure if Violet had some plants that died and no one brought in her mail, her cousin wasn't going to care. Violet was definitely past caring. According to the hospital, there wasn't anybody else to worry about.

I went back to the office in the basement and called Michelle Swanson. We'd gone to high school together, although it wasn't like we'd been friends. She ran in more of the cheerleader crowd. It wasn't a mean girl thing. It was just a different interests kind of thing. She'd done the college, marriage, baby thing and now had moved on to the realtor thing. I had done the college, career, fail publicly, and return home to work at the family business thing.

"Desiree, what can I do for you?" she asked. "Have any new murders I can help you solve?"

Michelle had provided the information that had broken

open the investigation into the death of Alan Brewer last July. I explained the situation with Violet Daugherty and her overstressed cousin. "She asked me if I knew a realtor that would be interested in selling the house. I'm going over there tomorrow. Want to meet me there and take a look? See if you're interested?"

"It's a date."

My phone buzzed again as I hung up. It was Nate. "I think I found something."

"What kind of something?"

"Something on Violet Daugherty." He sounded excited.

"Do you know why she passed out?"

"Not yet, but I think I might know how whatever it was that was administered to her. I found a spot on her back when I went over the autopsy photos." I could hear him rifling through papers on the other end.

"What sort of spot?"

"I think it might be an injection site."

"Injection of what? You said there weren't any drugs in her system."

There was a pause. "I know. I know. It has to mean something, though, doesn't it?"

"Could it be a spot where the EMTs or someone at the hospital injected her with something?"

"It would be a weird spot for that. It's right in the middle of her back."

That started me thinking. "I don't suppose there were any weird injection sites on Frank Fiore, were there?"

"On who?"

"Frank Fiore. The old man you looked at for me yesterday." I rolled my eyes.

Nate sighed. "I told you, Desiree. There was nothing strange about his death. And, for the record, no, there weren't any weird injection sites on his body. Everything was completely as expected and accounted for."

"Fine." Something still bothered me about the whole thing, but apparently I was the only one.

*   *   *

Upstairs, my sister Donna and her husband Greg were at the kitchen table eating dinner. Downstairs, we have a big kitchen for caterers to use when setting up for services. Upstairs, we have our own cozy little kitchen with a round oak table and glass-paned cabinets. I don't think the house had changed in all the time I remembered except for getting the occasional new coat of paint. I pulled up a chair and sat down. "Did you get hold of Violet Daugherty's next of kin?" Donna asked. She had her long hair pulled back in a braid and no makeup on. She still looked radiant. Pregnancy suited her, although to be honest, she'd always had a bit of a glow.

"Violet Daugherty? We're burying her?" Greg asked. Greg had always been a great match for Donna. A couple of inches taller than her so she never had to think about wearing heels, his hair was a few shades darker than hers, although pictures of him as a kid showed him to be a total towhead. They were a matched set, like salt and pepper shakers.

I didn't poke at him about the "we." Technically, Greg wasn't doing anything of the kind. He worked at an insurance agency in downtown Verbena. "Yes. I talked to her next of kin yesterday. She lives all the way in Maine. I'm not sure you could get farther away and still be in the continental United States. She asked me if I'd check out the house. Maybe help her find a realtor."

Donna furrowed her brow. "You're doing what? That is not a service we offer."

I drummed my foot against the rung of my chair. "I know. You should have heard her on the phone, though. She sounded so frantic and she asked so nicely."

Donna shook her head. "Pushover."

"Did Violet have any health problems?" I asked Greg. It was possible Greg might know something from seeing Violet every day that wouldn't have shown up in the autopsy. Maybe there'd be a simple explanation to put Nate's mind to rest.

"Not that I know of," he said. "At least not physical health problems."

"What does that mean?" I helped myself to a slice of meatloaf.

Greg shook his head. "She's gone now. There's no reason to discuss it."

"Why do you want to know?" Donna asked, her eyes narrowed.

I shrugged. "Something Nate said."

"About Violet? About how she died?" Greg asked. "I thought it was pretty straight forward. She had a car accident."

"Yeah, but she was the only one involved in the accident. According to the witness reports, it looked like she'd fallen asleep or passed out behind the wheel." I scooped some baby carrots onto my plate.

"And?" Donna asked.

"And Nate couldn't find a reason she would have done that. He didn't see anything that would have made her pass out." The carrots would be a lot better with some Ranch dressing. I went to the refrigerator to rummage around for some. Everything in there looked fearfully healthy. It had ever since Donna got pregnant. It was going to be a long nine months.

Donna picked up her fork and waved it at me. "Do not go pushing your nose into this, Desiree."

I clutched my hand to my chest. "Me? Why would you say that?"

"Because I know you. You see something that doesn't strike you as quite right and you won't let it go. Look what happened with the whole Alan thing," Donna said.

"You mean how I cleared the name of one of our dearest family friends and found the real culprit?" It all depended on how you framed the information. I, apparently, was framing it in a much more positive manner than Donna was. Or that Iris Fiore was, for that matter.

"See. I knew that would go to your head. I just knew it." She set her fork down.

I waved her away. "I'm not doing anything. I'm seeing if Michelle wants to take the listing. Once she takes over, the whole thing will be off our plate anyway."

Famous. Last. Words.

Chapter Three

Violet's house was a cute little Eichler in a neighborhood full of Eichlers. I recognized the style the second I pulled up and saw that entrance atrium that blurred the distinction between what was inside and what was outside. The roof was sloped and the façade was pretty plain. I knew it would be a different story once we got inside, though. There'd be a whole lot of plateglass and open areas. I'd put money on it having radiant floor heating. It sat back from the street with a brick path winding through a yard full of lavender and sage leading to the front door, where a BENVENUTI, AMICI! sign hung at a jaunty angle.

Michelle pulled up as I parked my car in front. "Nice neighborhood," she said as she got out of her SUV. She still had a bit of that cheerleader bounce in her step, but there was also a purpose to her stride. She had on one of those outfits that you see on the front of style magazines that looked somehow both totally casual and totally put together. Jeans. Boots. A cream-colored top with a sweater and scarf that somehow went with the boots without being too matchy-matchy. I looked down. I also had on jeans, boots, and a sweater, but it didn't seem to look the same way Michelle's did.

She'd been a huge help in solving Alan Brewer's murder. If I could throw a cute house in a nice neighborhood her direction as my way of thanking her, I might be able to even out the scales while doing something nice for Violet's overwhelmed cousin. Win-win, right?

"It's cute," I said, looking it over. I liked the clean modern look of the Eichlers. Scads of them had gone up in Northern California in the 1950s. They were sort of a poor man's Frank Lloyd Wright design, and by "poor" I mean middle class. Affordable housing. No discrimination. It was an Eichler thing.

Michelle gave me an appraising look. "You in the market?"

I shook my head. "I'm not sure how long I'm staying here." It had seemed like a huge investment to make over my childhood bedroom into something that made me feel less infantilized. A house? Well, that was just crazy talk.

Michelle rolled her eyes. "Always looking for greener pastures."

Before I could answer, a woman came rushing up to us from down the street. "Are you Violet's relatives? Are you taking over?"

"Not relatives," I said, holding up my hands. "Just trying to help the relatives out."

"Well, thank goodness you're here. I wasn't sure what I was going to do. I'm at the end of my rope." She pushed back the hair that had come out of her messy ponytail and wiped her hands on the oversized T-shirt she wore over leggings. I

39

thought she might have wiped them there before. She really did look like she was at the end of some kind of rope. "I thought maybe the people who were driving by the other night were the relatives, but they didn't really stop. Just sort of looked around and drove off."

That's when the barking started. Michelle's face went hard. "There's a dog?"

The woman nodded. "Oh, yeah. There's a dog. Kind of a puppy really." She marched up the brick path. When she opened the front door a very large ball of fur came bolting out, tail wagging and tongue lolling.

"That's a puppy?" I asked. The thing must have been fifty pounds.

She nodded. "Malamute and German shepherd mix. His name is Orion."

After racing out in the yard to relieve himself, he came back and sat in front of Michelle and offered his paw to shake. "Sweet," she said, in the same way you tell a mother that her ugly baby is darling. I didn't think Michelle was a dog person.

"He is sweet," I said. He turned to me and offered his paw. I shook it.

"I haven't known what to do," the neighbor said. "I heard about Violet's accident and started looking after him. I mean, who could let a dog starve to death right down the street, right? George—that's my husband—said I shouldn't stick my nose in, that someone would take care of it, but you should have heard the poor little thing howl. I couldn't do nothing, but now I'm doing everything and, well, I just can't anymore." She paused to take a breath, but it was a quick one. "I had her key and the code to her security system from when I watered her plants while she was on vacation. Although it's not like she ever said thank you or would feed our cat when we were away. I figured I should still be neighborly and all, but I don't want a dog. I can't have a dog. My husband's allergic. He's been sneezing all night long from me coming over here to feed Orion and walk him a bit."

Michelle put her hands up in front of her and said, "Do not look at me. I'll check out the house and see if I can help you out there, but I'm not getting a dog."

"Do you know where to take him?" I asked, reaching down to scratch him behind the ears. He thumped his leg.

"The shelter? I don't know." She stepped into the house and I followed with Orion, and the neighbor on our heels.

"Doesn't the shelter euthanize them after a while?" I asked, feeling a bit queasy as I looked down into Orion's big brown eyes. There was something about his face that made it look as if he was smiling.

Michelle sighed. "Yes. I don't think they want to, but it sometimes comes to that. I don't know what else to suggest. Can I look at the house now? That I can actually help with." She took a bottle of hand sanitizer out of her purse and, pushing up her sweater sleeves, disinfected herself up to the elbows. She really, really wasn't a dog person.

I shut up and let her walk through the house. The house was, after all, what I'd told the cousin I'd help with. Not a dog. Hadn't I heard a dog barking in the background at the cousin's house? She must be a dog person. Maybe she'd like a second one.

Inside the house was a lot more purple than I expected.

Lavender walls. Paintings of lilacs. Couch cushions that could only be described as amethyst. I supposed it made sense for a person named after a color. Maybe if Mom and Dad had named me Ruby, everything in my room would be red. Michelle murmured a lot, made some approving noises in the big open space that held the kitchen, dining room, and living room, then made a few clucks in the bathroom, all the while making notes on her tablet. I went into the kitchen and saw Orion's bowls were empty. I opened a cabinet, thinking it might be where the dog food was and found a complicated looking metal thing with a crank on the side, a tool that looked a lot like the wheel cutters quilters use, and some kind of fancy rack.

"If you're looking for the dog food, it's here." The neighbor who had followed us in pointed to a cabinet on the other side of the sink. Sure enough, it was there. I scooped some out into one bowl and filled the other with water. Orion raced over and crunched happily at the kibble. "What's all that stuff?" I pointed to the things in the first cabinet I'd opened.

"Violet was getting into pasta making. Something about getting in touch with her Italian heritage." The neighbor glanced at her watch. "I need to go. Thanks for taking Orion. Be careful. He likes to dig. He dug up Lorene Quinn's front yard right before this year's garden tour. Destroyed it. I thought she was going to have a heart attack."

Before I could protest that I had absolutely no intention of taking Orion anywhere, she was gone. "Well, buddy," I said to him. "We'll have to find you a new home."

He barked twice. I turned around slowly. Everything

was open. Light poured in from the windows that stretched from the tiled floor up to the peaked ceiling, glinting off the chrome legs of the coffee table. Violet's taste in furniture had run to midcentury modern, too, with a bright boxy sofa and two armchairs in the living room. It was a little stark for my taste, but I could see its appeal.

Michelle came back into the kitchen. "Give me the cousin's contact info. I'll have this thing gone in a New York minute." She snapped her fingers at me.

"What about the dog?" I asked, texting her the information.

She shrugged. "What about him?" Her phone booped and she nodded at me.

"I mean, what should I do with him?" He wagged his tail hard enough to make a thumping noise against the hardwood floor.

"Call the cousin. Ask her what she wants to do." Michelle put her phone in her purse, snapped her tablet shut, and marched out the door. "See you."

For the moment, I supposed Orion was coming home with me.

Once Michelle left, I nosed around a bit more looking for some kind of reason why Violet might have passed out behind the wheel. Besides a lot of pasta-related items, some very fancy olive oil, and a stovetop espresso maker, there wasn't much in the kitchen. Very little booze, just a bottle of Frangelico. No pills beyond the normal painkillers and cold medicine in the bathroom cabinets. Maybe she overdid it on the pasta and went into some kind of carbohydrate coma. I did find a laptop and a little notebook with passwords for different websites neatly noted down. That might come in handy for the cousin so I packed that up to take with me.

I scrounged around the house and found some dog toys, a leash, and a dog bed. It took a few trips, but I managed to shove it all into the car. "Come on, Orion," I called. "Let's go, buddy."

He trotted down the path and jumped into the passenger side of my Element as if we'd been going on road trips together forever.

A woman came out of the house next door as I went around to get into my side of the car. She crossed her arms over her chest and glared. I waved. She spun on her heel and went back in her house. Her garden was a magnificent riot of lamb's ear, sage, and big poofs of native grasses under a miniature windmill. There were rock formations dotted around in ways that looked natural, but somehow really tended. Probably Lorene Quinn of the apoplectic fit during the garden tour. I could see why. That thing must have taken a ton of work. No wonder she didn't want a dog digging it up.

"I'm afraid you didn't make a lot of friends in the hood here, buddy." I started the car.

He nosed the window and whined. I rolled it down and he hung his head out. As I pulled out of the neighborhood, he barked twice.

* * *

Sneaking a fifty-pound puppy into a house is not as easy as you might think. Orion and I barely made it up the back stairs to our living quarters on the third floor before Donna blocked our path, and she could do a lot of blocking these days. "What is that?" she asked, pointing at Orion.

He sat and put his paw out to shake. "Look how adorable!" I said. "I think he does that whenever he meets a new person."

"Who is he?" Donna asked, still standing in the door in a power position with her pregnant belly making her extra intimidating.

"His name is Orion. He was Violet's dog. The neighbor had been taking care of him, but was freaking out because her husband's allergic and Michelle wouldn't take him so . . . well, here we are." I sidled past her into the kitchen. "I'm going to call Violet's cousin and see what she wants us to do with him."

Uncle Joey was sitting at the kitchen table eating lunch. When he saw Orion, his eyes lit up. In a second, all two hundred and twenty pounds of him were down on the floor. "Puppy!" he yelled.

Orion went over to him, tail wagging so hard his back end waggled. Orion licked Uncle Joey's nose. Uncle Joey tussled with him, laughing the whole time.

I took Orion's bowls over to the sink and filled one with water. "Don't give me the stink eye like that, Donna. We're not going to keep him."

Uncle Joey peeked out from under all that fur and said, "We're not?"

"I don't have the time. Plus, Dad always said this wasn't the right place for a dog. That a dog might bark during a service or get out and jump on people when they were coming in or out." We had a lot of old people coming in and out of Turner's. Old people with balance problems. Old people who'd been whittled down to next to nothing. A dog Orion's size could probably take out two or three of them with one jump. More if he could set up some kind of domino effect. I set the bowl down in the corner and filled up the food bowl.

"Dad was right. Dogs don't belong at funeral homes," Donna said. "Do you have a plan?"

"No. Not yet. I have to see what Violet's cousin wants us to do with him. I'm sure someone will want him. He's super cute." I got a little pang in my chest. I rubbed at my sternum with my thumb.

"Fine. I guess he can stay if it's not for too long." She waddled out of the kitchen.

I opted not to ask for a precise definition of what "too long" might mean. I took Orion down to the basement office and called Violet's cousin. "Hi, Lizette. It's Desiree."

"Who?" I could hear banging noises in the background.

"Desiree Turner. From the funeral home."

"Oh. Yeah. Desiree, what's up?" she asked.

"So I checked out your cousin's house. I showed it to a realtor friend of mine. She'd be happy to help you with it." I gave her Michelle's phone number and e-mail address. "She said she'd be contacting you, though."

"Great. Thanks."

"Uh, one more thing," I said fast to catch her before she hung up again.

The banging had gotten louder. "What?"

"Violet had a dog. A puppy really. He's really cute. A

malamute-shepherd mix." Orion rested his chin on my leg. I scratched his ears.

"Oh, my God. He must be enormous."

He wasn't enormous yet, but his paws looked like dinner plates on the end of his legs. He had some growing yet to do. "Well, he's not small. Anyway, what would you like me to do with him?"

"Do?"

"Yes. With the dog. He can't stay at the house. There's not really anyone to take care of him." Orion rolled over on his back and I rubbed his belly with my foot. He wiggled. It was seriously the cutest thing ever.

Now there was a crash to go with the banging on the other end of the phone. "Well, I can't take him. I don't even know how I'd get him here."

I thought for a second. "I could maybe take some photos of him, put them up on the Internet and see if anyone here wants to adopt him."

"Oh, would you? That would be so great. Thank you." She hung up before I could say another word. I took a deep breath. That weird burning sensation I'd had in my chest had gone away.

Orion whined and pawed at the door.

"Do you need to go out?" I asked.

His ears perked up.

"Do you need to go for a walk?" That was a thing you did with dogs, right? Lola and Kyle were always walking their dogs, Maurice and Barry. Being a regular dog-walker had been part of how someone had almost framed Kyle for murder.

Murder accusations aside, if Lola and Kyle did it, it must be the right thing to do. I pulled out my phone and called Jasmine, my sister from another mister, my BFF since preschool, my bridge over troubled water. "Do you want to walk a dog with me?"

There was a pause. "Is that a euphemism or something?"

"What on earth would it be a euphemism for?"

"I don't know, but you don't have a dog so it was the only thing that made sense to me."

I laughed. "I have a loaner dog. Come walk with me and I'll fill you in."

"I need to get out of here anyway. I'll be there in ten."

* * *

Jasmine made it in five. She pulled her Subaru into the driveway and got out. "Who is this cute fellow?" she asked coming up the steps where we'd been waiting. Jasmine's mom was African-American and her dad was white. She had beautiful golden brown skin, cascading curls, and a body full of curves. She'd left Verbena when I had, but was also back, opening a therapy practice just outside of downtown.

The day had been bright and sunny and warm, but as the sun started to go down, the chill had come up. I'd thrown a fleece on over my regular clothes, but the breeze seemed to cut right through it. The light had gone from golden and warm to having a bluish tint and a definite bite to it.

Orion greeted Jasmine with his handshake routine.

She clasped her hands to her chest. "Oh, my God. He is charming!"

"I know. Let's take him for a walk and then take some

pictures of him to put up on the Internet. I know someone will snap him up." That weird pain in my chest thing happened again. I frowned.

"You okay?" Jasmine asked, looking up from petting Orion.

"Yeah. Just indigestion from something." What else could it be?

"Where did he come from?" Jasmine twisted her curls into a makeshift bun to keep her hair from blowing across her face. She had on what I thought of as her shrinking clothes. Not that they were getting smaller. They were the clothes she wore when she saw patients for therapy. Soft fabrics. Muted colors. Nothing that would show off her curves.

As I snapped on Orion's leash and we stepped down onto the driveway, I explained about finding Orion at Violet Daugherty's house after the cousin asked me to look into it.

"So you're helping the cousin deal with Violet's estate? Not exactly your job, is it?" Jasmine lifted her face to the afternoon sun.

"No, but it needed to be done and look at him. How could I leave him or take him to the shelter?" We stopped by a pile of leaves. "Oh, let's take his picture here. It'll be great with the leaves and stuff." I led Orion to the pile of leaves and told him to stay. Then I started snapping photos with my phone.

Jasmine looked over my shoulder. Orion crossed one paw over the other and cocked his head. "Oh, look. He's posing."

I also told her about Nate's suspicions about Violet and how I'd messed up big time with Iris Fiore.

"Ouch. Sounds like she was pretty upset." Jasmine made a face.

"She was. And all for nothing. Nate says there was nothing hinky about her father's death. He thinks I have Daddy issues." I made it clear how ridiculous I thought that was with my tone.

Jasmine pressed her lips together and said nothing.

Great. "You, too?"

She shrugged. "Let's face it, Des. You haven't exactly adjusted to your father's death very well."

"Because he isn't necessarily dead." I picked up Orion's leash and started walking. Fast.

"Slow down," she said, trotting up next to me. "I'm not trying to pick a fight. I just think if your father was really alive he'd be in touch. He was a good dad. He loved you guys. He wouldn't desert you for no reason."

Since finding the card that had said "sorry" and his appearance on our back porch, there'd been nothing. No little gifts left on my car. No skeins of yarn left for Donna. I'd made sure to leave my car in the parking lot by the trail, where the first charm had appeared, at least three times a week, and nothing. So someone was sorry for something. That was all I knew. "What if there was a reason?"

Jasmine pulled her sweater closed. "What kind of reason?"

"Maybe he was going into Witness Protection or something." Orion danced around me and tangled us both in the leash. I stopped to unwind us before we both fell flat on the ground. I was going to need to look into some puppy training classes.

"What do you think your dad could have seen that would put him in Witness Protection?" Jasmine stopped beside me and put her hand on my arm. "Have you seen something that might have put him in danger?"

I hadn't. "We see all kinds of things at the funeral home. We see all sorts of people's secrets." None of them that I'd seen rose to that level, though. Then again, I hadn't really been looking.

"Where are we walking anyway?" Jasmine asked.

"I thought we'd walk to the *Free Press* to drop off Mr. Fiore's obituary."

"And you wanted me there?"

I squirmed a little. "It's good to have a buffer." Rafe Valdez, the editor of the *Verbena Free Press*, and I had a relationship that was . . . complicated. There had been moments. Moments when it felt like there was something between us. But then there was Nate. There was definitely something there. Besides, Rafe was also my boss to a certain extent. I didn't work for the Free Press full time, but I'd started doing some articles for him. Longer things. Not quite the investigative journalism I had always wanted to do, but close to it. It was best to keep business as business. But sometimes, when it was only the two of us, the air seemed to warm up and there was this buzzing noise in my ears and . . . Well, it would be better if Jasmine was there, too.

"You're such a weenie," she said.

We walked into the paper's office. Rafe had actually managed to hire some staff. Vern Godfrey was now answering phones and taking ads, but Rafe still sat out in the open bull pen on the other side of the old wooden counter that ran the length of the room, right in the thick of things. Or as thick as things got in Verbena, California.

"Desiree," he said as I walked in. "And Jasmine, of course. So nice to see you both."

Orion barked and held up his paw to be shook.

"And who is this?" he asked, coming around the counter. Rafe kept his dark hair short and his jaw clean-shaven, but somehow there was always something about him that made me imagine him with his hair rumpled and stubble on his chin. He wore his usual dress shirt and jeans, loafers, no tie.

"Orion." I explained about taking care of him for a bit until we could find a permanent home for him.

"He's a cutie. You shouldn't have much trouble. Shoot Vern a photo and a little bit of copy. I'll run the ad for you gratis. You have papers and stuff for him?" He squatted down to pet Orion eye to eye.

"It's all probably in Violet's house. I'll ask her cousin if I can poke around." It hadn't occurred to me to look through her files for papers on him. Maybe there'd be something on her computer.

"I don't suppose you want to cover tonight's city council meeting?" he asked, looking hopeful.

"You supposed correctly." Council meetings were important to cover for local papers like the *Free Press*, but they were also boring as hell. "Send Vern."

Rafe glanced over to where Vern sat talking on the phone. He lowered his voice. "They're accepting the bids for the construction of the new bathrooms in the park. I'm not sure Vern's got the nose for it yet."

Did anyone have a nose for public bathrooms? "He'll figure it out. Or he won't. You should give him a chance."

Rafe straightened up and all of a sudden he was standing much closer to me than I realized. Apparently, that air-heating-up thing happened when Jasmine was there, too. "Please, Desiree? This is the kind of stuff that people in town really need to know about. It's their money. They should know how it's being spent. You of all people should want to cover it."

"What does that mean? Me of all people?" I took a step back, pretending to untwist Orion's leash to give myself some space.

"You're the one who's always concerned about the community. Look at all articles you write trying to keep people from dying." He pulled my article on drowsy driving and the one on not getting electrocuted at home out of the stack of papers and pushed them toward me. "Please?"

He looked so desperate. Over his shoulder, I heard Vern asking someone to spell zucchini. Rafe might have a point. Vern might not be ready for city council meetings. He also had a point about people in town needing to know what their elected officials were doing with their money. "Fine. I'll cover it. How soon do you need the article?"

"Can you get it to me before midnight for tomorrow's paper?" he asked, wincing a little since he knew what he was asking.

I couldn't help myself. I laughed. It was so Rafe. Ask for a favor and then expect me to expedite it. "Sure."

Jasmine and Orion and I walked out of the office.

"He totally has your number," she said, smiling. "He knows just what buttons to push."

*　*　*

I was on my way back to town when my phone buzzed.

The text was Nate asking if I could meet him for coffee. We changed course and headed downtown. I asked him to get us a table outside. He texted back: it's cold. I texted back: bundle up, buttercup, and ask Monique to set up a heater.

A few minutes later, I slid into the chair across from him and shivered a little. It was a little cool for patio sitting if you weren't in direct sunlight.

Nate cocked his head to one side and looked down at Orion. Orion cocked his head and looked up at Nate. "What on earth is that?" Nate asked.

"He's a dog." I picked up my menu even though I knew exactly what I was ordering.

"You don't have a dog," Nate said.

Orion offered up his paw to be shaken.

"Nope. I don't. This is Violet Daugherty's dog. His name is Orion." I shivered again.

Nate slipped off the fleece he was wearing and passed it across to me without looking away from Orion. "Interesting."

I slid into the jacket. It smelled like him. A little spicy. A little sweet. "So what's up?"

Nate finally looked away from Orion. "I figured out why Violet passed out while she was driving." He tapped the file folder on the table between us. "Insulin overdose."

That made me sit up. "Was she diabetic?"

"Nope." He looked pleased with himself.

"Why didn't that show up in all the tests you ran before?" Wouldn't insulin be pretty hard to miss in all that blood work?" I picked up the menu and looked it over even though I knew exactly what I wanted.

"It did show up. I didn't miss it." He leaned forward. "It's really common for people to be given large doses of insulin when they've had a traumatic accident."

"Why? That doesn't make sense." I shut my menu and set it down.

"It makes perfect sense. Think about it. When something bad happens, that fight-or-flight instinct kicks in. The body sends out adrenaline. The adrenaline causes cortisol to release into the blood stream and that makes blood sugar levels rise. When someone is in an accident, their body reacts as if they're going to have to fight off a wild beast. It thinks it needs the sugar to have the energy to battle a bear or a lion. But when they don't have to do that, they end up with these crazy high blood sugars and no way to use them. Insulin brings the blood sugar down. So when I saw the elevated insulin levels, I didn't think anything of it." He shoved his hair off his forehead.

Monique came over with a coffee pot and filled our mugs. "The usual?" she looked from one of us to the other. We nodded. "With a side of bacon for me, please," I called after her as she left.

I asked Nate, "Why do you think the insulin is an issue now if it all makes such great sense? What changed?"

Nate sat back in his chair looking very satisfied. "I went back through all the records. She was never given insulin."

Now I sat back. "Could someone have forgotten to put it

in the chart? Things probably get crazy at the scene of an accident and in the emergency room. Maybe somebody slipped up."

He grimaced. "There's always that possibility, but we have an awful lot of systems in place that are supposed to keep exactly that from happening. Let's say it's unlikely. Plus, there's the weird injection site on her back."

I took the saucer out from underneath my coffee mug, put it on the ground, and poured some water in it for Orion. "Could it have been the only spot they could get to? You know, right after the accident?" There might be a perfectly good explanation.

"I doubt it. If it had, there would have been other marks there, too." Nate pulled out a folder. "Let me show you."

It's not every girl who gets treated to photos of dead bodies on a breakfast date. I felt super special.

"So here are a bunch of areas where IVs were started and blood was drawn." He pointed to several bruised spots on her arms. "Here are the bruises on the backs of her hands that made me suspicious in the first place."

He wasn't joking. Her hands looked terrible. Black and blue and one pinky sticking out in a weird direction.

Then he showed me the photo of her back. The one little spot there was all by itself in a sea of unblemished skin. "See? There's nothing else here. There's no reason for anyone to have given her an injection there."

"So what you're saying is that someone injected Violet with insulin and that the insulin made her pass out." I shut the folder.

"Oh, yeah." He nodded. "It would have made her sweaty

and confused. She might even get combative. Eventually she'd lose consciousness and possibly have seizures."

Monique showed up with my pie with bacon on the side and Nate's cinnamon roll. I took one strip of bacon and fed it to Orion who licked my hand in gratitude. Monique bent down to pet him and got a kiss on the lips in response. She laughed.

"Did you talk to Luke?" I asked Nate.

He sighed. "I did."

"I take it that it didn't go well."

He shook his head. "He felt my evidence of foul play was 'weak sauce,' and I really couldn't fight him on that. The fact that she didn't have bruising on her hands where I think she should is one of those negatives that you can't use to prove a positive in a court of law."

"What about the insulin?" I asked.

"I think some of what I was telling him about that went a bit over his head. He still didn't think it was enough to open a criminal investigation into a single-car accident." Nate rubbed the back of his neck. "He had one other good point."

"What's that?"

"Why? Why would anyone want to kill Violet?"

*   *   *

By the time I got home from the city council meeting and had written up my notes, I was exhausted. I texted Rafe once I'd uploaded it. He texted back right away.

Rafe: I knew I could count on you.
Me: Jasmine says you know just how to manipulate me.
Rafe: Is that necessarily a bad thing?

Me: Depends. Are your intentions good or evil?
Rafe: Would good AND evil be possible?
Me: You're impossible.
Rafe: Yet here I am.
Me: Good night, Rafe.
Rafe: Sweet dreams, Desiree.

I was more than happy to curl up in my bed with a cup of hot chocolate, a book, and Orion who was better than a hot water bottle when it came to warming up cold feet. It wasn't long before I was doing the slow blink I'd warned people was a sign they should pull of the road. I shut my book, turned off the light, and was asleep in seconds.

Unfortunately, it felt like only seconds later that a loud noise woke me up. It hadn't been seconds. It had been closer to hours and I was seriously disoriented, trying to figure out where I was and how to make that damn noise stop. It took a few minutes, but I finally realized that it was coming from Violet Daugherty's purse that was hanging off the back of my desk chair. I grabbed it, opened it up, and pulled out her cell phone, hitting the buttons frantically to make it stop. By the time I did, Donna, Greg, and Uncle Joey stood at my bedroom door.

"Is everything okay?" Uncle Joey asked.

"Do you need help?" Greg asked.

"What the hell was that?" Donna asked.

I rubbed the sleep from my eyes and tried to focus on the screen. "It's the security system at Violet Daugherty's house. Someone tried to break in."

* * *

Fifteen minutes later, I was back in Violet Daugherty's front yard. This time I was with Carlotta Haynes, Verbena police officer and Jasmine's girlfriend. Carlotta was a whip-thin African-American woman, straightened hair pulled back into a neat bun. She actually made the uniform look pretty good. Not an easy feat. Carlotta shook her head. "Some people. They see the obituary and know the house is empty and decide to do a little breaking and entering."

"The obituary hasn't been printed yet," I pointed out. I pulled my fleece jacket tighter around me, wishing I'd put on jeans instead of leaving on my pajama pants and just jamming my feet into UGG boots to haul booty over there.

Carlotta shrugged. "You printed that article about falling asleep at the wheel. Someone could have seen her name in that and figured out her house would be empty." Her words made little puffs of steam in the air.

Or if someone had somehow orchestrated Violet's car accident as Nate suspected, they'd know the house was empty, too. Could someone have wanted her out of the way so they could steal something from her? I hadn't seen anything in the house remotely valuable enough for that. "You know, the neighbor down the street mentioned seeing a car drive by. Maybe it was somebody casing the joint."

"Listen to you with the cops and criminals jargon!" She smiled, but then turned serious. "Do you think you'll be able to tell me if there's anything missing?"

I shook my head. "I doubt it. I was only in the house once and I was mainly looking for dog food." I gestured down at Orion who had stayed so close on my heels as I got dressed that it had never occurred to me not to bring him with me.

"Let's look anyway."

I followed her around the back where someone had bashed in the window by the back door and reached in to unlock the door. I shined the flashlight from my phone on the broken glass. "Is that blood?" I asked.

Carlotta peered at it. "Probably. It's harder to bust in that way than people think. It's easy to cut yourself."

"You can test for DNA! Maybe the person will be in the system." Case closed. Problem solved. Perhaps even Violet's murder solved.

Carlotta stared at me. "It's a B & E, not a homicide, Desiree. I doubt our resources will run to DNA tests, especially if the alarm system scared them off and there's nothing missing."

I knew Luke wasn't impressed with Nate's theory, but maybe Carlotta could be swayed. "What if it *is* a homicide?"

"What? You think there's a dead body in there?" Carlotta turned around to stare at me.

"Not in there." I explained about Violet and the insulin in her system.

Carlotta listened, never interrupting. I got to the end. It didn't take long. "Nate explained all this to Luke, right?"

I nodded. "Luke didn't think there was anything to it."

She snorted. "For good reason, Desiree. That's a lot of random stuff to string together to turn a tragic car accident into a murder. Why would anyone want to kill Violet anyway?"

"I don't know," I admitted.

"Let's see what's inside," she said.

I tied Orion up to the table on the back patio. We walked in, crunching over glass. Whoever had come in had started pulling out drawers and emptying them before, I presumed, the alarm had started clanging. They hadn't gotten far, but the laundry room was a mess. Nothing else seemed disturbed.

"Okay. I'll follow up with the neighbor to see if I can get a description of the car she saw," Carlotta said.

"That's it?"

"You need to call an emergency window-repair place, but then yeah, that's it." She ushered me out the back door. "Whoever did this isn't somebody who's real experienced. It could even be kids. A professional would know how to break in without cutting themselves. In fact, a professional probably wouldn't break into a place with an alarm system."

Why would anyone break into a place with an alarm system? Even a bunch of kids would have seen the sign. I added it to my mental list of things that just didn't seem right.

Chapter Four

The Verbena Free Press
October 7
By Desiree Turner

City Council News and Notes

On October 6, Verbena City Council named the second week in April Verbena Safety Week and all voted in favor of Ms. Lombardi's fifth grade class's petition to name the double chocolate chip muffin the official muffin of Verbena. A letter from Kecia Wilcox was read into the record. Ms. Wilcox visited Verbena's sister city, Qufu, China. She liked all the bicycles, but China was more humid than she expected.

Bids were officially submitted by the Sterling Company, Winters Construction, Canty Construction, and Montgomery Construction Company for the contract to build new bathrooms in four of Verbena's parks. Fumiko Winters of Winters Construction said, "I feel like our bid is highly competitive. We'd bring fresh ideas to Verbena. Canty Construction renovated the Civic Center here and paved the Senior Center parking lot. I think Verbena's ready for some new blood."

The council will review the bids and vote on them in a special closed-door meeting on October 8.

* * *

I slept late the next day. I'd been up until the wee hours waiting for the window repair people. Orion and I had huddled together in the Element to keep warm. How had I survived all this time without a dog? How was I going to survive once he was gone? I needed to figure out a way to keep him around. If I could make Donna understand how useful he was beyond not having to sweep the kitchen floor nearly as often, I'd have a shot. Maybe I could get him to sit on her feet while she watched television. Her toes were always like ice cubes.

I'd only just finished drinking my coffee and eating breakfast when the doorbell rang. We don't get a lot of drop-ins at Turner. People usually call first to make an appointment. Plus it was Saturday. I assumed it was a friend. It didn't occur to me not to let Orion trot at my heels when I answered the door rather than putting him some place so he wouldn't disturb a client. We trotted down the stairs from our living quarters and I opened the extra wide front door.

The woman who stood in front of me was my age, maybe even a little bit younger. She had on Lycra biking shorts, the kind with the big pad in the seat, and a biking jersey that had a picture of Rosie the Riveter with the slogan "We Can

Do It!" on it. She was also clearly devastated. Her eyes were red-rimmed and puffy, her face blotchy. "May I help you?" I asked.

She fell into my arms and sobbed against my shoulder.

I guided her inside, her biking shoes clicking on the hardwood, and into the Lilac Room where we have some couches for people to sit on while they make their decisions. It is well stocked with tissues. Always. Keeping the tissue supply steady and swapping out the magazines and newspapers had been my first job at Turner back when I was in fourth grade. Dad paid me a dollar a week for it. I guided her to a couch, snatched up a cough drop that apparently Daisy Fiore must have dropped when she sat here last, helped my biker girl sit down, and handed her a box of tissues.

She blew her nose. "Sorry," she choked out.

"Don't be," I said. "Crying is pretty normal and it's way better than keeping it all bottled up." Whether it was normal to show up in bike gear to cry at a funeral home was another question, but I figured we'd get to that.

Orion went over to her and laid his chin on her leg. Her hand dropped to his head and he licked it. "Ohhhh," she gasped out.

I was about to drag him away, when she slid off the couch onto the floor next to him and buried her face in his fur. As she cried, he placed one paw on her leg and left it there, resting gently.

It took her a few minutes, but she finally calmed down enough to speak. "I didn't know you had a therapy dog," she said. "It's not on your website. You should totally tell people.

I wouldn't have even looked at any of the other places if I'd known."

I looked at Orion as he sat next to her, leaning the bulk of his body against her and letting her hold on for dear life. "To be honest, I didn't know we had a therapy dog either. We're just taking care of him for a little while for someone."

"Oh," she said, brushing at the tears on her cheeks. "Then he's a natural."

As intrigued as I was with the idea of Orion as a therapy dog, I felt we probably had some other business. "So what can I help you with? What brings you here today?"

My questions set off another bout of crying, but it was less violent this time. Orion stayed right where he was next to her. "It's my Blaine. He's . . . he's gone."

"I'm so sorry," I said. I reached out and put my hand on her shoulder, wondering why on earth she'd opted to bike here to make arrangements.

"Thanks. The people at the hospital, they said I needed to make arrangements." She had a hard time choking out that last word. "Your name was on a list of places they had. It was the only one I could bike to."

I wasn't sure I'd heard that correctly. "You biked here directly from the hospital?"

She nodded. "Blaine and I were out for a ride. We were going down the big hill over by the dam. He must have hit a rock or a pothole or something because all of the sudden he was flying over his handlebars." Her chin wobbled. "I told him not to take off his helmet, but he said he just had to feel the wind in his hair."

My heart clutched. The hill down from the dam was known as Heart Attack Hill to local cyclists, of which we had quite a few. It was seriously steep. The heart attacks came from trying to climb it. Going downhill was supposed to be fun. Usually it was smooth, but apparently not always. "You were there?" I asked. I cringed thinking about it.

"Right behind him." She blew her nose again. "Can you help me? Can you . . . can you pick him up?"

It was the absolute least we could do. "Of course we can. Do you want us to make arrangements with some place closer to where you live?"

She shook her head. "No. That's okay. I . . . I just want him cremated. No service or anything else. Can you do that?"

"Of course we can." I pulled out the folder of information and handed it to her. "Let's go over some of your choices here."

Once Annamarie, that was her name, knew all of her choices, we went through the process of filling out all the paperwork. "How are you going to get home?" I asked.

She gave me a funny look and looked down at her clothes and shoes. "I'll bike."

"Isn't Oak Pass at least fifty miles from here?" I wouldn't be able to walk after I'd ridden fifty miles, much less figure out how to grieve my husband who had died right before my eyes. "I could give you a ride." I was sure Donna and Uncle Joey would say it was okay and her bike could easily go in the back of the Element.

She nodded. "I'm sure. It'll give me time to process. You'll let me know when he's ready for me to pick up?"

I stood up to go downstairs and let Uncle Joey know we

had a pickup at the hospital, but I still felt uneasy. "Of course. Are you sure we can't call someone to give you a ride or something?"

She shook her head. "No, but can I sit here with Orion for a little bit longer?"

"Take all the time you need."

I stepped out to give her some privacy, then pulled out my phone and pulled up the search engine. I typed in "how to train a therapy dog."

* * *

Writing an obituary was a great way of getting to know someone, as long as you didn't mind them not being around to actually know. I was the official obituary writer at Turner Family Funeral Home. Cousin Lizette hadn't actually asked me to take care of the task for Violet, but it was generally part of the whole package. I'd be doing my job and finding out a bit more about Violet. Maybe there'd be an explanation of how she'd ended up with so much insulin in her system that she'd passed out and had a seizure.

I'd looked her up on social media. Her Facebook page mainly had shares of dog memes. She was a member of a lot of different groups: one for only-children, one for people with puppies, one for Zumba enthusiasts, one for Italian cooking, one for amateur photographers. She liked purple. She liked her dog. That wasn't much. I decided to drop by Greg's office to see what her coworkers might say about her. It was also a great excuse for finding out a bit more about who hated her enough to possibly orchestrate her car accident. Greg hadn't wanted to talk about her. Maybe there was a reason for that.

He wasn't one to spread gossip. Whatever. Everyone has their failings.

I parked on Sparrow Street, took Orion for a spin around the gazebo to stretch his legs, and then went to the You're Covered Insurance Agency on Oriole. No one heard the chime over the door tinkle as we walked in because there was a burst of applause as I opened the door. I looked around to see what I'd done, but then realized it wasn't for me. Most of the staff was gathered around an area in the back of the office, and people were clapping for something back there.

I found Greg standing on the edge of the group and walked up next to him. "Hi, Greg. What's going on?" I asked, keeping my voice low so as not to interrupt the party.

"Oh, hey, Desiree. Rachel got a promotion. We're congratulating her." Greg pointed to a pink-faced young woman of about thirty who stood in the middle of the group, beaming.

"Good for her! Congratulations, Rachel!" I called out.

Rachel turned to me and waved. "Do you want a piece of cake?" she offered.

I was about to say yes, but out of the corner of my eye I saw Greg give me a teensy tiny head shake.

"Uh, no thanks," I said. Was I getting fat? I patted my hips. "Watching my weight, you know."

"Oh, this has hardly any calories. It's vegan, sugar-free, and gluten-free." She lifted the plate toward me.

I looked over at Greg whose eyebrows had climbed up his forehead. "Oh, I really couldn't," I said.

I sidled over to the side of the group and Greg sidled with me. "Thanks for the heads up."

"No problem. It's like eating cardboard. They suck you

in with those pretty icing flowers. It's kind of evil. But it's what Rachel wanted. She could never eat the cake before." He looked down sadly at his plate. "So what are you doing here? You didn't just drop in to say hello, did you?"

"No. I was hoping someone might give me some material to put in Violet's obituary." I leaned against his desk.

Greg pursed his lips. "This might not be the exact right moment to ask." He gave a head nod toward the front and started walking. I followed him.

"What's up?" I asked, keeping my voice low.

"Rachel is being promoted into Violet's old position. It would be weird to talk about Violet when we're all so happy for Rachel," he said.

"Because people are also going to miss Violet and you don't want Rachel to feel bad?" That was nice. So typical that Greg didn't want to bring down the room when they were celebrating.

Greg shook his head. "Look. I don't like to trash-talk anyone and I especially don't like to speak ill of the dead, but Violet wasn't the most popular employee around here."

My eyes opened wider. "Why?"

"Can I tell you about it at home?" He looked around like he was about to get caught with his hands full of full sugar cookies.

"Sure. No problem." I had some time before I had to get the obituary in since there wasn't going to be a service. "Did she have any friends I could talk to?"

He thought for a second. "I think she was tight with Brandie Frierson over at the Mailbox Place. At least, they used to have lunch together."

I'd seen that name on Violet's Facebook page, liking her posts and commenting on them. "Great. I'll go talk to her."

He held up one finger. "Oh, one more thing. You're dealing with Violet's stuff, right?"

"Sort of."

He picked up a box and put it in my arms. "This is her stuff from her desk. Can you deal with it?"

I looked in it to see a framed photo of Orion, some painkillers, a comb, some honey lemon cough drops. It wouldn't be too hard to put it in her house with the rest of her stuff. "Of course."

Orion and I headed to the door. We were stepping out onto the sidewalk when Iris and Daisy walked toward us. "Oh, hi," I said. I was still feeling a little awkward about the whole kind of accusing them of murdering their father thing. "Fancy meeting you here." I cringed. I sounded inane.

Daisy nodded her head at me. "Desiree."

Orion sat and offered up his paw for her to shake. She reached down to pat him on the head and Iris made a noise in the back of her throat. Daisy straightened up, wiping her hand on her jeans. I guessed Orion knew better than to try to shake hands with Iris.

A man from inside came out and said, "Ladies, come in. There are a few papers to sign and we'll get your father's affairs all tidied up."

Oh. That's why they were there. Greg's firm issued their father's insurance. I waved as I left.

Orion and I stowed the box of Violet's things in the car and walked to the Mailbox Place to talk to Brandie. "Come on, boy," I said to Orion. "We'll walk to get our exercise in."

The corn maze was nearly complete, and banners advertising the pumpkin patch, the zucchini carving contest, and the ghost tours had gone up. Nearly every business in downtown Verbena had pumpkins or scarecrows or black cats decorating their doors. Except the Mailbox Place. Their door was decoration-free. Turner Family Funeral Home decorates for a few of the holidays. We have pine wreaths during the winter holidays, flags for Memorial Day and Fourth of July, a cornucopia for Thanksgiving. We do not decorate for Halloween. No one wants to go into a funeral home with a plastic skeleton on the door. I wondered why Brandie didn't decorate. Surely a few grinning skulls or bats with vampire teeth wouldn't put anyone off picking up their mail.

The Mailbox Place was a fairly small room. One side held a bank of post office boxes for rent. There was a display of packing supplies. Then Brandie presided behind a counter with a computer. She was a white lady with dark hair cut in a chin-length bob. Medium height and medium weight. Her one distinguishing feature was her facial expression. She pretty much always looked as if someone had farted near her. There was a line at the counter when Orion and I walked in. I scooted to one side by the boxes to wait until the place cleared out.

Brandie looked up. "No dogs in here." She made a shooing gesture.

"Oh, sorry. I didn't know." Orion and I stepped out to wait outside for the place to clear. Orion lay down on the sidewalk with a "hmmph."

"Nothing personal, big guy. Rules are rules." I watched through the window until everyone finished and it looked like Brandie had a minute and walked back in.

"I told you no dogs in here." She glared at me.

"But this is Orion. Violet's dog." If she was Violet's friend, then certainly she would know Orion. If nothing else, she would have seen photos of him on Violet's Facebook page. Violet was clearly crazy about him—who wouldn't be?—so her friend must have liked him, too.

"I know whose it is. No dogs." She gestured out the window. "You can tie him to the bike rack out there. You can still see him, but he's not in here."

Orion let out a sigh as if he knew what was coming. I did what Brandie suggested and left him on the sidewalk with a treat. I made sure that he could see me and I could see him once I was back inside. "Hi, Brandie. I'm . . ."

She didn't let me finish. "Desiree Turner. I'm aware."

"Oh. Okay." That brought me up short. "I understand you were close with Violet."

She crossed her arms over her chest. "We were friends."

"Did she seem okay to you in those last few days?" I asked. "Happy?"

Brandie's eyebrows went up. "As happy as any of us ever are. Is that all you wanted to know? If she was happy when she died?"

"Well, no. Her cousin doesn't really know her very well, and I was hoping to get some insight into who she was as a person and what you think her wishes might have been." I pulled out a little notebook that I used to keep track of things.

"I imagine she wishes she hadn't driven her car into an embankment." Brandie cackled. It was the first time I'd seen her smile.

People deal with grief in all kinds of ways. I'd heard

plenty of families make inappropriate jokes and laugh at things that really weren't funny. It was a coping mechanism. Some people laughed instead of crying. This didn't exactly sound like that, though. Those laughs tend to have a bit of a hysterical squeal at the end. This laugh sounded kind of mean, like she'd seen someone trip and fall and was pointing at them rather than helping them get up. "Oh, well. Yes. I'm sure she would wish that. I was thinking more about some kind of service locally or what she might want to do with any of her clothes or furniture." I took a deep breath, not wanting an answer for this last item. "Or her dog."

Brandie shook her head. "I have no idea why she wanted that damn dog. I mean, look at him."

I turned and looked out the window. Orion had crossed his paws in front of himself and was using them as a pillow. I almost ran back out to snap a photo of him. Too adorable. I didn't think that was what Brandie meant, though. "He's just sitting," I said.

"Sitting and smelling and probably having fleas." She shivered with disgust. The sour look was back.

Okay, then. I wasn't going to have to battle Brandie for Orion. "What about services? Do you have an idea of what she might have wanted?" I realized that not everyone has the "here's what I want at my funeral" discussion on a regular basis like some of us do.

Brandie screwed up her face. "She didn't really know that many people. She hadn't lived here all that long."

I hadn't realized that. "When did she move here?"

"About six months ago."

"What brought her here?" I asked.

Brandie shrugged. "She wanted a change of pace."

I thought about the blanks on our obituary form. "Did she have any hobbies or favorite charities?"

Brandie settled back onto the high stool she sat in behind the counter. "Why?"

"For the obituary."

She tapped her fingers on the counter. "She liked photography." She snorted a bit.

"Why's that funny?" I looked up from the pad where I was noting that down. I didn't see anything inherently funny about photography. Violet had been a member of a photography Facebook group.

She waved her hand. "No reason. No reason." Then she stopped still for a moment. "Have you found any of her photos or anything?"

"I haven't really gone through the place yet," I said.

"Oh, so you haven't gone through any of her files or anything." She cocked her head to one side.

Something about the way she was asking made me uneasy. When I got home, I'd go through her computer files. "No. Anything else you can tell me that would be good to have in her obituary?" I asked.

Brandie smiled. "Say that Violet was always interested in what was going on around her." Then her face fell a little bit. "And she was always trying to figure out how to be a part of it."

*   *   *

I'd only barely gotten settled at my desk when the doorbell rang again. I jogged down the steps and opened the door to a woman wearing what I could only describe as a power pantsuit. Conservative. Understated. It did nothing to hide her curves, which were impressive. Better even than Jasmine's and that's saying something. Somehow the suit conveyed all business, though. Her dark hair was pulled back in a sleek, but no-nonsense ponytail and she had on thick black-framed glasses. If this was a movie, she'd be the one to jump on the furniture, shake out her hair, and start dancing. The hot girl that no one knew was hot. The naughty librarian just waiting to have her books checked out, if you know what I mean. "May I help you?" I asked.

"Do you work here?" she asked, her tone brusque.

"Yes. I'm Desiree Turner."

She sniffed and adjusted her glasses. "Ah. Family member, then." She made a note on a clipboard. "Your role here?"

I crossed my arms and leaned against the doorframe. I didn't take particularly kindly to people asking me a lot of questions without saying who they were. I'd done it to quite a few people and I knew how that situation could turn on a person. "And you are?" I asked.

She gave a disgusted sigh and pulled a card from her suit pocket. "Zenia Morrow. I'm with the Department of Consumer Affairs. Cemetery and Funeral Bureau."

Uh-oh. I straightened up. The Department of Consumer Affairs oversees funeral homes in California. I didn't remember Donna saying we were having an inspection. Maybe this was a surprise spot check. "Please, come in."

I stepped aside and she brushed past, stopping in the entryway and looking around. I looked around with her. There's nothing like knowing you're being inspected to make you look at your own place—not to mention the jeans and cotton jersey top I was wearing—with different eyes. Was that a cobweb up by the chandelier? I hoped not.

As she stalked into the Magnolia Room, head darting like a small bird, I pulled out my phone and texted "911" to both Donna and Uncle Joey. Then I texted "Inspector." I slid my phone back in my pocket.

"Is there something specific you'd like to see?" I asked, walking up beside her where she stood at the cabinet where we keep our sound system. Were there regulations about those? I didn't remember any.

She turned back to me, her head at that funny little angle that made her seem a little avian. "You said you're Desiree?"

I nodded. I was pretty sure I wasn't getting that wrong.

"You work here as an assistant funeral director?" she asked.

I nodded again.

"Well, there's been a complaint."

"A complaint? Against me?" I squeaked.

Donna appeared from upstairs and Uncle Joey from downstairs as I said it. Uncle Joey froze. "Zenia?" he said.

She turned to him. "Hello, Joseph." Her face looked calm, but her voice wobbled a little and it sounded a little husky. Where had I put that cough drop that I'd found? Maybe Zenia could use it.

I looked back and forth between them. Something was going on there. I wasn't sure what. I looked over at Donna. Her lips were pressed together in a tight line and her hand rested on her bulging stomach.

"What are you doing here?" he asked, stepping toward her.

She pulled herself up even straighter. "I'm an inspector now. There's been a complaint. Someone claims they weren't given the full price sheet."

I shook my head. "I'm sure I've given everyone the full price sheet. We make up the packets beforehand. Donna double-checks every one." And if it was double-checked by Donna, it was right.

She turned toward me. Her blue eyes were unsettlingly bright. "Did you keep copies? With signatures?"

I nodded. "Always."

"May I see them?" She sounded impatient as if we'd been keeping her waiting.

Uncle Joey gestured for her to follow him to the basement office. Donna sidled over to me. "Where's Orion?"

"Back porch. Sleeping." Puppies apparently slept nearly as much as babies, which made sense when you thought about.

"Thank goodness." Donna brushed her back from her forehead.

"Is he against the rules?"

"Not in the living quarters. Probably should keep him out of the office, though." She cocked her head and gave me a hard look. "You're looking for a home for him, right?"

"Of course." No need to show my hand yet. I scampered upstairs to make sure Orion would stay put, while Donna followed Zenia and Joseph down to the basement. Orion was still asleep, dozing in the morning sun. I left a rawhide chew next to him and took the stairs two at a time to the basement.

I stopped at the bottom step. Uncle Joey had set Zenia up

at one of the long tables in the office with a stack of files in front of her. He looked up as I came to a stop and winked at me. A sign it was going to be okay. I felt air flowing back into my lungs. I tried to relax. I so hoped I hadn't screwed up. I'd screwed up so much in my life, I didn't want to screw things up in anybody else's life. I really didn't want to have performed the assistant funeral director version of a hot mic oops.

"I'll need to go through all the files for the past month," Zenia said. "It will take some time."

"Can I get you something to drink?" I offered. "Water? Coffee?"

She turned those bright blue eyes on me again and I felt my heart beat faster. If she was birdlike, it was because she was like a bird of prey. "No thank you."

Uncle Joey made a little shooing motion to Donna and me and we took the hint and went upstairs.

"Who is she?" I asked. "How does Uncle Joey know her?"

"Zenia used to have her own funeral home over in Santa Linda," Donna said as she pulled herself up the stairs.

Santa Linda was basically one county over from Pluma Vista. Close, but not too close. Uncle Joey would know anyone who worked in his industry there. "What happened?"

Donna shrugged. "I'm not entirely sure. I know she ended up selling to one of the big corporate outfits, though."

It was the fate of a lot of small family funeral homes. So far, we'd avoided it, but the specter always hung over us. "So what's the deal between her and Uncle Joey? Is it just me or did it seem like there was something going on there?"

"It's not just you." We made it to the top floor and Donna

flopped down on the couch in the living room. "She was our competition for quite a while. It was friendly, I think. They were all in the same bowling league. But it was hard to compete with Dad, you know?"

I did. Dad had been a charmer. "And she decided to stop competing? Were there hard feelings?"

"That's what I'm not so sure about. There might have been an argument. I know Uncle Joey stopped going to bowling on Tuesday nights for a while." Donna slipped off her shoes and put her feet up on the coffee table, wiggling her toes as if they were dancing at being free.

"It had to be a pretty serious to get Uncle Joey to not bowl." Uncle Joey loved bowling. He was good at it, too.

Donna leaned forward over the pillow she'd pulled into her lap. "I know, but nobody would talk about it. Not Joey. Not Dad."

"Do you think we put her out of business?" I sat down on the other end of the couch.

Donna bit her lip. "Maybe."

"And now she's here inspecting us?" I shook my head. "That doesn't seem like a good idea."

"It's how things go. The state always hires from within the trade and the people within the trade who are available are often people who are out of business." She rubbed at her stomach again.

"Shouldn't there be some kind of conflict of interest that we can point to?" I asked. "Get a different inspector?"

Donna reached over and put her hand on my arm. "Don't borrow trouble. Let's wait to see what she finds before we start accusing her of anything."

"Well, I can't sit here waiting for the axe to fall. I'm taking Orion out." I got back up.

"Have you put up the ad yet?" she asked.

"The what?" For a second, I didn't know what she was talking about.

"The ad. You know, to see if someone will adopt him. In the paper? On the Internet?" She shifted around on the couch, trying to get comfortable.

"Oh, yeah. Not yet." That weird indigestion started up again. Both of us rubbed at our stomachs.

Donna raised an eyebrow.

"We had a service yesterday and now I can't use the computer downstairs while Zenia is inspecting us. I'll do it this afternoon." There might have been a bit of bite to my words.

Donna held up her hands in front of her. "Okay. Okay. Relax, will you?"

Orion was done with his nap and ready for another walk. We traipsed along through the sunshine. Mornings were already chilly, but afternoons still warmed up into the seventies and were pretty much perfectly Californian. Light breezes. Bird song. I wasn't sure which one of us enjoyed it more. When we got back, Zenia's Saab was still parked in the drive, though. How long was it going to take for her to go through those files? "Let's go upstairs, boy."

We tiptoed up the back stairs and to my room. Violet's laptop sat on my desk. I plugged in the laptop and flipped it open. I took out the notebook and found the password and typed it in. Everything whirred to life. First I launched her e-mail program. A ridiculous number of e-mails started to download. That was going to be a lot to go through.

I clicked on her Internet browser and it loaded Facebook right away. Violet had forty-two notifications. Then I went back to her e-mail. She had notifications of some bills to be paid.

I called Lizette.

"Hi, Lizette. It's Desiree at Turner Family Funeral Home again."

She made a weird noise. Kind of like a strangled growl. "What now?"

I held the phone out from my ear. She sounded irritated. I was pretty sure I was the one doing her the favors. What did she have to be irritated about? "I found Violet's laptop and a notebook with her passwords. I, uh, thought maybe you should go on Violet's Facebook page and let people know what was going on. She seems to have been pretty active there."

"How on earth would I do that? I'm not her Facebook friend. I didn't even know she existed until she didn't any-more." Definitely irritated.

"Well, it's not that hard. You just . . ."

"If it's not hard, would you mind taking care of it?" There was a bit more honey in her voice now. I was noticing a pattern.

I hesitated. I wasn't crazy about her previous tone. "Look," I said. "You're her actual relative. It seems a little strange to have me announcing her death to people."

"Isn't death stuff what you do?" The edge was back. "Like as your job?"

She had a point. "Yes, but this is more of a personal thing, something that should be handled by family."

She heaved a sigh that could probably have been used as a leaf blower. "Look. I didn't know her. I don't know her friends. I'm not even sure how we're related. Just post something if you think that's what should be done, okay?"

It seemed ridiculous to argue about it. She was right, in a way. What did it matter if I posted about Violet's death or a cousin who didn't know her did? "She also had some notifications about bills needing to be paid."

"You have her laptop and all her passwords, right?" she asked.

"Yes."

"Pay the bills. You can probably pay them online, right?"

"Is that even legal?"

"Who's going to turn you in? Look. I've got to go. Call me if there's any problem paying the bills."

She was gone. I clicked to Violet's profile page and posted a brief announcement informing everyone that Violet had passed away.

I started going through Violet's e-mails, deleting the obvious spam, political e-mails, and sales notices. I didn't think Violet wanted to buy any crafting materials or enlarge the size of any of her organs, including ones I was pretty certain she didn't have.

It didn't leave much. There weren't many actual e-mails really to her. There were two from something called Helix Helper. I opened the first one. The subject line was Question Regarding Relative Search. Inside, the e-mail read:

Hi, Violet,

We hope you enjoyed your DNA profile. As to your question about our Relative Search option, you will get notifications that certain possible relatives exist, but you won't be able to contact them unless they, too, have made their profiles public and available. Even if their profile was originally public, you won't be able to contact them if their profiles are now private. There is no way to force them to reply to any messages you might have sent them. Like you, they have an expectation of privacy unless they specifically choose to give that up.

Let us know if you have any further questions or concerns,

Helix Helper

That was interesting. I'd thought Violet didn't have any relatives besides the cousin in Maine. I clicked the link. Three people showed up as possible relatives in the Helix Helper database. None had made their profiles public. They hadn't even posted photos of themselves on their profiles. According to Helix Helper, their possible relationship to Violet was listed as "extremely high." I wonder if I could post some kind of plea to them. Maybe I could find someone besides the snotty cousin in Maine to help sort everything out. I didn't really want to deal with Violet's belongings or her bills or her house. I didn't want to deal with anything. Well, anything except Orion. I'd still deal with him. I mean, that just made sense. I was here on the ground, after all.

It was sad, really. Violet clearly had been looking for some place where she belonged. All those Facebook groups? Trying to find distant relatives? It all pointed to someone who was trying to find her people, her tribe. I'd spent a good portion of my life trying to get away from my tribe, but I'd had the luxury of belonging in the first place.

I continued deleting the ads and the spam and the special offers. Then I hit one that didn't seem to be any of the above. The e-mail address didn't have a name attached to it or any signature line inside the e-mail. The subject line read: Back off. Inside it read: Leave me alone if you know what's good for you. The date on the e-mail was October second. The day of Violet's accident.

I forwarded it to Nate with a note saying, "Looks like somebody hated Violet." Before I could decide what else to do, my phone buzzed. It was Uncle Joey asking me to come back downstairs.

I told Orion to stay. He gave me a hurt look, but curled up on the rug by my bed. I went back to the basement, slowing with every step I took. Zenia, Donna, and Uncle Joey were waiting for me at the bottom of the stairs.

"I've looked over the files and I don't see any discrepancies or other wrong-doings," Zenia announced.

I blew out a breath. That was a relief.

"It's been a while since you've been inspected, though. I'll be back on Wednesday to do a more thorough inspection." Her words were clipped and sharp. I wasn't sure if the inspection was a promise or a threat.

"I'll walk you out," Uncle Joey said. He put his hand on

the small of her back to usher her out. She must have been cold. I thought I saw her shiver.

I watched as he followed her up the stairs, then Donna and I both looked over at the piles of files that Zenia had left on the long table. "I suppose I better get started refiling those," I said.

"Would you?" Donna leaned on the back of one of the chairs. We'd had a little scare early on and we'd thought she might lose this baby, too. She'd even been on bed rest for a while. The doctor had loosened things up as Donna had improved. She could help in the office and with anything that wouldn't put her on her feet for too long. Things had mellowed out, but we still didn't want to overtire her.

"Sure. You can go upstairs and rest." I hesitated. "Can I bring Orion down here?"

"You already have been." She made that older sister face at me. The one that said she knew what I'd been up to, even if I hadn't told her.

Whatever. "I know, but I wasn't sure if it was okay."

Donna shrugged. "I don't think there's any actual rule against it."

I went upstairs with Donna. She stayed upstairs and Orion came back down with me. "You can keep me company while I file," I told him.

He yipped, then settled onto my feet under the table as I sorted through the files. They were all from the past fourteen days. Somewhere in there was whoever had made a complaint against us. I scanned the names to see if I could figure out who. I didn't spot anyone whose service or burial or cremation hadn't gone as planned. Things had been running really smoothly. I hadn't screwed anything up in weeks.

Then my hand stopped on the file for Frank Fiore. I remembered Iris's angry face as she told me off for looking into her father's death. Could she be the one who filed the complaint? It didn't matter if she was. Nothing had been found. The inspection would be a bit of a hassle, nothing more. I refiled Mr. Fiore's folders.

Then another thought struck me. If Dad had seen something that made him need to disappear, it would probably have been in one of the services he'd handled right before then. If he had seen or had heard something that was bad enough that he'd felt he had to somehow disappear, he wouldn't have told us. That would have put us in danger, too. He might be out there trying to resolve whatever it was.

That might explain why he would make his presence known after all this time. He wanted me to know he was still here. He knew if he did that then I'd want to find him. If he wanted me to find him, though, maybe he also wanted me to find what had made him disappear. I hadn't been looking into that angle. I'd only been looking for him. Maybe letting me know he was still around was his way of getting me to step up and do some digging. I chewed on my lower lip. If there was anything to that hypothesis, the start of my answer would be in whoever's funerals we had held around the time he disappeared.

We keep our physical files alphabetical, but there are, of course, computer files as well that can be sorted by any number of criteria. After I finished filing the ones that Zenia had looked through, I tapped a few buttons on Uncle Joey's computer and pulled up the names of the funerals that had been held in the two weeks before Dad had disappeared.

There had been four. Detra Shively, Kenyatta Westfall, Jerrod Dew, and Broderick Gunter. Nothing about them jumped out at me right away. I pulled their physical files and sat down in the spot where Zenia had been conducting her audit. I went through each one. Detra Shively had been a bookkeeper for the school district before retiring. She'd been eighty-one when she died of congestive heart failure. Kenyatta Westfall had been a wildlife biologist. She'd died too young. She'd only been fifty-two when breast cancer had won out. Broderick Gunter had worked construction for Canty Construction and had had a heart attack. Jerrod Dew was a software engineer for the state of California and had had MS.

They were regular people who had had regular jobs and had died in regular ways. I refiled the folders, feeling unsatisfied and unsettled.

There wasn't anything in the notes on any of the funerals to make me think that something could have been wrong. Maybe Dad hadn't wanted to put anything in writing, though. I scratched Orion behind the ears. "What would he have done if something had been bothering him?" I asked him.

He looked up with his big brown eyes like he'd answer me if he could.

The first person Dad would have talked to was Uncle Joey. He clearly hadn't done that. Maybe he hadn't wanted to involve his brother. Who else would he have confided in?

The answer came to me in an instant. I made a call and invited myself for breakfast the next day at Kyle and Lola

Hansen's house. I could ask them if Dad had said anything and maybe get some bonus dog-raising hints at the same time.

Before I could set my phone down, it buzzed again with a message from Rafe. The city council was ready to announce who had won the bathroom bid.

Chapter Five

The next morning, Orion and I got into the Element. I rolled the passenger window down and Orion stuck his head out. As we left town and picked up speed, I could have sworn I heard him laugh.

I pulled up into the driveway at Kyle and Lola's house. Kyle and Lola were my dad's best friends. They'd been fixtures in my life ever since I could remember. If I had a second Dad, it was Kyle. Lola was the one who'd inspired me to become a journalist. She'd been the one to notice my writing while I was in high school and had helped me navigate my way through the world of journalism. She'd also been the one to tell me to come home after I'd torpedoed the whole thing. It made me sad that their gate was locked, but I understood why. I glanced up the road at the neighboring property with its prominent FOR SALE sign out front. Apparently, people weren't keen to buy a place that had been the scene of a murder. Well, that and one where chickens had apparently been allowed to live in the house.

Lola walked down the driveway, her step light, with her

Australian shepherds, Maurice and Barry, cavorting around her. She looked tall to me again. For a while there, she had seemed to shrink as evidence had mounted up against Kyle. Who could blame her, really? Her husband had been accused of murdering a neighbor. Everyone had thought he was guilty. Well, everyone except Lola, and their lawyer Janet, and me. Together we'd figured out who had really done it and made sure that person went to jail. I'd help remove that burden from Lola's shoulders and that thought made me stand a little taller, too. She opened the gate, but held up her hand for me to wait. "I thought it might be best if the dogs all met out here, not quite on our property. Then nobody has to get defensive."

I bowed to her greater doggie wisdom. I opened the door and slid out, then called Orion. He came to the edge of the seat and looked down. His eyes got wide then he looked at me. "It's okay." I said. "They're friendly." I hoped I was right.

Then Barry did that thing dogs do where they stretch their legs out in front of themselves and wiggle their butts up in the air that seems to be a universal invitation to come play. Orion's ears perked up and he leapt from the car. In a second, the three dogs were chasing each other around in circles.

"I think it's going to be okay," I said to Lola.

She laughed. "Apparently."

She opened the gate and we all went in.

"So how did you end up with this dog again?" she asked.

She motioned me to their deck where Kyle waited with coffee and muffins. "Just guarding the snacks," he said.

"Smart move. Orion stole a cookie out of my hand yesterday. He did it so quickly and gently, I didn't even know it was gone until I tried to eat another bite of it." I was kind of proud of him. It had been a slick move. I also hadn't thought it was possible to feel so much affection for a being who had stolen my Snickerdoodle, but here we were.

Kyle motioned for me to sit. "When did you get Orion?"

"He's not really mine. I'm fostering him until the person who inherited him figures out what to do with him. She's all the way in Maine and didn't really know the person who died. It's been hard." I grabbed a poppy seed muffin and took a big bite.

"He's gorgeous. Why don't you keep him?" Lola sat down and poured herself a cup of coffee.

"I'd like too, but Dad always said a funeral home was a terrible place for a dog and Donna agrees with him." Again with the indigestion! I set the muffin I'd been about to eat down. Maybe too much sugar on an empty stomach was causing it. I rubbed at my sternum. According to what I'd read about training therapy dogs, I'd have to start with some special puppy training for Orion. I'd have to look into that next.

"So what else brings you out here?" Kyle stood up and threw a ball for the three dogs to chase. It bounced off their deck and down the long slope toward their stand of olive trees. Their branches drooped with fruit. Harvest time must be right around the corner. We—and thirty or so of Lola and Kyle's closest friends—would spent most of the day picking and then be rewarded with a truly astounding meal and a bottle of oil that came from the olives we'd picked ourselves. "What did you need to ask?"

I pulled out the list of four names I'd made the day before

and pushed it across the low table to Lola. "Did Dad ever have any issues with any of these people?" I asked.

Lola picked up the paper and looked over the list. Kyle looked over their shoulder. They both snorted at the same time.

"What?" I asked.

"Well," Lola said. "Everyone had trouble with Jerrod Dew. He was an ornery old coot."

"What kind of trouble?" Maybe I was on to something.

Kyle broke off a piece of blueberry muffin and chewed for a moment. "The get off my lawn kind of trouble. Nothing big. Why?"

"Yes." Lola shook her head. "Not that I know of. What are you up to, Desiree?"

I slumped back in my chair. "I'm not sure."

"Walk me through it." Lola tapped me on the knee and it was like I was back in high school trying to figure out how to write an article for the paper.

"These are the last four people whose funerals Dad oversaw before he disappeared. I thought maybe he might have stumbled across something that would make someone get rid of him or make it so he needed to disappear." I kicked at the leg of my chair. "It might explain where he is and why he had to go there."

Lola was shaking her head before I even finished speaking. "No. Stop this. It's not good for you. It's not good for any of us."

I felt tears filling my eyes. Suddenly, Orion was back on the deck and sitting on my feet. I reached down to scratch him behind his ears. "I can't. I can't drop it. Until I know what happened, I can't let it go. I swear I feel his presence sometimes."

Kyle sighed and scratched at his beard. "I know. I get the same feelings. I want so much for him not to be dead that I entertain all kinds of thoughts about how he might have survived and what he might have been doing all this time. Sometimes I even convince myself that I can feel his presence nearby, too. It's because we miss him so much. It's magical thinking. He would have told you the same thing. You know how he was about ghosts."

I did. This was different, though. "I don't think he's a ghost, Kyle. That's why I'm looking into this. I think he's here. Really."

Kyle leaned forward, elbows braced on knees. "We've been over this so many times. Your dad's gone, Desiree. I don't like it any better than you do. At least he got to go out doing something he loved."

"What about the tape?" I asked. I'd installed a security camera over our back door. I had tape of the person who'd left the note for us. We couldn't see that person's face; he'd had on a baseball cap pulled low. We could see his general build, though. "How can you ignore that?"

Lola put her hand over mine. "That tape was like photos of the Loch Ness Monster or Big Foot. Yes. The man who left that note on your back porch was the right height and general weight as your dad, but you really can't see anything else. You can read all kinds of things into that tape."

"The handwriting?" I pressed.

"A lot of people around your dad's age made their Ys like that. It's how they were taught to write cursive in elementary school. You had Luke dust the note for fingerprints, didn't you?" she asked.

I nodded. "There were none. Totally none. Like someone had wiped the paper clean with something and then worn gloves whenever they touched it." I'd been so hopeful when I'd brought it to him. I'd have proof. My dad was alive. The results had been more than disappointing. "So if that guy wasn't my dad, who was he?"

Kyle threw his hands in the air. "Who knows? None of it makes sense, Desiree. None of it."

I tore up my muffin into pieces. "I feel like there's more to this story."

Kyle said, "I feel like if he wasn't dead, he'd be here with his daughters. Not running around leaving weird notes and creepy gifts. You know how important family was to him."

He had a point about that.

* * *

Jordan Giroux had a heart attack and dropped dead on the kitchen floor while his wife, Reita, was playing bridge like she did every Tuesday night. It wasn't a total surprise. It wasn't Jordan's first heart attack and he hadn't exactly been living life the way his doctor wanted him, too.

Reita, a tiny woman of Mexican descent with neatly cut graying hair, patted his hand inside the coffin. "He did it all on his terms," she said. "If he couldn't have a beer or eat cheese, he didn't want to live. It may have shortened his life, but at least he was happy while he was here." A little sob wracked her.

"Oh, here." I guided her to a seat and settled her. I felt as if I could pick her up and carry her, her bones seemed so fragile and light. "Can I get you anything? Some water?"

"Would you mind?" She looked up at me, her brown eyes starting to swim with tears behind her glasses.

I brought her a cup of water, which she gulped down greedily. "Are you taking care of yourself?" I asked. "Are you eating and drinking enough?"

She looked up at me as if those words didn't have meaning. "I think so."

"But you don't know so?" It was easy when you were grieving to forget about such ordinary things as eating and drinking. I was certain Reita wouldn't starve herself, but it was easy to get dehydrated and that didn't help anything at all. "I'll get you another cup."

I got her another cup of water and then the guests began to file in. "I'm worried about Reita," I told Olive as I took her walker. "I'm not sure she's taking care of herself."

Olive looked over at Grace. "We've got this," she said, taking her walker back. All three of them shuffled over to sit around Reita, patting her shoulder.

There was a time that I thought Olive, Grace, and Henrietta's presence at every funeral was ghoulish. I couldn't decide if they were lording it over the dead that they were still alive or faced with their deaths coming closer they had an unhealthy fascination with it. Dad had explained that it was none of the above.

"When someone passes, there's a hole in the community. The community needs to mourn that. These days, people are too busy. Everyone is going a million directions at once. Olive, Grace, and Henrietta come to represent the community so the family of the person who passed knows they're not alone," Dad had said.

I hadn't totally bought it at the time. They liked to throw a little too much shade to be seen as entirely benevolent. Seeing them surround Reita now, I thought maybe he had a point.

When the service was done and people had filed out, Reita came over to say her final good-bye.

"I knew when it happened, you know," she told me.

"You did?" I'd thought she wasn't home at the time. Maybe I'd heard wrong.

She nodded. "I didn't know what it was, but I felt it. I thought it was one of those little earthquakes. You know, the ones that you barely notice, but still wake you up at night or knock a picture off the wall."

I knew exactly what she meant. Pretty much anyone who lived in California for any length of time knew what she meant. You found yourself sitting bolt upright in bed and you wouldn't even know why until you read the newspaper the next morning. Or maybe you thought you heard the sound of a really big truck going down the street, but there was no truck there. "I asked the other ladies at the bridge table if they'd felt it, too, but they all said no. I thought I was just a bit more sensitive than the rest of them." She looked up at me. "I always have been," she said. "I've always been a bit more sensitive than everyone else."

"Do you really think it was the exact time?" I asked. "How do you know?"

She nodded. "I looked at my watch. You know, so I could look it up later and say I told you so to the other ladies about feeling the earthquake at the exact time and Jordan smashed his watch when he fell down in the kitchen so we know when that happened, too." She gave another little sob. "Maybe if I'd run home right then, they'd have been able to bring him back like they had before. I felt it and didn't listen to whatever forces were telling me that he was gone, that our connection had been severed."

Their connection. She was talking about that emotional and psychic link that some couples had. I'd seen it between Donna and Greg and I was pretty sure I'd seen it between Carlotta and Jasmine. I'd bet Reita never had to ask Jordan to pass the salt. I wracked my brain for something to say to comfort her. Something Dad would have known to say. "If the connection was severed, he was really gone," I said. "Gone past bringing him back."

"Do you think so?" she asked. Something in her eyes behind the tears gave me courage to say more. I wasn't sure what the something was. I thought maybe it was a tiny bit of hope.

"I do. I really do." I closed the coffin lid and helped her outside to go to the cemetery.

Jordan Giroux's graveside service took place under blue skies with hardly a trace of cloud. As the coffin was beginning to be lowered, a perfect V-formation of geese flew overhead, heading south. I saw Reita look up and then her hand went to her chest. I thought she'd been hit with a surfeit of emotion. I knew how she felt. There was something about the perfection of those moments that stirred me, too. Then her legs crumpled beneath her.

I dialed 911 as I rushed to her side. "We need an ambulance at Lawn of Heaven," I said.

There was a moment of silence, then the dispatcher said, "Isn't everybody there already dead?"

"Not yet, but maybe if they don't get here soon. Reita Giroux just collapsed."

"Oh, poor thing. I'm sending them now."

Sure enough, I heard the sirens within a few minutes.

* * *

After the paramedics left with Reita, Luke strolled over to me. "Hell of a way to drum up business, Desiree."

I glared at him. "Show some respect for Reita and Jordan, Luke."

To his credit, he looked a little bit embarrassed. "Gonna need a statement from you." He pulled out a pen and a notepad.

"Right here?" I asked, looking around the cemetery at the people still milling around not quite sure what to do.

"Unless you want to come down to the station." He looked at me over the top of his mirrored sunglasses.

I didn't want to come to the station. I wanted to go back home, find Orion, and have a good cry with my face pressed into his neck. I definitely didn't want to make a statement here at the cemetery. "Let me make sure people know they can go home, then I'll meet you at Turner, okay?"

He thought for a second. "Yeah. I can make that work."

I went around to the other mourners, suggesting that they go home. Many wanted to know what they could do and I really didn't know what to tell them since I didn't know what to do in these circumstances. I'd never had anyone have a heart attack at a graveside service before. At the moment, I was mainly relieved that she hadn't tumbled right into the open grave with the coffin. Once everyone was gone, I got back into my car and headed back home.

I saw Luke in his police cruiser parked in front as I pulled up. I waved and drove around back, went inside through the back entrance, went to my room, changed my clothes, found Orion, and then went downstairs to let him in.

"Took you long enough," he said, looking me up and down.

I'd put on a soft cotton tunic, jeans, and fuzzy boots. I needed comfort. "This way." I nodded with my head toward the Lilac Room.

I settled myself on the couch where we usually seat our clients. I shuffled today's newspaper that was on the coffee table over to one side. Luke sat down across from me in the straight chair I usually sat in these days. I plucked a tissue from the box and Orion put his head on my knee.

"Hey, who's this?" he asked, pointing at Orion.

"Luke," I said. "Meet Orion. He was Violet Daugherty's dog." We did the handshake routine. "I'm taking care of him until I find a home for him."

"The cousin didn't want him?" Luke asked.

"She already has a dog. She thought a second one would be too much." It wasn't really a lie. I was pretty sure that was what she'd meant when she hung up the phone on me.

"How could you be too much?" Luke leaned down and rubbed his head against Orion's. "You're too cute to be too much."

He was awfully cute. Orion. Not Luke. Although I suppose some people might think Luke was good looking.

"So what happened with Reita?" Luke sat up and asked.

"I don't really know. One minute we were standing there. Then Reita looked up as some geese flew over and crumpled to the ground." I scratched Orion behind the ears. He licked my hands.

"What do you think happened?" he asked. "Do you think it's goose-related?"

I looked up. He was willing to entertain the possibility of a goose-related death, but not one caused by insulin? "Earlier she seemed a little dehydrated. I gave her some water. I'm hoping it's just that."

"Uh-huh." He made a note. "So you don't think it's another murder?"

There was a gloating smirkiness to his tone that I didn't like. The goose thing was a joke. It wasn't funny. Then again, Luke rarely was. "Is that really all this is to you? An opportunity to bust my chops?"

He shrugged. "When something drops into your lap like this, you gotta take advantage of it."

"Luke Butler, a member of our community has been rushed to the hospital and all you can think of is scoring points in an argument?" Every once in a while, I warmed to Luke. I started to think he was okay. Then he proved to me he wasn't.

"Hey, who's busting whose chops?" He snapped his notepad shut. "You never come to me for those quotes you put in your articles. You always talk to Carlotta. And you and Johar are the ones trying to tell me I'm not doing my job."

He was jealous that I'd quoted Carlotta and not him. How old was he? "Well," I asked. "Are you?"

"Of course I am."

"Then have you looked into what Nate found out about Violet Daugherty? That she had high levels of insulin in her blood when she crashed her car?" I started to get up, but Orion put his paw on my leg and I settled back on the couch.

"No. Because that's a bunch of nonsense." He waved me away.

"How do you know it's nonsense? You haven't looked into it at all."

"Because there's no reason to! The woman lost control of her car and it went into an embankment on a twisty country road at a time of day when the sun is setting and gets into people's eyes. It's tragic. It's sad. It's not murder." He shook his head. "Somebody forgot to write down something that was done in the field in a moment of high pressure. I'm sure that's it."

That was just supposition. Not fact. Not investigation. "But you don't know, do you?"

"I do know." I hated how confident he sounded, how confident he always sounded. I'd felt that confident at one point in my life. I missed the feeling.

"What about that e-mail? The nasty one. Nate said he told you about it. Maybe there are other people with grudges against her."

"Oh, no, no, no," Luke said, sitting up straight. "You're not playing detective again, are you?"

"I'm not playing at anything," I said. "I'm keeping my eyes open and seeing a lot of connections. I'm a reporter. It's what I do. If that also makes me a detective, then I guess I'm a reporter-detective. I'm not so bad at it, if you'll remember."

Luke's eyes narrowed. "Solving one murder doesn't make you a detective."

I leaned forward. "Yeah. How many have you solved?"

He leaned forward, too, so we were nose to nose. "I solve what needs to be solved and there's nothing here to solve. There are no murders to be solved here. None. Chick fell asleep while driving her car and rammed into an embankment. It was a single-car accident. No skid marks on the ground. There's not a lot more to discuss." He sat back and wagged his finger at me. "You are skating on thin ice, Death Ray. Don't think I didn't hear about your little to-do with Iris and Daisy Fiore."

I decided to ignore Luke going back to using my old grade school nickname. He knew how much I hated it. He was only doing it to get a rise out of me. "That was a mistake," I said. I looked down. I still felt bad about it. Every time I thought of it, I saw the tears in Iris's eyes when she talked about what it took to be a good daughter. I was embarrassed that I'd made her feel bad when she was already grieving. Embarrassed enough that I hadn't talked to anyone about it, except Jasmine. I sat up straight. If Luke had heard about it, someone was talking about it. The only other people who knew were Daisy or Iris. They had to have been spreading it around. What possible reason would they have for that? "Who told you about it anyway?"

Luke puffed up his cheeks and blew out a breath. "Someone at the coffee shop told me. No idea who told her."

So weird. Why would Iris tell anyone? But back to the

matter at hand. "If there aren't murders to be solved here, what does it matter if I poke around?"

"You're pissing people off," Luke said, sounding as if he was one of the people I was doing that to.

The feeling was mutual. "You're pissing me off. Do you have to stop what you're doing?" I said.

He stood up, too. "I suppose so. I'll see myself out."

I couldn't help it. I stuck my tongue out at his retreating back as he went out of the room.

Donna slipped into the room and cuddled into the couch with Orion. Perhaps he was already growing on her. I sat back down. I was not going to miss a group cuddle. "What did Luke want?"

I told her what happened at Jordan's graveside service. Her hand went to her mouth. "That's terrible."

"I know. I feel awful." I did, too. Now that my self-righteous indignation from talking to Luke was burning out, the sorrow over Reita came back to the fore.

"It's not like you did anything wrong." She paused. "Did you?"

Her tone made me think of Daisy asking Iris what she'd done. "Of course not!" I shrunk down in my corner. "At least, I don't think so."

"Well, then we're fine." She patted me on the knee and left to go back upstairs.

I didn't feel like we were fine, though. I felt like there was some kind of disturbance in the field. Things were off kilter. I'd felt that way for a while, too. First Dad, then Kyle being accused of Alan Brewer's murder. It had felt like something had happened to my community, something had knocked it out of balance, had put on a blot on it. Now there was Violet Daugherty, too. Something wasn't right there, but Luke refused to see it. I needed to find something to force him to open his eyes.

Chapter Six

The Verbena Free Press
October 9
By Desiree Turner

Bathroom Contract Awarded to Winters Construction

Verbena City Council voted unanimously to give the contract for new bathrooms in four area parks to Winters Construction.

Fumiko Winters, owner and CEO of Winters Construction, said, "I'm so pleased to be part of adding these necessary services to such a great town."

Luckily, I had the perfect opportunity to snoop around a bit more in Violet's life the next day. I'd made arrangements to meet Michelle at Violet's house that afternoon. "You have the key?" she asked balancing a box and some garbage bags on her hip as we walked up the front sidewalk. Orion pranced around, clearly happy to be back in his own yard. I took off his leash and he took off running in a giant circle around the yard. Then he made a beeline for the crabby neighbor's yard. I dropped the box and stopped him before he dug up a lavender plant and dragged him back. I snapped his leash back on.

I opened the door and turned off the alarm system. There's a particular silence about a house that has been empty for a while. If people have just stepped out, there always seems to be some echo of their presence, a warmth to the air, a scent. Violet's house was truly empty. It gave me a bit of a shiver. Orion whined and tapped me with his paw. "What's up, boy?" I asked.

He trotted over to a corner of the living room and curled up on the rug by a fuchsia wingback chair, chin propped on his crossed paws. The chair looked like a good place to sit and read. I could imagine Violet sitting there with Orion beside her. Maybe Orion had felt the chill of Violet's absence, too. Sometimes I wondered if Dad was wrong about ghosts.

"So what did you need to talk about?" I asked Michelle.

"We need to talk about staging." She started walking through the house. "This has to go. This has to go. All these have to go." She touched several framed photographs and prints and gestured to everything on the kitchen counter.

"And this has to do with me how?" I had a bad feeling about what was coming.

"Lizette said you'd volunteered to help her deal with all these things." Michelle looked surprised, as if we'd all discussed this before.

"I volunteered to get a few things started for her, not to act as her dogsbody." Orion yipped. "No offense," I said.

She frowned. "Well, I don't have time to do it and Lizette certainly isn't going to come out here to do it."

I started to protest, then changed my mind. I'd get to go through all of Violet's things looking for clues and be doing a good deed at the same time. I wasn't sure anything could be more win-win than that. "Fine," I said. "Tell me again what stays and what goes."

Michelle left me with a preprinted checklist that she'd annotated. "You want the space to be aspirational, but still relatable."

I had no idea what that meant, but I figured I could follow a simple set of instructions. I wasn't really set up to do much, but I could at least do the first thing on the list. Gather up all personal photos and remove them. There weren't that many of them. There was a studio portrait of a much younger Violet with an older woman. I was pretty sure it was her with her mother. Then there were some vacation-type photos. Violet on cross-country skis in the snow. Violet with a lei around her neck sipping a drink that had fruit and umbrellas sticking out of it. Violet in front of a huge fountain. It was always Violet alone in every shot. Then there were a few photos of Orion as a much smaller puppy. There were a couple more photos sitting out in the kitchen. These were a few group shots. Violet and her mother were in them with other people. I squinted at one of them. The man in the photo with his arm around Violet's mother looked familiar. I couldn't quite place him, though. He was a nice-looking guy with a full head of dark hair and a flirty smile, one of those guys who maybe wasn't traditionally handsome, but had a joie de vivre that I could see even in the snapshot. I put those photos in the stack, too.

I carried that set of items out to my car with Orion at my heels. The wind whipped up. Orion lifted his head and sniffed. I wished I'd brought a sweater with me. The breeze had a dampness to it that crept down the collar of my shirt and made me shiver. Fall was on its way and maybe that storm was finally coming.

"Okay, then," I said to Orion, pulling out the checklist that Michelle had given me. It was broken up by room, which was handy. First on the list was the kitchen. Job one was to empty the refrigerator. I grabbed a garbage bag and opened up the fridge, wincing away before I even got a good look. Orion lay down, whined, and put a paw over his snout. There was a definite smell. It was coming from the crisper where a head of lettuce had pretty much become water and half a red pepper was growing what was either an alternate life form or penicillin. It all went into the garbage. I pulled the drawer and put it in the sink and gave it a good scrub.

There wasn't much else in the refrigerator, but I seriously didn't want to encounter much more like that. It felt wasteful, but I decided the best thing would be to simply throw it all out. I swept everything into the garbage bag. Everything until I picked up a can of soda from the far back corner of the fridge and found it to be nearly weightless. I gave it a shake and something rattled inside. I turned it and twisted it and shook it. Finally, I grabbed it in both hands and gave a forceful twist and the top popped off. A key rolled out.

Keys are like loose change in most people's lives. They seem to accumulate. I'd found one in my father's desk a few months back that opened a storage locker we hadn't known about. Random keys, however, weren't the ones you hid inside fake soda cans in the back of your refrigerator. That kind of key was to something important. The question was what.

I looked around the kitchen. I looked in every cabinet and the stove and even managed to slide the refrigerator out a tiny bit to be sure there wasn't anything hidden behind it. Nothing but dust bunnies.

Next, I searched the area off the kitchen that Violet had set up as her office with a desk and a two-drawer filing cabinet. I sat down behind the desk and turned back and forth in the chair. I went through the papers on the top of the desk. The usual stuff. A water bill that needed to be paid. I set those aside. Some solicitations from people who wanted to feed hungry children and others from people who wanted other people to stop abusing animals. All good causes, but definitely not what I was looking for. Nothing that needed a key. All the desk drawers opened. All the filing cabinet drawers opened. I went through all the drawers of the desk and found nothing more interesting than a tape dispenser in the shape of a high-heeled shoe. I started through the filing cabinet. Tax returns. Bank statements. Owner's manuals for the refrigerator and stove and washer and dryer. I looked underneath to see if there was some kind of hidden compartment. No.

Next I went to the dining room, taking down wall decorations to see if there might be something behind it. I did the same in the dining room, both bedrooms, and the bathroom. I struck gold in the laundry room behind a wall sign that read TANTO AMORE. Built into the wall behind it was a small safe. I stuck the key in. It turned easily. Inside was a shoe box. I shook it. It rattled.

Outside, the rumbling sound of thunder echoed through the town.

I spread the contents of the safe out on Violet's dining room table. There were photos and thumb drives and a DVD and some cards encased in plastic with fingerprints on them. I started with the photos to see if there was anyone I knew.

There were. Some only by sight, but I knew them. I wasn't certain I understood what some of the photos meant. For instance, there was one of the neighbor who had come out to give Orion and I the stink-eye the first time I'd been at the house. She appeared to be scattering something into a garden. I could see the front of the house and it wasn't one of the ones on this block with their striking Eichler profiles. This was a different neighborhood. It wasn't a McMansion like Michelle's either. I'd bet Michelle would be able to identify it, though. Others were a little more obvious. There was one of a woman working out with a well-built man, then another of the same two still in the gym, but in a more compromising position. I would never look at a lat pull the same way again.

Then there was a series of photos of our illustrious mayor accepting envelopes from a man in a suit. I recognized the man. I'd seen him at the city council meeting I'd covered for Rafe, the one about the bathrooms. His name was Titus Canty and he'd been one of the people submitting bids. You couldn't tell from the photographs what was in the envelopes, but I had a feeling they weren't greeting cards. It was certainly worth looking into. It was definitely worth looking into why Violet would have photos of the two men together tucked away in a safe.

I chewed my lip. I'd seen Canty Construction's name somewhere else recently, too. It was the company that Broderick Gunter worked for. Broderick had been one of the people Dad had buried in the weeks before his disappearance. Could this all be linked? Could Dad have heard or seen something to do with Canty Construction while taking care of Broderick Gunty that would make him want or need to disappear?

I looked at the items spread out in front of me. Had this been what Brandie Frierson had meant when she said Violet's hobby was photography? If it was, no wonder she'd snorted. The next question, however, was what had Violet been doing with these photos? And could it have led someone to pump her so full of insulin that she'd pass out behind the wheel of her car and slam it into an embankment?

I shivered. Orion set his head in my lap and whined.

"I know, boy. I know. We've got some digging to do and it's not the kind that ruins someone's garden."

* * *

Back home, I opened up my laptop and typed in Canty Construction. The first thing that came up was the company's website. Might as well see what they wanted their public face to be. There was a big banner with the company name, then underneath was a scrolling set of images of things they'd built. I clicked over to the "About Us" page. There was a nice big photo of Titus Canty wearing a hard hat and pointing upward while holding a blueprint. Another man in a hard hat stood next to him looking like Canty was giving the directions to the fountain of youth.

According to the copy, Canty's father had started the company way back when. Titus took over from Canty, Sr. about five years ago. He had a degree in Construction Engineering and an MBA. Apparently, he'd been groomed from birth to take over this company.

The next three hits for Canty Construction's name were not so glowing. All three involved ethics violations. It wasn't Canty that was being charged, though. Four members of the school board in Santa Linda were put on administrative leave after it came out they had accepted gifts just before awarding Canty a contract to build additional classrooms at the junior high. The gifts looked pretty good, too. Trips to San Francisco. Tickets to Hamilton. A ski weekend in Tahoe. The obligatory golf outing to Pebble Beach. I wasn't sure they were worth ending your career in ignominy, but that's a tough mathematical equation to put into play. People didn't expect to get caught. They didn't think anyone was watching and with no one watching . . . well, not everyone wanted to be good for goodness' sake. Sadly, some people needed oversight.

The other two stories were much the same. Gifts to public officials followed by Canty Construction getting contracts.

What if Dad had overheard something or seen something during Broderick Gunter's funeral that would lead to Canty being charged with a criminal offense like bribery? Or for the mayor being charged for accepting bribes? It was one thing to pay fines. It was an entirely different thing to go to prison. I could see it being enough to make sure someone didn't come back from surfing. Or possibly to threaten that and then Dad would feel he had no choice but to disappear. I pulled out the photo of the mayor accepting that envelope from Titus Canty again. It really could be anything. A thank you note. A party invitation. A valentine.

But then why did Violet have the photo in a box that she kept in a safe hidden behind a cheesy Italian phrase sign in her laundry room? It had to mean something.

I picked up my phone and called Rafe.

"What?" he asked. "An actual phone call? Not just a text? This must be serious."

"I think it is. I think I've got a story. If I do, it's a juicy one."

"Meet me at the office in fifteen."

*   *   *

Rafe looked at the photos and print outs I'd spread across his desk. He had on a sweatshirt and jeans and his hair was damp as if he'd just gotten out of the shower. I could smell the citrus aroma of his shampoo.

Vern was gone for the day and most of the lights in the office were out. We huddled in Rafe's office, a pool of light shining onto the treasures I'd accumulated, Orion curled up on my feet.

"Let's walk through this again, okay?" he said, leaning back in his chair. The sweatshirt stretched against his chest in a way that was distracting although admittedly not as distracting as his jeans had been as he'd walked in front of me into the office.

That, however, was beside the point. Way beside the point.

I took a deep breath and thought about the most linear and logical way to present the information. "You know Canty Construction, right?"

He nodded. "Absolutely. They do a lot of work around here."

That was true. Now that I thought about it, I'd seen their signs all over the place. "These are photos of Titus Canty, head of Canty Construction, handing an envelope to our mayor."

"But we can't see what's in the envelopes, right?" He tapped on one of the photos.

"No. We can't." I admitted. "I think it's worth asking a few questions, though, don't you?"

"What kind of questions?" he countered.

"How much does the Mayor get paid?" I asked.

Rafe squinted his eyes as he thought. "Hold on." He turned to his computer. I watched as he tapped at the keyboard for a few moments. He cocked his head to one side. "Not much. About twenty thousand a year. There are some benefits, too, though."

Twenty thousand would not go far in California, even in a small town like Verbena. "Does he do anything else?"

"He used to do some consulting of some kind, but I haven't heard much about it lately." He turned back toward me, the light glinting off his dark hair.

"He has a very nice house." I chewed on the edge of my thumb. "But I think it's been in his family a long time. Maybe he's really frugal."

Rafe nodded. "Maybe."

"Or maybe he's found a way to supplement that income." My heart thudded a little, the way it did when I was on to something good, something interesting, something the public needed to know. It had been a good long time since I'd felt that particular thud. I'd missed it. Orion whined and I reached down to scratch behind his ears.

"But the bathroom contract didn't go to Canty. It went to Winters," Rafe said. "Shouldn't it be a photo of Fumiko Winters handing the mayor an envelope if he was being bribed?"

That part bothered me, too. "When was the decision made?"

"Yesterday."

"So it's pretty fresh." Way fresher than Violet was at this point. The bids had come in and the contract had been awarded after she'd hit that embankment.

"As fresh as a bunch of freaking daisies." He leaned forward. "What do you want to do next?"

Possibilities raced through my mind. Would the mayor have wanted to get rid of any evidence that he'd accepted bribes? Would he have wanted to do it badly enough to actually murder Violet? Or at least set up a situation where she'd be likely to have a car accident? Or maybe Titus Canty had done that dirty work. His family seemed to have a way of escaping charges being filed against them even as the public officials they'd bribed lost their jobs and were brought up on corruption charges. Did Violet's death somehow free the mayor from making good on whatever it was Canty wanted from him? "I think I need to get a quote from Mayor Wilburn," I said, standing up.

"Want me to go with you?" he asked. "Just in case?"

I'd known Mayor Wilburn since I was a kid. He'd been friends with my dad. Did their friendship end when Dad found out that Wilburn was accepting bribes from Canty

Construction? Had something happened at Broderick Gunter's funeral that clued Dad in? Had he confronted Wilburn and ended up being disappeared while he was surfing? Maybe it would be better to have a little back up with me.

At the very least, Wilburn deserved an opportunity to comment on what we'd found. I didn't think showing up at his office was a great idea, though. I wanted our conversation to be private and I wanted the element of surprise, too. I went to his house. I loved his neighborhood, probably because it was a lot like the one Turner Family Funeral Home was in. It was one of the old areas rebuilt right after the fire of 1913. Everything had that Craftsman look to it with built-in bookcases and fireplaces and lots of wood and stone and brick. It was definitely more upscale than Violet's neighborhood. Maybe she thought he had deep pockets and pressed him for money he didn't have. Maybe he decided to get rid of her, too.

Cars came in and out of the neighborhood as people returned home from work or left for evening activities. Orion and Rafe and I passed the time sharing a bag of pretzels. We added a very cute peekaboo game to Orion's list of tricks. I'd say "peekaboo," he'd cover his eyes with both paws, then he'd get a pretzel. He really was the smartest and cutest dog ever. It was nearly seven o'clock when Mayor Wilburn pulled his Buick into the driveway of his house. "It's show time, boy," I told Orion as I snapped on his leash. Rafe and I agreed that I should talk to Wilburn on my own first. He'd be more likely to open up to me. I started to open the car door when I saw someone getting out of a car parked up the street, walking with a lot of purpose and determination toward the Mayor. "Was that car here when we got here?" I asked Rafe. It seemed like we weren't the only ones waiting for the mayor to get home so we could have a private chat.

He shook his head. "I'm not sure."

Orion whined in my ear, anxious to get out of the car. "Just a minute. Let's see what this is." I rolled my window down to listen.

"Hey, Wilburn!" the man said. He stepped into the light of the street lamp. It was Titus Canty, owner of Canty Construction, hander out of mysterious envelopes.

Mayor Wilburn looked up from his mailbox. He took a step backward toward his house when he saw who it was. "Titus," he said. "What can I do for you?"

Canty balled his fist into his hand. "You can explain to me what the hell happened last night. That bathroom project was supposed to go to Canty Construction."

I started to open the car door wider, but Rafe put his hand on my arm. "Hold on a second. This is good stuff."

Wilburn shook his head. "I couldn't do it, Titus. I told you it wasn't going to happen. It's . . . it's not right. I'm sorry."

Canty took several more steps toward Wilburn. He was taller than the mayor by quite a few inches. Broader and younger, too. "Yeah. You're right. You're going to be sorry. Very, very sorry."

Wilburn took a few more steps back. "Let's talk about this, Titus. We can work this out. After all, I gave you back the money. All of it. Every cent."

"I didn't want the money. I wanted the project." Canty continued to advance. "And we're gonna work it out all right, Wilburn. Right here. Right now."

The mayor tried to back up more, but stumbled and fell backward. Canty reached down and grabbed him by the front of his shirt with his left hand, his right hand pulled back in a fist. I unsnapped Orion's leash and threw open the car door. "Go, boy," I said.

As far as I knew, Orion had never bitten anyone, but he did like to run once that leash was off. I figured sixty pounds of unknown dog charging at you out of the dark would make anyone pause. If all the dog did was try to shake your hand and play peekaboo with you once he got there, well, you wouldn't know that was the case as he raced toward you. Sure enough, Canty dropped the mayor and backed up against the Buick. "Shoo!" he yelled at Orion. "Go home."

I walked up from behind Orion and offered Mayor Wilburn my hand to help him get up. "Everything okay here, Mayor?" I asked, keeping my eye on Canty. Once the mayor was up, I snapped Orion's leash back on.

"F-f-fine, Desiree," Wilburn stuttered out.

"Yeah. We're fine. Just having a chat," Canty said. He smiled at me with a smile that was all teeth and no warmth. A shark's smile.

"Oh, really? I was hoping to chat with Mayor Wilburn, too. I'll just wait right here until the two of you are done." I leaned against the mailbox and patted Orion on the head.

Canty looked at me with narrowed eyes. I smiled back. I was pretty sure my smile was all teeth, too. Whatever it looked like, it was clear Canty didn't much care for it. He turned back to the mayor. "We'll talk later, Wilburn." He marched past us, giving Orion a wide berth.

Mayor Wilburn stumbled over to his car and leaned against the trunk.

"Are you really okay?" I asked, wondering if I should call 911.

"I'm fine. Fine." He held up his hand as if to stop me. "How much of that did you hear, Desiree?"

"Enough. I have this, too." I handed him Violet's photo.

"Ohhhhh," he said, sounding like air going out of a bounce house. He sagged a bit more. "I can explain."

I crossed my arms over my chest. "I'm listening."

He turned toward the house and gestured for me to follow. "Come inside. We'll sit down."

I shook my head. "No thank you. I'd prefer to stay out here." It wasn't as if there would be witnesses, which had been what Canty was counting on, but I felt better knowing I could run if Mayor Wilburn started brandishing syringes at me. Plus, this way Rafe could hear everything from inside my car.

"How much do you know?" he asked, turning back around to face me, his face spotlighted in the glow of the streetlamp. He looked old. Tired.

I shrugged. "I know that you've been taking bribes to throw projects Canty Construction's way. That Violet Daugherty had a photo of you accepting one of those bribes. That she's dead now and that seems to have freed you from giving those contracts to Canty. Or is it just that Fumiko Winters offered you more money?"

"It sounds pretty bad when you put it like that." He rubbed his hand across his face.

"I'm pretty sure it is bad," I said. "Imagine what that would look like splashed on the front page of the *Verbena Free Press*."

"Trust me. I've been imagining nothing but since Violet approached me with that photo." He hung his head, the streetlight making his bald head shine.

"What did she want from you?" That was another piece of this whole puzzle that I didn't understand. What did the mayor have that Violet wanted? I wanted him to spell it out for me.

"She wanted help with a dispute with her neighbor." He leaned against his car, sounding weary.

Not a typical shakedown, then. "That's all?"

"She hinted that she might need my help again in the future, but yeah. For now that was it." He actually laughed. "Ridiculous, right?"

It didn't sound like a reason to kill someone. At least, not yet. "So what did you do?"

"The neighbor had complained about Violet's dog." He paused and looked at Orion. "That's him, isn't it? How did you end up with her dog?"

"It's a long story. Explain about the neighbor." I pressed.

"The dog had gotten loose and dug up the neighbor's yard. The neighbor was furious. It was right before the garden tour and, well, the dog pretty much ruined the neighbor's chances of being named Best Verbena Garden."

Ah. I knew which neighbor he was talking about now. The sour faced one who'd given us such a dirty look. "What did Violet want you to do?"

"Well, obviously to not fine her or anything like that for

the dog getting out, but also to find a few code violations at the neighbor's house. You know, to make her think twice before complaining to the authorities about Violet." He rubbed at his jaw.

"And did you?" I asked.

He dropped his head again, refusing to look me in the eye. "I did. I'm not proud of it, but I did."

Some of this was not computing for me. "So if you'd already done what she asked, why did you return the money to Canty?"

"I can't live like that, always looking over my shoulder, always wondering if I'm about to be exposed." He shook his head. "I dug myself into a hole. Financially." He gestured back toward his house. "I'd already mortgaged this place to the hilt. I didn't see another way out. So I accepted a few gifts for nudging contracts in Canty Construction's direction. What harm was there in it, really? They did a good job. Their bids were competitive. I wasn't hurting the city. At least, not much. And I could do so much more good for Verbena as mayor. It seemed like the good outweighed the bad."

Sure it did. It was a pretty high class justification, but that's all it was. A justification.

"Then Violet approached me with that photo. All I could think about was what would happen if she went public with it. Everything I'd ever done for this town would be meaningless. All anyone would remember was that I'd been a crooked politician. Everything I'd worked for would be ruined. I realized that what I thought was a way out was getting me deeper in the hole. I was desperate, but I didn't see a way out. I was getting pressure from two different directions, Canty and Violet. Then . . . then Violet died. I thought it was over. I could return Titus' money and get back to living the way I was supposed to." His head came up and he glared at me. "It didn't occur to me that anyone would try to pick up where she left off."

My cheeks flushed with indignation. "I'm not doing that. I'm not interested in blackmailing anyone. I do want to know who killed Violet, though."

"Killed Violet?" Wilburn made a face. "She died in a car accident."

"Brought on by an overdose of insulin," I said, watching his face.

It went a little white. "Does Luke Butler know about this?" he asked.

"Luke doesn't think there's any reason for anyone to kill Violet so he's not really interested in investigating." Now I made a face. I'd found him a darn good reason that someone would want to kill Violet. Would he listen to Nate and me now?

Wilburn rubbed at his face, looking weary. "You're not planning on blackmailing me for anything?"

I shook my head. "No. Not my style. I'm much more likely to write an article about you than blackmail you." He was trying to turn it around, to go straight. I had some admiration for that. The taking bribes in the first place thing wasn't so admirable. Realizing you'd made a mistake and trying to make up for it had some merit. "What are you going to do now?"

"I'm not sure. Probably sell this place." He turned to look at the house behind him.

I had a moment of imagining selling Turner and how much that would hurt. "I'm sorry, Mayor Wilburn."

"Me, too, Desiree. Me, too." He hung his head again. "What are you going to do?"

"About?"

"About me. About the bribes. You were right when you said it would be quite the splash on the front page of the *Verbena Free Press*." He settled his shoulders as if he was steeling himself.

He was right. It would be a big splash. It also would be a service to the community. An elected official taking bribes? It really didn't get much more on the side of right than that.

"Desiree." His voice shook. "Can we come to some kind of compromise? Being mayor is all I have. It's all I've ever been and all I've ever wanted to be."

"Any compromise we come to has to somehow include you telling the truth about what's been going on. The town deserves the truth." I knew that was true. I also knew that Wilburn had been a damn good mayor for Verbena and that it wasn't an easy job.

Wilburn staggered against the car and I made sure my phone was available to call 911, just in case. Orion looked over his shoulder at me and then tugged on his leash to get closer to Wilburn. I let him. He sat down next to the mayor and leaned against his legs. Mayor Wilburn took a couple ragged breaths. "It'll be the end of me."

I thought for a moment. "Maybe. Maybe not. I used to overhear the PR people talking when there was a scandal brewing. They always talked about getting ahead of the scandal, controlling the narrative. You could do that." I paused. "I could help."

"Why? Why would you do that?"

"I'd do it because people deserve second chances. And because I'd like to see an official investigation into Canty Construction started. I think it's possible they may have had something to do with father's disappearance." I heard Rafe getting out of the car behind me.

"Why would your father know about any of this?" Rafe asked.

I turned. "He buried Broderick Gunter a few days before he disappeared. Gunter worked for Canty. I think there might be a connection there. Maybe Dad knew something that Canty didn't want him to know." Maybe Dad had figured out the corruption scheme and had confronted Canty instead of Wilburn.

"And you think Canty killed him?" Mayor Wilburn's voice was horrified.

I shrugged. Could my dad be chopped up into tiny pieces and distributed in the concrete of a dozen construction sites in northern California? Could that be why we never found him? "Maybe. Or maybe Dad felt like he had to make it look like he was dead to keep himself and us safe."

"No, Desiree. No." Wilburn crouched down to pet Orion, color returning to his face.

"Are you saying that because it couldn't be true or because you don't want it to be true?" I asked.

"I don't know. One thing I've learned is that we're all capable of things we didn't know we could do. I never thought I'd do anything to hurt this town, but I have. And now I have to pay for it. When do we get started on this staying ahead of the scandal?" he asked.

"There's no time like the present, right?"

Chapter Seven

The Verbena Free Press
October 10
By Desiree Turner and Rafe Valdez

Mayor Confesses to Wrongdoing

Mayor Wilburn has revealed that he has accepted money and other gifts in exchange for steering construction contracts toward Canty Construction in a long and detailed interview. Speaking to *Free Press* reporter Desiree Turner, Wilburn said, "I'm so terribly ashamed. I love this town and everyone in it. I've let them down."

When asked why he had accepted the gifts, he said, "I don't make much as mayor and it is pretty much a full-time job. For a while, I made it with my savings, but those are running out."

According to Wilburn, he returned the last attempted bribe. "I couldn't keep living like this. I'd done wrong and

I had to stop. I returned all the money and the contract went to a different construction company."

Wilburn says that he plans to step down from his office and sell his home. "I hate the idea of leaving Verbena, but I don't feel I can show my face on the street anymore."

*   *   *

The next day, we put Frank Fiore to rest. As always, after Uncle Joey had wheeled him in, I did a quick check to make sure everything looked right before his daughters arrived. He looked pretty darn good for someone who had been as ill as he had been. Daisy came in while I was checking. I steeled myself for getting reamed out for suspecting her sister of doing something wrong, but either she had forgiven me or Iris hadn't said anything.

She put her hand on his shoulder. "Aw, Dad. I'm sorry."

I looked over at her. "He had a hard time at the end, didn't he?"

"Yes. It seems so unfair. He really suffered." She cocked her head to one side. "He was such a good dad. He made me feel so special all the time. He used to call Iris and me his little flowers."

"Those are good memories to focus on." I had more than a few of those. Hiking with Dad at Cold Clutch Canyon. Surfing. Him cheering for me at volleyball games as if I was in the Olympics. I smiled, then bit back a yawn. Rafe and I had been up late the night before finishing our article about Mayor Wilburn to make sure it was part of the morning's paper. It had been close to two o'clock when he'd pulled a bottle of Wild Turkey out of his lower desk drawer and we'd toasted our scoop.

The bourbon had warmed my stomach and given me a tingle or was that because Rafe had come around from his side of the desk to sit closer to me? "Strong work, Turner," he had said. "Very strong."

"You weren't too shabby yourself." I'd clinked my glass against his. Orion had gotten up from where he'd curled up in the corner—on a blanket Rafe had put out for him—and had pushed against me, clearly ready to go home. All he'd done, however, was somehow push me until I was off balance and tip me right into Rafe.

Rafe's eyes had widened in surprise and, for a second, our faces were inches apart. Orion barked and I'd put down my glass and said I needed to get home.

I shook myself back into the present.

Daisy said, "I don't really want to remember this last bit too well. He looks pretty good now, though."

"He must have been really handsome in his younger days." He had a strong nose and a cleft chin. It was a handsome face.

"Oh, yeah. Totally like that guy from *Under the Tuscan Sun*. Raoul Bova?"

I looked in. "I can see the resemblance." I also noticed something wrong with his hand. His pinky finger stuck out at an odd angle. Uncle Joey didn't usually make mistakes. I reached in to straighten it, but Daisy stopped me.

She held up her hand. Her pinky finger went off in the

same direction. "It won't straighten," she said. "It's genetic apparently."

"Interesting," I said. "If you don't need anything right now, I'm going to go check on the guest book and the programs."

I left her gazing at her father. I checked on everything else and greeted people as they came in. Olive, Henrietta, and Grace arrived and took their usual spots. I folded up their walkers to lean them against the wall out of the way.

"Frank's getting a nice showing," Olive observed.

"He always was popular," Grace said with a chuckle.

Olive gave her hand a little slap. "That was years ago. Frank hasn't had the energy to flirt for years."

"People remember even if you've been sick a long time," Henrietta said. "And he certainly was."

"He was lucky that Iris was willing to give up so much to take care of him. She did a beautiful job. Anywhere else, he probably wouldn't have lasted as long as he did," Grace said.

I felt extra bad that I had suspected her of wrong-doing.

"I'm not sure she did him any favors," Olive said. "He might have been better off if he'd checked out a little earlier."

"She certainly would have been," Henrietta said. "I can't imagine how much money they ran through keeping him alive. She'll be lucky if there's a pot left to pee in when it's all settled."

"Don't know what she'll do if there's not anything there. She hasn't worked as anything but his caretaker since before she came back home and I doubt that deadbeat of an ex-husband of hers will help with much." Grace shook her head.

All three clucked their tongues.

"Nice article this morning, by the way, Desiree," Olive said nudging me with her elbow. "Quite the scoop you and Rafe cooked up. I don't think anyone even suspected the mayor hadn't been thoroughly on the up-and-up."

Except Violet, of course. She'd suspected enough to have a photo of him accepting bribes. She'd known who to watch and how to watch them. Maybe it was part of always looking for a way to fit in. "Oh, I'm sure there were other people who were starting to nose around. We just got there first."

"That's not the scuttlebutt that's going around," Grace said.

I snorted. Scuttlebutt moved faster than wildfire around here and wildfires could move damn fast. "Oh, really. What does the scuttlebutt say?"

"That you stumbled across some kind of clue that someone else might have just tossed aside, but you followed it up instead." She looked up at me, one eye squinted shut. "They're not quite sure where you stumbled across that first clue, though. Care to share?"

I shook my head. "A reporter never reveals her sources."

"Fine." Olive sniffed. "We'll figure it out, though. Just you wait and see."

That worried me a bit. The last thing I wanted was for the three of them to somehow put themselves in danger by poking into Canty Construction's business. It might very well be the reason my father had never come back from his early morning surf. "I promise I'll share as soon as I can, okay? Until then, maybe stay away from this one. Titus Canty might be more dangerous than he seems."

"What does that mean?" Grace demanded.

"It might mean nothing. I just want you three to stay safe, okay?" I pointed to my eyes and then to them to indicate that I'd be watching them then went back over to the front where a crowd was beginning to bunch up near the entrance. Daisy was in the center of the crowd. I made some subtle suggestions for people to move to their seats and the crowd broke up a bit.

"It's always been like that," Iris said at my elbow.

I jumped. "I'm sorry. What has?"

"Daisy. She was born first and she makes sure she stays first in everything." Iris shook her head. "Everyone always flocks to her. I'm always the one coming up behind everyone and mopping everything up. Doing what needs to be done while nobody even notices."

I could relate to that. "People notice," I said. "I've heard a number of people talking about what good care you took of your father."

Iris gave me a strange look and seemed about to say something when were were interrupted by a teenaged girl coming up beside Iris. She had that leggy gazelle look that a lot of teenagers have. Her hair was glossy and her eyes were bright. "Mom?"

"Where are you going to apply for school, Rose?" An older gentleman asked the girl.

She smiled, revealing a set of braces. "I'm looking at Stanford, Berkeley, and UC Santa Barbara right now."

"Good schools," he said.

"She's got great grades and test scores. She won the regional science fair, you know. All about genetics. I think she has a good chance," Iris said, puffing up a bit.

"Oh, I'm sure. Maybe she'll get a scholarship. Some of

those places are so expensive these days." The man shook his head. "Of course, you'll have some money from Frank to help with that."

Iris suddenly looked like she was barely keeping her temper. "I have it covered," she said. "I can take care of my child."

"Of course. Of course." He started to cough. Daisy came over and said, "Oh, Uncle Leo, let me help you find a seat. Do you need a cough drop?" She pulled one out of her pocket and they walked away on a cloud of honey, lemon, and menthol.

Rose looked at me and rolled her eyes a bit.

"Is everyone asking you the same set of questions? Where are you applying? What do you want to study? I remember my senior year here. I felt like I should wear a sandwich board with the answers to those two questions on it." One more of the reasons I'd been happy to skedaddle out of here.

"The questions do get a little repetitive. I get it. They're important decisions. It doesn't help that much to keep talking about it, though." Rose shook her head and laughed. "Cool article in the paper this morning."

I laughed. "Kids read newspapers still? I thought print was dead."

"I read it online," she admitted. "Still, who knew Verbena had so much crazy stuff going on? I mean, Mayor Wilburn? Taking bribes? Crazy."

I knew what she meant.

A young woman I didn't recognize came in. White, tall, and thin, with an athletic grace to her movements. Iris's hand went to her mouth. "Oh, Jenny, you didn't have to come."

The woman put her arms around Iris. "I know. I wanted

to, though. I've been with you guys so long you feel like family. You know Frank was one of my favorite patients, too."

I looked over at Rose. "Hospice nurse," she mouthed. I nodded. That was nice of her to come to the service.

"He loved you, too, Jenny," Iris said, her voice quaking a bit.

"Are you okay? Remember to take care of yourself." Jenny held Iris out from her and looked her up and down. "You were such a dedicated daughter, so conscientious, so scrupulous. Absolutely fastidious. I know it was exhausting. Be sure to pamper yourself a bit now."

Iris laughed. "Somehow getting a pedicure doesn't seem high on my priority list right now."

"Well, then take a walk or a nap or a trip to the coast. Anything. Promise?" Jenny asked.

Iris nodded. "I promise. Just as soon as I get Dad's affairs squared away."

Pastor Campbell came in. I ushered everyone to their seats and the service started.

Olive was right. Frank did get a good showing. I moved over to the side of the Magnolia Room. Out of the way, but around in case I was needed.

*　*　*

The last twenty-four hours had been a whirlwind. Finding Violet's blackmail photos of the mayor, figuring out what the photos meant, confronting Mayor Wilburn, writing the article, then Frank Fiore's funeral. Fatigue dragged at my legs, making every step seem like a huge effort. Orion looked even more tired than I felt.

After I got back from the Lawn of Heaven Cemetery where Frank Fiore was laid to eternal rest, I headed straight up to my room and collapsed on the bed. Orion curled up on the rug. I set the alarm on my phone for twenty minutes and shut my eyes, still with all my clothes—even the pantyhose!—on. When the alarm went off, it felt like I'd only closed my eyes for seconds, but I knew from experience if I slept much longer than that, I'd never get to sleep that night. I hauled myself upright. Orion lifted his head, sniffed the air once, then set his head back down and closed his eyes.

I stripped out of my clothes and took a quick shower. With my hair still wrapped up in a towel and the rest of me wrapped up in a terrycloth bathrobe, I snuggled back under the covers. I wasn't quite ready to go back out and face the world yet. My eyes lit on Violet Daugherty's shoebox. I hadn't had a chance to go through the rest of it. What other treasures did she have in there? I snagged it from the top of my desk where it sat and pulled it over to me on the bed and flipped the lid open.

There were the photos of the very flexible couple on the lat pull and the grumpy neighbor. There was also a photo of a man sniffing a shoe followed up by one of him licking the same shoe. I set those aside. I didn't know him and I doubted it would be at all newsworthy. Dad used to say that pot had its lid. Maybe ever shoe had its sniffer, too.

The other items were more mysterious. I looked at the thumb drives and the DVD. I hesitated to plug them into my own laptop. What if there was a virus or something on them? Violet's laptop? I had fewer qualms about that. I did my contortionist maneuver again to get the laptop and fired it up, then I plugged in the DVD. It took a second to come up, but then I saw video of a woman pulling up to a curb in a minivan, letting her children out, then taking a little glass bottle out of her purse and dumping it into her travel mug before driving off. In fact, there were three sequences of the same thing on what looked three separate occasions. I recognized the street she was driving on, too. If you squinted, you could see the roller slide at Manor Park in the background. It was the park right next to the elementary school. This took place right here in Verbena. After watching them, I backtracked and zoomed in on the bottle. Video quality got decidedly worse the closer I zoomed in, but I was betting on vodka. Everyone always said it was odorless. That had not been Jasmine's and my experience when we'd tried to sashay past her mother after an evening spent drinking out by the edge of the creek with a bunch of other high school seniors. We'd both been grounded for weeks.

I typed diabetes and alcohol into a search engine, curious to see if there might be some connection that would explain Vodka Mom having insulin as well as a minivan. I sat back, chewing on the side of my thumb as I read. There was definitely a connection. There were several ways drinking too much alcohol could trigger diabetes in a person. Booze can make a person's body less sensitive to insulin and cause them to develop type 2 diabetes. Drinking way too much can cause an inflammation of the pancreas, which can then trigger diabetes. It wasn't any kind of proof, but it did give me some ideas.

I picked up the fingerprint card. That one was still baffling. I put that with the photos. Then I put in one of the thumb drives. A whole set of photo icons came up. I started clicking on them. Most of them were of people I didn't know. I didn't even recognize them. A lot of them were of people doing what looked like pretty ordinary things, then again the mayor accepting an envelope from a guy in a suit looked pretty ordinary when you didn't have context for it. Once you knew that the man in the suit was the head of a construction company known for bribing city officials, it looked a lot different. It still wasn't proof of anything, but it had been enough to get us asking questions.

I was about halfway through the photos when my phone buzzed. It was a photo from Jasmine of a wine bottle sitting on a café table. A message followed it. "How fast can you get here?"

I snapped Violet's laptop shut. "Twenty minutes."

* * *

I met Nate and Jasmine at Tappiano's for Hometown Happy Hour where drinks were half price if you could point to your photo in any one of the dozens of Verbena High Year Books that Mark Tappiano kept around. We sat out on the patio so I could keep Orion with us, a light breeze playing across us and rustling the leaves of the linden trees planted along the sidewalk. Monique had brought out a water bowl for Orion as well as wine for us. Jasmine raised a glass of Zinfandel and said, "To our very own Christiane Amanpour. Everyone's talking about your article."

I tried to keep the smile off my lips. After all, it wasn't good to find corruption in your town. I couldn't help it, though. It was a solid article. "Thanks."

"How did you figure it out?" Nate asked, clinking his glass against mine, too.

I shook my head and mimed locking my lips with a key and throwing it away.

He sighed. "Fine. Have you found out anything more about Violet?"

I bit my lip and didn't say anything.

Jasmine set her glass down with a bump. "They're connected, aren't they?"

"I didn't say that," I protested.

"You didn't have to. It's written all over your face. And in your whole body, to be honest." Sometimes it really sucked to have a best friend who's a therapist. She was way too good at reading me.

Nate leaned in. "Violet knew about the mayor?"

I looked around to see who else might be listening. Nobody was near. "She did. I found some . . . something in her house that pointed me in that direction. Mayor Wilburn confirmed it. She was blackmailing him."

"Blackmail? Do you think Mayor Wilburn killed her to keep her quiet?" Jasmine's brown eyes were huge in her face.

I shook my head. "No. You should have seen how fast he folded when Rafe and I confronted him. I don't think he has that kind of nerve."

Luke Butler slid into the fourth seat at the table as if we'd been expecting him and signaled Monique for a beer. Yes. A beer at a wine bar. That was Luke all over. He leaned down and said, "You still haven't found a home for Orion?" he asked.

"Not yet."

Jasmine looked at me through narrowed eyes. "Have you run an ad about him yet?" she asked.

"Not yet. It's been busy. I haven't had time to put it together. I need to sort through all those photos we took to pick one or two. It's going to be hard. Each one is more adorable than the last." I didn't meet her eyes.

She picked up my phone and hit a button so the screen came alive. She pointed at the photo of Orion with his paws crossed in the leaves, which was now my screen background. "What about this one?"

"The focus isn't good. I need to retake it." I grabbed my phone back from her.

Jasmine took a sip of her wine. "Mm-hmm. What about a Facebook post or a tweet?"

I'd spent more time on Violet's social media than I had on my own. "Not yet."

"You're keeping this dog, aren't you?" Jasmine asked.

I shrunk down in my chair. "Maybe."

"Donna's going to hate that." She took a sip of her wine.

I knew Jasmine was right. "I think I might be able to talk her into letting me keep him. He's really friendly. He seems to like everybody and everybody likes him. You should have seen him with this one client. It was like he knew exactly what to do to comfort her. She thought he was a trained therapy dog."

"Maybe he is," Nate said. "Who else would know besides Violet?"

Violet knew about a lot of things, a lot of things no one else seemed to have noticed around this town, things that other people should have noticed. I turned to Luke. "You were on the force when my Dad disappeared, right?"

He gave me a wary glance. "Yeah."

"Did anybody look into the funerals we'd had right before it happened?" I asked. It was always possible that someone had done that kind of due diligence. It wasn't likely, but it was possible.

"Why?" he asked.

Monique came out and set Luke's beer in front of him. I waited until she'd gone back inside. "It's possible that he found out something about someone and they made him disappear to keep that secret."

Luke looked confused. "But they'd be dead already."

"Not them. Their family maybe. Or their employer." I rolled my eyes. What would it be like to be that literal?

Luke gave me a funny look. "What were you thinking? What kinds of secrets?"

"My dad buried Broderick Gunter right before his disappearance. Gunter worked for Canty Construction, the same Canty Construction that has just been exposed for bribing our mayor."

"So you think your father figured out something like that while arranging Gunter's funeral, threatened to expose people, and someone murdered him to cover it up?" He tapped on the table for a second. "I thought you said your dad was alive still. That you saw him on your back porch in a video."

"I did," I insisted. "Maybe someone made him disappear. Or he disappeared himself. Maybe he did it to protect us, to keep us safe."

Luke looked over at Jasmine and then at Nate. Nobody would meet his eyes. "Desiree, I get it. You want your father to be alive. I saw that video. It's way too dark to know if that's your father or not. As to your father's disappearance, there was absolutely no evidence of foul play. Nothing was missing. There were no signs of violence."

"There wasn't any evidence of anything," I broke in. "An absence of evidence doesn't prove anything. He was just gone and I don't see how that could happen." My voice broke. I cleared my throat to cover it, but I didn't think anyone was fooled. Orion's ears perked up and he got up from where he was lying on the sidewalk and rested his chin on my leg.

Luke put his hand over mind. "Desiree, your Dad wasn't murdered. No one was murdered. He didn't stumble onto a big conspiracy and go into witness protection. He went surfing by himself and he didn't come back. End of story."

"You know what, Luke?" Jasmine broke in. "Not end of story. Desiree has been right about so many things since she got home. She was right about Kyle and you didn't want to listen to her. Nobody knew about the mayor and she figured that out, too. Maybe it's time you listened to her, don't you think?"

I stared at her, my mouth open a tiny bit. We'd always had each other's backs before, but I'd felt pretty isolated out there with my theories about my dad. Apparently I wasn't so alone anymore. "How about you listen to Nate and me about Violet Daugherty, too?" I asked.

Luke hit the table with his fist, making our wine glasses jump and making Orion yip. "Absolutely not. You're seeing murder everywhere. You're riling everyone up, getting every-one upset. People are afraid you're going to randomly accuse them of something. I won't have it."

"I haven't randomly accused anyone of anything. If any accusations have been made, there have been reasons." I pat-ted Orion to calm him down.

"Well, stop looking for reasons, okay? Everything was easy here before you came home. Everything was calm. I want it to go back that way." He flung himself back in his chair and crossed his arms over his chest. I half expected him to stick out his lower lip.

* * *

Nate walked Orion and me home. The sun had started to go down and our shadows stretched before us, snaking along the road. The temperature had started to drop, too, and the wind picked up. It smelled like rain again. It seemed like a storm was coming, but nothing had yet appeared. Orion lifted his head, sniffed at the air, and gave a happy bark.

"Do you think we should drop the Violet thing?" I asked. "Luke was getting pretty upset."

He looped his arm over my shoulders. The warmth felt good. "Since when do you care if Luke is upset or not?"

I slipped my free hand into his back pocket. "I don't. Well, I don't care if he's upset with me. I can ignore him if I want to. You actually have to work with him from time to time, though."

He pulled me a little closer. "I can handle Luke."

There was a little more steel in his voice than I was used to hearing. I glanced up, but his expression remained impassive. I'd known this man nearly my whole life and I still found him impossible to read. "Okay then."

We got to Turner Family Funeral Home and walked up the back stairs. Nate brushed away the hair that the wind had whipped across my face and leaned down to kiss me. I stepped into the kiss, to get closer, but Orion had other ideas. He nosed his way in between us and barked.

Nate leaned down and scratched behind Orion's ears. "No need to get jealous, buddy boy. We're all here together."

Once I was inside, I refilled Orion's bowls and then rummaged in the refrigerator for leftovers of whatever it was Donna and Greg and made for dinner. Chicken. There were even some mashed potatoes left. I made a plate to put in the microwave.

Donna came in and sat down heavily at the table. "Don't bother laying out the programs for the Dickerson service. They canceled."

"What?" Nobody canceled. Once people signed in, they generally did not sign out. We were like Hotel California.

"Yeah. It was weird. We already did the cremation so they'll be by to pick up the ashes tomorrow. She said they decided to go a different direction with the service." Donna leaned back and put her feet up on the opposite chair.

"Okay, then." It was unusual, but not crazy. Sometimes people realized they wanted to wait to have a service until more people could be there or until the mourners were a little more together. The microwave dinged. I pulled my plate out. "We still have the Sizemores tomorrow afternoon, though, right?"

Donna nodded. "Yep. You good to go on that one? I e-mailed you the video."

"I've got it. I think I'm set." Ironically, Zenia's review of our files had bolstered my confidence.

*   *   *

I felt a whole lot less confident when Orion woke me up barking and growling. I rolled over and looked at the clock. It was after one. "Hush, boy. It's time to sleep."

He grabbed my blankets in his teeth and pulled them off the bed. Then he started barking again.

"Make that dog be quiet," Donna yelled from her room.

"I'm trying," I yelled back.

For a second Orion hushed and that's when I heard it. A crashing sound. Glass breaking. I flipped on the light. Orion ran to the door of my room and barked at it until I opened it, then he rushed downstairs. I followed flipping on lights as I went.

By the time I reached the ground floor, I could hear Uncle Joey thundering after me. I was about to head into the basement, but Orion took a sharp right turn when we passed the Magnolia Room and headed into the kitchen we use when we're setting up for a reception.

There was glass everywhere. I snatched up Orion—no easy feat considering how much he weighed—to keep him from cutting his feet.

Uncle Joey came up behind me, breathing heavily. "What happened?"

"Someone tried to break in." I gestured with my chin toward the side door. Its panes had been smashed in.

* * *

DeAndre of Roosevelt Window Repair put the last pane into place. "That should do it for now, Desiree. I'll come back tomorrow to make sure everything is set right."

"Thanks. Maybe I should apply for a frequent flyer discount." I rubbed my eyes as I watched DeAndre put away his tools. DeAndre had been the one to replace the glass at Violet's house, too.

DeAndre laughed. "Trouble does seem to follow you, doesn't it?"

Donna kicked me lightly under the table. "That's exactly what I've been saying for years."

"You don't have to wait up," I told her. "Especially not if you're going to assault me."

"I wasn't assaulting you. I was making a point." She stuck out her tongue at me.

"With your foot." I kicked her back. Just a little.

DeAndre laughed. "You two crack me up. You remind me of me and my sister. Always squabbling, but take after one of us. Look out, man."

Carlotta stretched and yawned. "Why would someone break in here?"

"Whaddaya mean?" DeAndre said. "People are dying to get in here."

I smiled, but not with a lot of enthusiasm. It wasn't the first time I'd heard that particular joke.

DeAndre shook his head. "Tough crowd." He snapped his tool box shut. "See you tomorrow."

Donna walked him out.

"Have you had a lot of break-ins recently?" I hadn't been

reading the police blotter lately. Maybe there was something going on that would make a good article.

"Not really. Just the one at Violet Daugherty's and this one." Carlotta considered for a moment. "Whoever did this one did a much more professional job. They used the same technique, but they were a lot more careful. Better prepared. They didn't even cut themselves. I'm actually surprised you heard it. It was probably pretty quiet."

"I didn't hear it. Orion did." I patted his head.

She turned slowly around in the room. "Any idea what they might be after?"

I was about to say no, but then I remembered the shoebox, the one that had contained what I'd needed to expose the bribery scandal. There were lots of things in that box. Lots of people who Violet might have been blackmailing. Maybe one of them figured out that I had her stash and wanted it back. It seemed like too much of a coincidence to have the only two break-ins be at Violet's and then at Turner's, especially when the technique used to break in was the same.

"Desiree?" Carlotta pressed.

"Let me think about it," I said. I wasn't quite ready to hand that box over to the police yet. I wanted a few more answers myself first. "By the way, did you ever talk to the neighbor about the car she saw cruising in Violet's neighborhood?"

Carlotta nodded. "Yeah. She wasn't totally sure. She thought it was some kind of Honda or Toyota."

"What color?"

"Green."

The woman with the vodka in her thermos in Violet's

photos had a dark-colored car. It could easily be a green Honda or Toyota. I could see a person who was a little drunk thinking they might be able to get away with breaking into a place with an alarm system like Violet's and then maybe sobering up a bit and doing a better job on the next place they broke into.

Perhaps it was time to have a little chat with Vodka Mom.

Chapter Eight

The next day, Orion and I hunkered down in the Element and watched the parade of minivans and SUVs driving up to the school, pausing for a minute, then driving off. I kept looking at Iris's photograph and up at the line, hoping I'd be able to pick out Vodka Mom from the pack.

A knock on the window make me jump. Orion barked. I accidentally hit the horn. I turned, ready to start cursing at whoever had snuck up on us. Then I saw who it was. Luke freaking Butler. I rolled down the window. "What are you doing here?"

He leaned onto the door with his elbows and said, "That's exactly what I was going to ask you. We got a report of someone lurking on the side streets near the school watching the children go in and out."

I looked around. Who had reported me? I saw a curtain twitch at the house across the street. I made a mental note of the address. I'd find out who the busybody was and I'd . . . Well, I didn't know what I'd do. That was for later, though.

I needed to get Luke away from me now in case Vodka Mom showed up. "I'm not lurking. I'm sitting."

"Apparently that looks pretty lurky to some people. Why are you sitting here anyway?" He peered into the car as if there might be some contraband.

I slid the photo of Vodka Mom under Orion. "Just reliving the glory days of elementary school."

He squinted at me. "Well, relive them someplace else. You're making people nervous."

That was the moment I saw Vodka Mom pull up. At least, I thought it was her. It looked like the right van. Green minivan with a slight dent in the left front fender and a scrape on the back. Maybe driving around sipping vodka out of your travel mug led to some fender benders. "Okay. I'll go." I pushed at his elbows to get them off the door.

"What's your hurry?" He didn't budge.

"Oh, I don't know. Being accused of being a pedophile. I figured it would be best to leave the situation." Vodka Mom had pulled up to the curb.

"No one said you were a pedophile. They said you were lurking and watching the kids." Luke made a face. "You always overreact."

"And what did you think they meant?"

He stood up. Finally. I put the Element in drive. He shook his head. "Desiree Turner, if you're up to something . . ."

I waved and pulled out into the intersection as Vodka Mom pulled away from the curb. "That was a close one," I told Orion. He settled down onto the photo.

Vodka Mom drove exactly like a mom should. She signaled every turn and lane change. She came to a complete stop at every Stop sign. She drove the speed limit. She certainly didn't drive like she was drunk or even buzzed or about to bounce her dented minivan off of anything.

She drove down Oriole and turned onto Sparrow and then into the Civic Center parking lot. I drove past the parking lot—no need to tip her off that I was following her—and went around the block. I managed to see her going into the Civic Center as I pulled into the lot. She looked different than the photo, somehow. I pulled it out from underneath Orion. In the photo, she looked a little bleary. Her hair hadn't been combed and I was pretty sure that day old mascara was smeared underneath her eyes. I'd seen it enough times on my own face to recognize it. Today, she had her hair pulled back into a sleek ponytail and there was a bounce in her step that didn't gibe with smeared mascara, uncombed hair, and vodka instead of sugar or cream in your coffee. She had on exercise clothes, but not necessarily the kind you would really exercise in. Cute capris, a zip-up-the-front hoodie, and sneakers. Athleisurewear. I parked across the lot from her van and waited a minute or two to be sure she wasn't coming right back out. She didn't.

"Wanna go for a little walk?" I asked Orion.

He barked twice, which I took as his universal sign of yes. We got out of the Element and I snapped on his leash. We had a bad moment when I walked toward the Civic Center and, for some reason, Orion thought we were headed to sniff every tree in the square, but once we got that straightened out we made it to the door of the Civic Center.

I'll admit. I didn't have the best associations with the place. Some things had gone down there that still gave me bad dreams. In those dreams, the place had gone up in flames with me trapped inside, fighting to get out and failing. In the dream, no one had come to save me, and I burned with the sound of someone's triumphant cackle sounding in my ears over the roar of the fire. I gave myself a little shake and I pushed the door open. It was only a dream. It wasn't what had happened. I'd kept the place from catching on fire and a whole crowd of people had come to aid me. Jasmine and Nate and Luke and Carlotta and Rafe. They'd all been there for me. My town had my back.

Inside, the hallway was lit only by natural light coming through a skylight and there wasn't a huge amount of it. It gave the hall that weird ghostly feeling, like when you'd walk into your school after hours and everyone was gone. Like maybe if you listened hard enough, you'd hear ghost children chanting nursery rhymes and the creak of swings going back and forth in the breeze with no one on them. Halloween was clearly getting to me. Orion whimpered as if he'd felt it, too, or maybe caught a case of the creeps from me. I bent down to pet him and absorb a little warmth to get rid of the goose bumps that had risen up on my arms. As I listened, I heard the sound of people all speaking in unison for a moment and then stopping. What had I stumbled on? Some kind of weird cult or something? I crept along the hallway to the source of the chanting. It wasn't in the main hall. I was just as happy to not go in there. It came from one of the smaller meeting rooms.

There was a sign on the door. AA MEETING 8:30 AM.

No wonder Vodka Mom didn't look quite like her picture. She wasn't Vodka Mom anymore.

* * *

I went back home, unsure of what to do next. Did Vodka
Mom still have reason to want Violet dead if she was now
Not Vodka Mom? I had a while to think about it. Zenia was
scheduled to return for our inspection.

I took Orion on a long walk so he'd be mellow and sleepy.
I put on my most beige assistant funeral director clothes. I
walked through the place trying to find every speck of dust
and cobweb. Uncle Joey and Donna were doing the same
things. Uncle Joey had trimmed his beard and put on dress
shoes and a tie. He looked quite dapper. When it was time for
Zenia to arrive, we were lined up in the hallway like maids
and butlers at an English country estate waiting for the Lord
and Lady to arrive.

Zenia pulled into the driveway at exactly five minutes to
ten. She sat in her car and made notes on a clipboard until
one minute to ten when she got out and walked to the door.
I reached for the door to open it before she knocked, but
Uncle Joey put his hand on my arm to stop me. He shook his
head. Once she knocked, he let go of my arm and nodded.

Zenia walked through the funeral home with her clipboard in hand making notes here and there. Her heels clicked
on the hardwood floors. Uncle Joey followed after her, hands
shoved into his back pockets. Donna and I trailed after him
for a while then gave up and walked up the stairs to the second floor.

"Should we be doing something?" I whispered to Donna
from where we sat on the top of the stairs. We'd eavesdropped
on the adults our whole life on this perch. I looked over at
her bulging stomach wondering who this little one would

cuddle with as she tried to decode what the grown-ups were talking about. Maybe she could cuddle with Orion.

"We should be doing our jobs all the time," Donna whispered back.

I thought we were. I hoped we were.

Uncle Joey and Zenia left the ground floor and headed down to the basement where the office and embalming room were. Donna blew out a breath. "How did she seem? Do you think she seemed okay?"

"I'm not sure how to tell," I said. We crept down further. "She's a little hard to read. I could pretend to go get some paperwork or something from downstairs to see what they're doing."

"No. It'd be too obvious. Let's just wait."

We didn't have long. Uncle Joey and Zenia walked back upstairs and to the front door. Zenia pulled some pages off her clipboard. "These are the notifications of violations, Joe."

Uncle Joey glanced over the list and sighed. "I see."

"They're all pretty minor," she said, smoothing her hair. "But they need to be seen to."

"I understand." He folded the paper into thirds, nodding gravely.

"Is two days sufficient time to tend these items?" Zenia asked, her lips slightly pursed.

Uncle Joey thought for a moment. "Should be."

"Fine. I'll see you then. Let me know if you have any questions before then." She clipped out the door. Uncle Joey followed her. Donna and I rushed to the window at the stairs landing where you could see out onto the drive. He helped her into her car, then chatted for a moment. They shook hands. He shut the car door, then Uncle Joey slouched back in, hands firmly back in his back pockets.

"What do you think of that?" I asked.

"I'm not sure. Let's go ask." We scampered down to the basement where Uncle Joey whistled as he pulled a filing cabinet away from the wall.

"Everything okay?" Donna asked.

He shrugged and pointed to the papers on his desk. "Few little things here and there like cleaning behind these cabinets. Shouldn't take me more than a few hours to deal with it all."

"Then what happens," I asked.

"Zenia comes back and double-checks that we've fixed everything to her satisfaction." He took off his tie and rolled up his sleeves.

Uncle Joey prided himself on his work. He took pains to always do everything the correct way. He was looking at a list of things he hadn't done right and he was whistling. Something wasn't adding up. "Do you need any help with any of it?" I asked. "Are there things I can do?" I wasn't as proficient in all things funeral as Donna and Uncle Joey were. There were things I couldn't take care of, but there was a lot I could. Cleaning behind cabinets seemed like one I could do.

He shook his head. "No worries. I'm on it."

He sauntered off, still whistling. He seemed awfully happy for a guy who was just told he had a bunch of infractions to take care of.

* * *

Nothing was scheduled for the afternoon. We'd originally been scheduled for a pick-up, but it had been canceled. That didn't happen often, although apparently that was changing. I seized the opportunity to get out of the house. I took Orion for a hike through Cold Clutch Canyon. It renewed my spirit and energized me. It had been one of the special places I'd gone with my father. As I sat up on the ledge sharing some string cheese with Orion, I thought about what Dad might have done if he'd seen something. Would he have gone to the police? I'd certainly not had good luck with that. Dad was great at reading people. He might well have known exactly how Luke would react. Dismissive. Disbelieving. Disappointing.

So what would Dad have done? If he had evidence, he'd have put it in a secure place. He wouldn't have kept it at home. He wouldn't have wanted to put us in danger. It hit me like a lightning bolt. His storage space. Months after he'd disappeared, after I'd come home, I'd found a key to a storage space a few towns over. I hadn't seen anything important in it when I'd looked in it, but maybe I hadn't known what to look for. Maybe I'd find whatever evidence he had on Canty Construction or the mayor there and I'd be able to prove to everyone that the cases were connected and that my dad hadn't simply vanished at sea.

"Come on, boy. We've got work to do."

Orion stood up and shook himself as if he was gearing himself up for a chore.

* * *

The rain that had been threatening finally came as Orion and I drove to Pluma Vista Storage. I lowered the windows a crack. I loved the smell of the first rain after a long time, that scent of the dust being washed away. It would make the corn maze smell funny, but I was too old for corn mazes anyway. The hair on the back of Orion's neck stood up and he growled deep in his throat. "What's the matter, boy?" I asked as I turned on the windshield wipers. His head followed the blades back and forth a few times as if he was at a tennis match and then he barked.

It finally occurred to me that he might never have seen rain before. Spring and summer in this part of the country are notoriously dry. If we had any rain at all, it wouldn't have been much more than a sprinkle. This was the first good soaker we'd gotten. Orion wasn't even a year old yet. It might really never have rained here in his whole life. I reached into the backseat and put my hand on his back and made what I hoped were comforting noises. The barking and growling lowered to more of a whine, then he curled up on the seat.

We pulled into the storage facility. I punched in the code and drove around to the stairs closest to Dad's space. Orion nearly leaped from the car when I opened the door. He sprung out into the rain, snapping his teeth at it. Suddenly, he stopped. He sniffed the ground. He looked over his shoulder at me. I motioned for him to come under the eave where I was standing. "You're getting all wet."

He lifted his head toward the sky and opened his mouth, letting the rain fall on his lolling tongue. Then he did a little doggy dance before following me up the stairs. Apparently, rain was now fine with him. It was good to be flexible.

I got to Dad's space dragging a dolly I'd found at the top

of the stairs, pulled out the key, undid the lock, then pushed up the garage-like door, mentally calculating how many trips I'd have to take up and down to get everything into the Element. No way was I going to go through it all here. Four trips. Five at the most, I thought.

Then the door went up and we stepped inside. It was going to take me fewer trips than I'd thought. The space was completely empty.

*　*　*

Talking to the guy in the office at the storage facility was a complete waste of time. No, he didn't know when the space had been cleaned out. No. He still didn't know who had rented the space, just that it had been paid for in cash.

Rafe called as I drove back to Verbena. "Ready for some good news?" he asked over the swish of my windshield wipers.

"More than ready." Things had been on a bit of a downward swing for the day.

"Our article got picked up by the wire services."

That was good news. That meant people thought it was important enough to spread around. It would reach more people. Get more attention. "Nice," I said.

"And it has apparently triggered a Federal investigation."

Even better. That meant we didn't have to count on Luke to look farther than the end of his nose at anything. It also meant that if there were any connections between Canty Construction and my father, someone would unearth it. "Excellent."

"Does that mean you're now in a good mood?"

A gust of wind rocked the car. Orion lifted his head up and whined. "Why?"

"I have a favor to ask."

"Mm-hmm." I wasn't going to help him.

"You know those great articles you do about the town, the ones that give all the local color and showcase how Verbena is so special?"

I sighed. "Stop buttering me up. What do you want me to do?"

"I want you to interview Tamara Utley about her Ghost Tour."

No way. "Make Vern do it."

"He's swamped right now and he has no nuance and zero sense of whimsy. Please?"

"Why can't you do it?" I sounded almost as whiny as Orion.

"I'm swamped, too. Come on. It's right up your alley. All that small-town charm and stuff."

I sighed. I did love the small-town charm and stuff. I just didn't love Tamara Utley. Dad had really not liked her. It predisposed me against her. Of course, Rafe didn't say the article had to be flattering, now did he? "Sure," I said.

"Great. Meet her at the cafe at four."

"Do I get to expense my coffee?"

"Of course."

"And pie?" I'd almost certainly be hungry by then.

He sighed. "Pie, too. Geez. Get one article picked up by national press and suddenly you're a diva. Good thing you're worth it."

I hung up with a smile on my face.

*   *   *

First, however, I wanted to understand what was going on with Not Vodka Mom. I went back to the elementary school at release time. I parked on a different side street—no need for Nosey McNoserton to call Luke on me again. I knew what I was looking for this time. Orion and I got out and strolled down the sidewalk looking for that blue minivan. The rain had stopped, but the sky was still overcast and a gust of wind flopped one of Orion's ears over to one side. I spotted it about three quarters down the line of minivans and SUVs. When I got there, Not Vodka Mom—still in her athleisurewear, I knew it was too cute to actually work out in—was looking at something on her smart phone. I leaned in the open window on the passenger side. "Something interesting?"

She jumped. I felt a momentary pang. I hadn't liked it much when Luke had done that to me. She put her hand to her chest. "Who are you?"

"My name is Desiree Turner," I started.

"From the funeral home?" She put her phone down. "Are you trying to cause more heart attacks to drum up more business? I mean, I'd heard you guys were having some trouble, but that's pretty tacky."

"I did not cause Reita Giroux's heart attack," I said. "And what do you mean we're having trouble?"

She shook her head. "Never mind. What do you want?"

I took out my phone, pushed play on the video of her pouring vodka into her thermos for her, and held it through the open window.

"Damn it! When I heard Violet had died, I thought this was all over. So is this how you're going to save your funeral home? By taking over Violet Daugherty's blackmail business?" She smoothed her already smooth hair into its ponytail. "Because you can forget about it."

"No!" I said. Why did everyone think I was itching to become a blackmailer? "No. I don't want to blackmail anyone. Can we talk?"

She sighed. "Sure. Get in." She unlocked the door. Orion jumped into the back and I got into the front passenger seat. "Now, please tell me what you really want."

"Where were you on October second?" I asked.

She picked her phone back up and hit the calendar app. "Driving field trip. We went to the Rosicrucian Egyptian Museum in San Jose. They've been studying Egypt. We didn't get back until nearly seven."

"Driving sober?" I asked.

She looked me straight in the eye. "Always sober now. Always."

"Are you diabetic? Or is anybody in your house diabetic?" I asked.

She leaned forward and squinted her eyes at me. "What does that have to do with anything?"

"Just answer the question, please." I tapped my phone with the video on it.

"You know what? Keep that video. Do whatever you want with it. I don't care who knows I had a problem. They probably already knew anyway. I thought I was being so slick. I didn't think anyone knew. People probably suspected, though. It's not like they would have let me drive field trip back then. Oh, no. They would have found an excuse. It was a matter of time before something happened. Something I couldn't get back from." She shut her eyes and took a deep breath. Orion stuck his nose in from the back seat and whined. She opened her eyes and gave him a pat, then reached into her purse and, after a moment of fumbling around, pulled out a token, and held it up. "Violet did me a favor."

"What's that?" I pointed to the token.

"That's my three-month sobriety chip." She tucked it back away in her purse. "Violet blackmailing me was a wake-up call. When I realized how ashamed I was of what I was doing, I knew that I needed help. The day after she approached me with that video was the day I attended my first AA meeting. I've been clean and sober ever since."

"That's impressive," I said.

She shook her head. "Nope. It's all about taking it one day at a time, one moment at a time. Now I'd really like you to get out of my car."

I started to shift toward the door and stopped. "What did Violet want from you?"

A flush crept up her neck. "She made me run her errands."

I almost laughed. "What?"

"She said as long as I was driving around in my van getting my drink on, I might as well pick up her dry cleaning and go to the library and post office for her." She shook her head, making her ponytail bounce.

"You're kidding." Violet had a lot of nerve and she was one of the wackiest blackmailers I'd ever heard of. Code violations at your neighbor's house? Errand running?

"I wish I was. It was . . . humiliating. At least, at first." She shrugged and smoothed the already smooth ponytail again.

Something wasn't quite adding up. "Why did you keep doing it if you'd stopped drinking?"

She hesitated. "I felt like I owed her. I don't know what would have happened if she hadn't made me take a good hard look at myself and what I was doing. Something horrible could have happened." Her voice sounded thick. "I could have hurt someone, my kids, someone else's kids. The drinking was hell on my marriage, too. Violet saved me. She didn't mean to, but she did. Half the time I had errands in the same places she did anyway. It felt like a small price to pay to the woman who made me get my life back."

Two kids with enormous backpacks appeared in the door of the van. "Mom! Did we get a dog?"

Not Vodka Mom shot me a look. "I need you to go before I have real trouble."

I got out of the car. Orion followed. Of course he shook hands with the two kids, which set off a riot of oohing, aahing, and petting him. While the kids were distracted, I turned back to Not Vodka Mom. "Violet might have set you on the path to where you are right now, but you're the one who actually forged the path and stayed on it. It can't have been easy. Remember that before you go giving Violet too much credit for what you did for yourself and your family."

Then we left.

*　*　*

It was time to meet Tamara Utley at Cold Clutch Canyon Café. It was too cold and wet to sit outside and I knew I'd be pushing my luck if I tried to bring him inside. I called Jasmine. "Any chance you're available for some dog sitting?"

"For how long?"

I thought for a second. "No more than an hour or so."

She sighed. "Fine. Bring him over, but I'm not picking up any poo."

"I can work with that."

I scooted into the parking lot across from the house where Jasmine rented office space, gathered up some things, and we went into her office. Orion pranced around her as if she was a long lost relative he'd suddenly found hidden in some couch cushions. "Hey," I said. "Remember that storage space of my Dad's I found?"

"The one with photos of you and Donna and your mom and the little charms and stuff?" She crouched down to let Orion lick her face.

"Yeah, well, it used to be the one with the photos and the charms and stuff. It's empty now."

She looked up at me sharply. Orion licked her chin. "Like someone emptied it?"

I nodded.

"Who?"

"No one seems to know."

She stood. "Desiree, that's weird."

"I thought so, too. I mean, who empties out the mystery storage space of a dead man?" I glanced at my watch. "I've got to go. Can we talk later?"

She nodded. I left her with some treats and a leash and a poop bag just in case and walked over to the Cold Clutch. Tamara was already sitting at a booth in Monique's section, a cup of tea in front of her. She really wasn't the kind of person you'd expect to talk to ghosts. Her hair was gray and short and tidy. She never wore flowy skirts or scarves on her head. I turned over the upside down coffee mug on the saucer at my place and motioned to Monique.

"Nice to see you, Desiree," Tamara said, taking a sip of her tea.

"Lovely to see you, too, Tamara." I pulled out my notebook and a pen. "Shall we get started?"

First, we covered how Tamara had gotten started in the Ghost Tour business. "Not everyone has the sight," she said, folding her hands in front of her. "People aren't aware of how many spirits are around them. They want to know, but they can't see them."

"But you can?" I asked.

She nodded. "Ever since I was a little girl. My parents thought I had a series of imaginary friends. You know, how kids do. Then I walked into my great-aunt's house after she passed and went directly to the empty Folgers can in the back of the cabinet where she'd hidden her diamond earrings. My mother and her sisters had been searching for them for weeks." She smiled.

Okay, then. We moved on to the ghosts of Verbena. It turned out they were all over the place. At the schools. In the churches. Standing around on street corners. And they all talked to Tamara.

"So why do these ghosts contact you?" I asked.

She shrugged. "People have messages. They need someone to communicate them. Once they know I can see them, they pester me until I deliver them."

Yep. Sure. Of course. "What kind of messages?"

"Oh, you know. Different things. Where a key might be hidden. Who to trust. That they love you. That they're okay."

"How often do you get these messages?" I sipped my coffee, not even bothering to pretend to take notes.

"All the time." She folded her hands in front of herself on the table. "I'm getting one right now."

"Who's it for?" I almost rolled my eyes.

"You."

I leaned back and set my coffee cup down very carefully so she wouldn't see that my hands had started to shake. "You have messages for me?" There was one person who might be dead - or might not be - who I would have really liked to hear from. Could Tamara be talking to my dad?

Tamara nodded. "I do. I'm not sure. I understand. But something about thanking you for taking care of the stars."

Well, that made absolutely no sense. That didn't sound like Dad at all. "Who's the message from?"

"I'm not entirely certain. It's a woman. I know that. She passed on recently. Her name is a color."

I knew a recently dead woman whose name was a color whose business I was all up in. The hair on my arms began to stand up. "Violet? Is her name Violet?"

Tamara shrugged. "Possibly. It's hard to know for sure."

The stars? What could she be talking about? Then it hit me. Stars. Constellations. Orion. Orion was the hunter in the winter sky.

My heart raced. I leaned forward. Violet was sending me a message? "Does she have anything else to say?" Maybe she could give us a hint as to who might have shot her up with insulin. Maybe she could tell me who had killed her.

Tamara tilted her head to one side and looked at a spot over my shoulder. I swiveled around to look. There was nothing there except a view of the pie case. "No," she said. "The stars are the only thing that's important. Everything else is trivial, according to her."

I rubbed my arms. If someone had killed me and I had a chance to tell someone about it, I'm pretty sure I'd be naming names. Trivial shivial. "Nothing about what might have caused her accident, then? Nothing about any person or people I should talk to?"

Tamara shook her head then leaned back in the booth. "Sorry. No. She's gone now."

I felt a bit like the air had been let out of me and slumped back, too. "So a lot of deceased people contact you?"

She smiled like it was a treat. "Yes. Quite a few."

"Anyone else I would know?" Could she have heard from Dad? Would she be able to give me some kind of message that could either put my mind at rest or tell me to keep looking?

"Are you asking about someone in particular?" she asked.

I was. She knew it, I was sure. She was going to make me come out and ask, though. "Tamara, have you ever heard from my father? Does he have any messages for me?"

She put her hand over mine. "I'm sorry, but no. I've never gotten one word from your father and I tried to reach him."

"You did?" Dad had never had much nice to say to Tamara. I wasn't sure why she would want to keep talking to him.

"I thought maybe if I could help you find his body, you

could have some closure so I reached out to him. Several times. I used the tarot and the runes and the tea leaves. He never answered. I'm sorry." She really looked as if she was.

So much for hoping that Dad would let me know what was up with the storage space from the beyond even if I didn't think he was actually there. "That was nice of you. You didn't have to do that."

She smiled. "I know. It did occur to me that I'd have a little bit of satisfaction in telling him "I told you so" about whether or not ghosts exist. He was so adamant that they didn't. We argued quite a bit about it."

Well, that made a bit more sense. I couldn't imagine her really wanting to talk to him otherwise. "So you haven't sensed anything about my father."

"No. Not a thing. It's like he's not dead at all." She let go of my hand and finished her tea.

I had enough for my article so we said good-bye. I saw Michelle sitting at another table as I headed to the door. She was busy typing on her tablet. I walked over to say hello. "Hi, Michelle. What are you doing here?"

"Meeting a client," she said, barely looking up.

I was about to leave her to it when Iris Fiore came in and walked up to the table. "Hi, Michelle."

I didn't miss that I was left out of the greeting. I decided the best—and possibly most annoying—thing to do was to pretend like she had actually said hello to me and was happy to see me. "Hey, Iris! How are you? Has Rose decided where she's going next year yet?" I asked.

Iris looked like she might pretend that she hadn't heard

me, but somehow breeding took over. "Not yet." She glanced at her watch. "Should we go, Michelle?"

"You're looking at houses?" I asked.

"Iris is looking into selling her father's place and getting something smaller for herself. She'll be an empty nester next year," Michelle said as she packed up her laptop. "Might as well be in something that doesn't require so much upkeep. She'll probably be able to pull quite a bit of cash out of the house, too."

"Sounds smart," I said.

Iris smiled tightly at me again. "Michelle?" She tapped her watch.

Michelle stood, shouldering her bag. "Bye, Desiree. Stay out of trouble, okay?"

"I'll do my best."

I walked back to Jasmine's office, thinking hard. Jasmine was with a client when I came in. I could tell because she'd put the Do Not Disturb sign on her office door. I went outside to my car to wait. It's a small town. No one wants to see anyone they know in their shrink's waiting room. I sent Jaz a text so she'd know where I was when she was done with her session. I slid down in the seat of the Element and closed my eyes.

I must have drifted off because next thing I knew Jasmine was knocking on the window and Orion was leaping up beside her barking his head off. I scrambled out of the car. "It's okay. I'm okay. It's all right." I held him until he stilled.

Jasmine shook her head. "There is no point in either of

you pretending that you haven't developed a bond. What are we going to do to convince Donna that you need to keep this dog?"

"I'm serious about training him as a therapy dog," I said. "I'm going to sign him up for the puppy training that starts next month." We walked back into her office. She sat down behind her desk.

"He is a natural," she said. "You should have seen him with my client. He just sat down next to him and leaned against his legs. You could watch the guy's tension drain away." She typed on the computer for a moment. "First step then is this puppy class." She pointed at her computer screen.

"Click the button. Let's register him." I reached over her shoulder to do it myself.

She grabbed my wrist. "You sure you want to do that before you talk to Donna?"

I sighed. "I have so many things to talk to Donna about right now that Orion is going to have to be close to the bottom of the list." I walked back around the desk to sit down in one of the big comfy chairs Jaz's clients sat in. Orion came over and put his chin in my lap. "Do you believe in psychic connections?"

I told her about how Reita and known the moment Jordan had died and how Tamara hadn't been able to reach my father in the afterlife. I leaned forward, elbows braced on knees. "I don't know what to think. I never put a lot of stock in all the woo-woo stuff. But maybe there is something to it." I looked up to see Jasmine brush something bright off her cheek. "Are you crying?"

She straightened quickly. "Of course not. Don't be

ridiculous. I, uh, I just have to call Carlotta in a few minutes. Okay?"

I nodded. "Sure. Thanks for dog sitting. See you later." I started to get up.

"Wait, Desiree," she said. "What are you going to do next?"

"I don't know. I don't know where to look next for any connection between Canty Construction and my dad and I'm hoping the federal investigation will turn up something. In the meantime, I need to do a little research for this article I'm writing about Tamara and her ghost tours."

Jasmine got up and came around the desk. She put her arms around me and held me for a second. "We'll figure it out. I'll pump Carlotta for information to see if there's anything in the investigation into Canty Construction's bribes and your dad, okay?"

"That'd be great."

Chapter Nine

The Verbena Free Press
October 12
By Desiree Turner

Annual Ghost Tour Plans in Place

The first time a ghost spoke to Tamara Utley she was only seven years old. She didn't think anything of her dead great-aunt telling her where to find the diamond earrings everyone was looking for. Since then, all kinds of people have contacted Utley to send messages to their loved—and not so loved—ones here on this mortal plane.

"I generally don't pass on anything threatening," she said in a recent interview. "I don't think it's nice."

She will, however, show everyone the best places in Verbena to contact the spirits. Tickets for her popular Verbena Ghost Tour will go on sale starting on October 17. The tour will begin at the Lawn of Heaven Cemetery and range through downtown Verbena to historic sites and contemporary areas where ghosts have reportedly been seen and heard. Meet ghosts old and new and learn a bit about Verbena history at the same time.

The final stop will be at the corn maze. Town legend has it that the maze is built each year on top of the site where Iddell McCrary and Jonas Purdy killed each other in a duel over ownership of a horse in 1898. Utley claims phantom neighs can be heard on nights with a full moon.

Taylor Nieves of Taylor's Corn Maze said, "Every year Tamara tries to drum up more business for her gosh darn ghost tour by telling people my maze is haunted. It's not. There's nothing out there but good old-fashioned dirt and corn."

Further research has not been able to prove that either Mr. McCrary or Mr. Purdy actually lived in Verbena at all.

* * *

Thurman Sizemore had died of an infection that had run rampant through his body.

"They say it started with his tooth," Olive said as she took her usual place.

"Really?" Henrietta said. She clucked her tongue. "How bad do your teeth have to be to kill you?"

"Not even that bad," Grace said. "Think about how close your mouth is to your brain."

Henrietta's hand went to her cheek. "Remind me to buy floss on the way home."

I went to stand next to Thurman's husband. He was a

white man in his midfifties, his head shaved clean. Well, clean except for the very neatly trimmed goatee. He didn't look entirely comfortable in his suit, although it was pressed and neat. "Is everything okay?" I asked.

He jumped as if I'd poked him. "Yes. It's fine. Everything's totally fine."

"Well, let me know if you need anything." I made my rounds, making sure the guest book was out and the right music was playing. Everything was going smoothly. Everything had been going smoothly lately. I hadn't screwed anything up. There'd been no fistfights and no one had tried to climb into a casket. The flowers had been set up were they were supposed to be and the right cookies had been placed on the right platters. So why was he so nervous?

I made my way back to Grace, Olive, and Henrietta. "I guess this is the last time I'll be seeing you three this week. We've had some cancellations," I told my trio of little old ladies.

The three of them exchanged some glances. "So we heard," Grace said and then pressed her lips together in a tight line. I couldn't tell if she was trying to keep more words from slipping out or showing disapproval.

Whichever it was, it made me go cold inside. I'd been hoping the mass cancellations were a coincidence, one of those flukey things that happens from time to time. Based on Grace's expression, that wasn't the case. "What have you heard?"

Henrietta looked at Olive, and Olive looked at Grace who unpressed her lips. "Nobody wants to be accused of murder," Grace said.

"What?" The cold feeling inside spread to my extremities. A very big uh oh was forming in my brain. A huge uh-oh. An uh-oh the size of a redwood.

"Well, apparently you accused Iris and Daisy of giving Frank a little nudge into the grave and now you're running around poking into Violet Daugherty's car accident." Henrietta looked up at me, one eye squinted shut as if she was about to start my portrait.

I sat down next to Olive because my knees felt wobbly. "I didn't accuse Iris and Daisy of anything! I just wanted to be sure everything was okay before Uncle Joey embalmed Frank."

"Why wouldn't it be okay?" Olive asked.

I decided to keep what I'd overheard to myself. It seemed stupid now. "No real reason. Just being extra sure. Doing my due diligence and all that."

"And Violet?" Olive pressed.

"I've been helping out her cousin since she lives so far away." No good deed went unpunished, I guessed. "And I may have found a few things that need a bit more explanation. Nate's not satisfied that it was just a car accident either."

They exchanged looks again. "Do you think someone's been up to no good?" Henrietta finally asked.

I did. Unfortunately, that person was Violet. "Violet Daugherty might have done some things to make her less than popular." I traced the pattern on the carpet with the toe of my sensible pump.

"Dying while unpopular doesn't make you a murder victim," Olive said. "If it did, Luke Butler would be a lot busier."

*   *   *

When I got home from the cemetery, I found Donna and Uncle Joey seated at the kitchen table. It was almost funny to see them across from each other, their profiles with their Norwegian ski slope noses nearly identical. I probably would have at least smiled, but the expressions on their faces told me that wasn't such a good idea.

"Sit down, Desiree," Uncle Joey said. It was a totally different sounding invitation than the one to grab a plate and start eating roast chicken that I'd had the night before.

I sat.

"You have to stop looking into Violet Daugherty's death," Donna said, her voice flat. "In fact, you have to stop looking into any deaths."

That cold sliver of ice that had been in my stomach since Grace, Olive, and Henrietta had made their comments grew into more of a cube. "Where's this coming from?"

"Those cancellations we had? The slowdown in business? It's all about you and your meddling." Uncle Joey leaned back in his chair.

I looked over at Orion. At least now I had a dog to go with my meddling self. "How do you know?" I asked. "Did someone tell you that?"

"Thurman Sizemore's husband told me he was relieved that he wasn't accused of murder before the service was done," Donna said. "And I had a call from Jackson's Funeral Home over in Ardilla asking what was going on. That he was hearing rumors."

"I don't have to tell you how bad your timing is for this,

Desiree. We're being inspected." Uncle Joey looked down at his hands.

This wasn't a small deal. This was our livelihood. "What if I'd been right about Mr. Fiore? What if he had been murdered and it was only because of our thoroughness and interest that anyone found out?" I asked. "Wouldn't that have gotten us good press?"

Donna blinked a few times and then her eyes narrowed. "This is about all the attention you got for solving Alan Brewer's murder, isn't it?"

"Of course not!" I'd gotten more than a few pats on the back for helping find the person who had really killed Alan Brewer, but it had been nerve-wracking and it had taken weeks for my eyebrows to grow back in.

Uncle Joey shook his head. "I don't think it's an attention thing. She just likes to be the person who fixes things."

Donna weighed that for a moment. "I can see that. She had a real thing about fairness the whole time we were growing up."

"Hey," I said. "I'm right here."

They turned to look at me as if that surprised them. I wondered how long they had been sitting at the table talking about me before I came in. "Whatever your reasons, no matter how altruistic or well-meaning, you need to drop all this investigative stuff," Donna said. "Capisce?"

I bit my lip. It's not like I wanted our family business to suffer, but there were questions that still needed to be answered. I told them about going to Dad's storage space and finding it cleaned out. "So if there was something in there that implicated Titus Canty, it's gone now. I just have to figure out where."

"No," Donna said. "That's not your job. The FBI is looking into the corruption. It's their job. Let them do it."

"I can't," I said. "At least, not totally."

Donna knocked her forehead on the table a couple of times. "Why?" she asked. "For the love of God, why?"

"Give me a second. I'll show you why." I went upstairs and got Violet's shoebox of shame and my laptop, came back downstairs, and put it all down on the table.

"What's that?" Donna asked, pointing at the shoebox.

"I found this in a safe hidden in Violet Daugherty's laundry room behind a sign with an Italian saying on it." I flipped the box open. First I put the pictures of the mayor with Titus Canty out for them to see.

"Oh," Uncle Joey said. "That's how you knew. What's the other stuff?" He pointed at the DVDs and thumb drives.

"I haven't had a chance to look through all of it."

Donna pounded her fist on the table. "I don't care. I don't care who did what to whom. All I care about is this family and this business. You need to keep your nose out of everyone else's in the hopes that we can salvage the reputation of this one." He face turned red.

The last thing I wanted to do was get my pregnant sister upset enough that she ended up back on bed rest or worse. I looked over at Uncle Joey. He didn't meet my eyes.

"What's more important to you, Desiree?" Donna gestured at the laptop and the box. "What all these people have been doing that they should have been doing? Or your own family?"

I hadn't thought about it like that. "My family," I said.

"Then you have to drop all this. If Nate feels so strongly that there's something wrong with Violet's death then let him deal with it. No one else cares."

It was true. No one was mourning Violet Daugherty. The more I learned about her, the less I liked her. She exploited people's weaknesses. Even in the case of the mayor's corruption, she didn't use the information she had for good, to protect the community. She used it to torment a neighbor who had spent time, energy, and money into turning a yard into a work of creative genius. When she discovered that someone was driving around town drunk, she didn't move to protect the people who could have been injured. Instead, she had used the information to winnow down her to-do list. In the end, what did it matter how she'd died? Especially if looking into it was going to hurt people I did care about. "Fine," I said. "I'll drop it."

Donna scowled at me. "Promise?"

I held out my hand, little finger extended. "Pinky swear," I said.

She locked her pinky with mine. "Double," she said. We shook.

* * *

I took Violet's laptop and her box o'blackmail and my dog (he was my dog now—no one was going to separate us) up to my room. I called Nate. "I'm dropping the whole Violet Daugherty thing."

There was a pause. "Why?"

I explained about the cancellations and Donna's red face.

"I promised Donna and Uncle Joey I would drop the whole thing."

"Then what am I supposed to do?"

"Give it to Luke. I don't think there's anything else for us to do. He's the police. He's the one who's supposed to investigate murders." Orion jumped up on the bed next to me, turned around once and settled at the foot of the bed. I slipped my feet under him to keep them warm. "Or ask Carlotta."

"Luke doesn't even believe there is a murder. And if Carlotta started investigating something knowing he didn't want it investigated? Well, I can't imagine that would be good for her career. It's got to be us."

"It can't be us. Or, at least, it can't be me." I had double pinky swore.

"So people are dropping you because they think they'll be accused of murder?" Nate asked.

"Pretty much," I said.

"And they think that because you questioned Frank Fiore's death and now are nosing around Violet's death."

"Yes."

"They think that you randomly accuse people of murder."

"Yes. That's the point." I should have put it together sooner. Not Vodka Mom had said something about needing to drum up business. Luke had said something about me pissing people off. It was possible I hadn't wanted to see all the connections.

"Well, I think the best way to disabuse them of that notion is to prove that Violet was murdered and by whom.

Then they'd know that they'd only be accused of murder if they were murderers and your sister doesn't want murderers' business anyway."

It made a certain amount of sense, but only a certain amount. "I don't know. I don't think Donna and Uncle Joey would go for that."

"They don't have to know about it until it's a done deal. Then what are they going to say? That you shouldn't have sought the truth?" he asked.

I knew I was being manipulated. The trouble was that I was being manipulated into doing what I already wanted to do. "You think so?"

"Sure. If you prove that you're not just randomly accusing people of murder, you seem less crazy."

Less crazy was good. I could always use a dose of being seen as less crazy. Plus, if people found out I wasn't crazy about Violet's death, maybe someone would believe me and think I wasn't crazy about my dad either.

"I think you should at least think about it. Sleep on it. We can talk tomorrow. Okay?"

"Fine," I said. "But I'm not changing my mind. You wouldn't either if you could have seen how upset Donna was."

"Tomorrow," he repeated.

Now it was my turn to sigh. "Tomorrow."

We hung up and I stood to pick up the laptop and the box. I stood for a second with the whole armful poised over the garbage can. The little angel on my right shoulder whispered, "drop it." But the little devil on my left whispered, "just take one more peek." The little angel asked, "do you really need to know people's secrets and shames?" The little devil asked, "what if there's more corruption there? More people like the mayor?"

I told the angel that I was only going to look through the rest of the material to be sure there wasn't something I should do that was on the side of the angels. She made a raspberry noise at me then flitted off. Better angels have said a whole lot worse to me in the past. I could take it.

I opened up the laptop and put the thumb drive with all the photos on it into the machine and started clicking. I recognized a few faces, but couldn't figure out what they might be doing that they shouldn't. There was one of Jasmine and Carlotta holding hands as they walked down the street. Did Violet really think that was blackmail material? If so, I almost felt bad for her. It must be uncomfortable to have such a tiny mind. There was a photo of the young woman who had offered me cake at Greg's office sitting at a desk with a metal box in front of her and another of Carol Burston high-fiving a young man right after crossing a finish line at a race. It occurred to me that maybe Violet didn't know what might be wrong with the photos either. Maybe she just went around snapping photos knowing that people being people, at some point someone would do something they wouldn't want anyone else to know about.

I kept clicking. An older man at a grocery store. Maybe he was shoplifting? Who knew? A photo of people at the dog park. Perhaps they weren't picking up after their pets? I clicked more. Then a photo came up that made me freeze. I must have gasped because Orion got up and wiggled closer to me.

It was a photo of my father putting a surfboard on top of

a gray Element in front of a house I'd never seen before. Next to him stood a little girl of maybe ten or eleven.

I slammed the laptop shut as if closing it could erase what I'd just seen. It didn't. When I opened the laptop back up, it was still there. My father might be one of Violet's blackmail victims. Would that mean that my father might have a reason to kill her? There was really only one way to know for sure and that was to figure out who had really done it.

I texted Nate: I changed my mind.

He texted back a smiley face.

Chapter Ten

I didn't sleep much that night. I kept opening Violet's laptop and staring at the photo of my father. It was clearly him. This was no fuzzy security video. It was crystal clear. His back was to the camera, but he was looking over his shoulder at the little girl, the wide happy smile I associated with how he'd look when he saw me or Donna walking into a room plastered on his handsome face.

Then there was the car. Dad loved the Element. This one was gray, not black, but maybe he wasn't being a funeral director anymore. Maybe he toned it down to move onto whatever new life he was apparently leading. Could it be the same gray Element I'd seen in the Cold Clutch Canyon parking lot all those months ago? The one that had been parked there when someone had left a hiking boot charm for me and when I'd felt my father's presence so strongly on the hike that I felt like he was looking over me?

There wasn't any date on the photo. It wasn't too old, though. You could easily see the little bald spot that was starting to form on the back of Dad's head. You could see the laugh lines crinkling at the corners of his eye.

There would be no way Donna could dispute that it was him and that it could easily have been taken since his so-called death. Then I thought about how she'd react when I showed it to her. I thought about her red face the night before and how precarious the balance of her pregnancy seemed to be. No. I needed more than just this one photo to show her.

Where was I supposed to find that one more thing, though? Bleary-eyed and still half-asleep, I shoved my feet into boots and threw on a sweatshirt over my jammies and took Orion outside. He nosed at the gate from the backyard clearly suggesting that we take a walk rather than just taking care of business. "Later," I told him. He sighed, but acquiesced. We went back upstairs where I fed him and then went to get myself ready to face the day.

I took another look at the photo before I got in the shower. I didn't recognize the house or the neighborhood. It wasn't like I knew every neighborhood in Verbena, but I knew most of them. I knew I could probably show Michelle and she'd have an idea, but then she'd see the photo of my father and I wasn't ready to share this information yet. There could be darn good reasons that he didn't want us to know where he was. Until I knew those, I needed to keep this information as much on the DL as I could.

I could see a tiny fragment of the address on the mailbox, but I wasn't sure how the first two digits of a street number were going to help me if I wasn't even sure what town it was in.

Everything was all mixed up in my head. Violet. My dad. Canty Construction. I needed to slow down and think. First things first. Someone injected Violet with insulin. Who has insulin? Diabetics do. Who might have had something against Violet and was also diabetic. I froze, my hands in midshampoo. Someone at Greg's office needed a sugar-free cake. Was it because that would make it diabetic-friendly? Who had he said needed it? The one who offered me cake? Whose photo was in Violet's secret stash?

My first instinct was to leap from the shower, throw on clothes and run to Greg's office. Then I remembered that I was supposed to have dropped all this. I needed to act in a way that didn't arouse suspicion. Screaming into Greg's office with my hair still full of shampoo didn't sound like a good way to do that. There was absolutely no way Greg wouldn't rat me out to Donna either. I finished washing my hair, conditioning it, washing my face and all major body parts, and then leaped out of the shower. I didn't shave my legs. It was like I was a total rebel.

I made myself breathe and breathe deeply as I dried my hair and got dressed. "Wanna go for a walk?" I asked Orion.

He rolled his eyes as if to say he had made that perfectly clear earlier.

"Going out," I called to Donna as I slipped out the kitchen door. If I didn't hear her ask where, I didn't need to answer her, right?

I pulled my fleece jacket tighter around me as we walked. The mornings had gone from crisp to downright cold, at least for this California girl. Leaves swirled around our feet and Orion pranced down the street as if he was on a doggie

If the Coffin Fits

runway. Well, he did until he saw a squirrel and then he took off after it so quickly that he nearly pulled me off my feet. When I finally got him back under control, I gave him a dirty look. "We are so starting those puppy training classes next week."

He jumped up and licked my face. It was impossible not to laugh.

When we finally got to Greg's office, we'd both calmed down a little. I went in, wracking my brain for a reason to ask the questions I wanted to ask.

"Hey, Desiree," Greg said, standing up and coming out from his glassed in office at the back of the space. "What are you doing here?"

I glanced around at the people with their heads bowed over their work, tapping on computers, talking on phones. The woman who had been celebrating her promotion when I'd been here on Monday reached for a stapler on the edge of her desk. The sleeve of her sweater rode up. There was a bandage on her arm.

"Desiree?" Greg repeated.

I snapped back to the moment. "What's the name of the woman who's replacing Violet?"

His face darkened and he motioned to his office with a jerk of his head. I followed him in and he shut the door behind us. He didn't sit down. He turned to face me, hands on hips. "I am under strict instructions to not aid or abet you in any kind of investigations you might be undertaking."

"Who said it was an investigation?" I blinked my eyes, trying to look innocent.

"Your sister. She said you'd still be poking around."

"I'm not poking. I'm asking for the newspaper." I crossed my fingers behind my back. "Rafe likes to congratulate people who've received promotions. It's a nice community-centered thing for a local newspaper to do."

"Oh." Greg blinked and pointed out the window. "Sure. Her name is Rachel. That's her right there. It was a big jump for her, but she's a fast learner."

"Thanks." With a little wave, I left his office then stopped at Rachel's desk. "Hi, Rachel. I'm Desiree Turner."

She looked up from the spread sheet in front of her. "Yes? How can I help you?"

"I was hoping to take a photo of you for a new column we're doing at the *Free Press*. We're going to be congratulating people who get promoted in local businesses. You'd be one of our first subjects."

She blushed. "Really? That's so cool. Sure." She looked around. "Where would you like to take the photo? Over by the sign?" She pointed to a sign on the wall by the water cooler.

No way did I want to ask her the questions I wanted and needed to ask in the middle of her coworkers. "I was thinking of something with a bit more atmosphere. Could we meet after work today? Do you have some nice trees or something in your yard?"

She nodded. "Sure. That'll work."

I got her address from her and we set a time. "See you there," I said and left.

It had been a week since someone had broken into Violet's house, someone looking for something. A week was a long time for a cut to still need a bandage, but not if you were diabetic. They healed a little slower than the regular population. Someone at the office was diabetic. Someone had needed the celebratory cake to be sugar-free. I thought I might have found who had broken into Violet's house and who had tried to break into Turner's. Someone who learned fast from her mistakes like maybe how to break a pane of glass and reach through it without cutting herself. Someone who worked with Violet and might have had reason not to like her too much. Someone with access to insulin.

* * *

I texted Jasmine to see if she was available for coffee. I'd steamed out this morning without a caffeine jolt and there was no way I was going to be able to do everything I wanted to do without some support from my dark mistress. She texted back that she was already at Cold Clutch and to come right over. When I got there, I found her seated outside, bundled up in a wool jacket with a scarf, Carlotta at her side. I waved through the window at Monique who lifted the copper thermos coffee carafe she was carrying and nodded. I sat down with them. Jasmine took a sip of coffee and sighed. "I needed this."

Orion curled up beneath my chair. I was dying to show Jasmine the photo of my father, but I didn't want to do it in front of Carlotta. She was The Man, after all, and I wasn't sure what that photo of my father meant. Had he been mixed up in something illegal? Something that would make him blackmail worthy? Was he still alive? Did Violet Daugherty have proof? Or had he gotten caught up in the Canty Construction conspiracy?

"Long day already?" I asked Jasmine. It was only around ten after all.

"One of a series," she said. "We're heading into my busy time of year."

"I didn't realize shrink work was seasonal," Carlotta said. She was in her police uniform. "Based on my experience, people are crazy year round."

Jasmine looked at her over the rim of her mug as she took another sip. "Holidays are coming."

"It's only October!" I protested.

"Go to the stores. Places already have Christmas decorations out." She spread her hands out as if she was offering me the whole holiday season on a tray.

I grumbled. "I hate that. They should wait until the day after Thanksgiving."

"And people should put their grocery carts back in the cart corral and use their directional before they change lanes, but they don't," Carlotta said.

She was right. Especially on that directional thing. Half the drivers in California felt like using their directionals was tantamount to signaling the enemy. I wasn't always sure they were wrong. "So the second the decorations go up, you get busy?"

Jasmine stretched. "I have clients who go into full-blown panic attacks at the first sight of Santa."

"Because he's terrifying." I didn't know who thought little children would want to hear stories about an old man who broke into their house in the middle of the night.

"You're weird." Carlotta moved her chair a little away from me and, not coincidentally, closer to Jasmine. Carlotta's hand found Jasmine's and they interlaced their fingers.

I shrugged. She might be right. I might be weird, but not because Santa gave me the heebie-jeebies. "So everybody freaks out when they know Christmas is coming."

"Pretty much. Everybody realizes that they're going to have to see those same relatives at Thanksgiving and Christmas or Hanukkah or whatever that they saw last year and that they still haven't dealt with any of the issues that got brought up then."

"Fun."

She smiled. "Actually, it kind of is. Every once in a while, I get someone to look at something in a different way and instead of dreading being with their family, they can at least go in feeling at peace with themselves. Or even better, I manage to give them some kind of coping strategy that works. Families are hard."

"Speaking of family," I said. "Have you ever used one of those genetic testing sites?"

"For what?" Jasmine turned back to me.

"Oh, you know. People do them now to see what their ancestry is or if they're prone to have some kind of disease, but you can click a button to see if you have any relatives around." It was too bad Violet hadn't been able to contact any of those relatives while she was alive. Maybe she'd have had something to do besides take photos of people in compromising positions.

Jasmine's brows went up. "I pretty much know most of my relatives."

"Me, too. I'm living with most of them," I said.

"Besides, you might not always want to find relatives you didn't know you had." Jasmine took another sip of coffee.

"There have been some cases where people have found out things they didn't want to know."

"Like what?" Carlotta asked.

"Like their dad isn't really their dad or that kid in the next town is really their half brother. Like that." Jasmine shook her head.

"That would shake a person up," I said. I thought about that little girl, the one that my father was smiling at in the photo. Did she look like Donna or me? Was there something about the shape of her ears? Or her eyes? Did I have a half sister? Would doing a DNA test help me find out?

"Worse even than a giant blowup Santa at Costco in October," Jasmine said.

Carlotta's radio buzzed. She stepped away from the table to check in.

"I have something I need to show you," I whispered to her.

"What?" Jasmine leaned in, brown eyes wide.

I pointed my chin at Carlotta. "Later. Not in front of the fuzz."

Jasmine's eyebrows went up. "Seriously?"

Carlotta came back, gave Jasmine a quick kiss on the cheek, and said, "Gotta go. They need me down at the station."

"Big trouble?" Jasmine asked.

"No. But they need another pair of hands." She waved as she walked away.

"So spill," Jasmine said as she pulled a small pot of lip gloss out of her bag and reapplied it.

I pulled out the printout I'd made of the photo of my father and set it on the table. A range of emotions moved across Jasmine's face. Confusion. Concern. Consternation.

I'd been through pretty much the same set so I recognized them. "When do you think this was taken?" she asked.

I shook my head. "I'm not sure. There's nothing really to indicate the date."

"Who do you think the girl is?" She lifted up the photo.

"Not a clue." I paused. "Do you think her ears look like mine?"

"Her ears? Why her ears?" She picked up the photo as if she might be able to see the girl's ears more clearly.

"Something Olive said to me about my ears looking like Donna's ears."

"You think if her ears are like yours, she could be your sister?"

"Half sister?"

"Your dad never even dated, although I think there were quite a few ladies who tried. Remember how Chrissy Rinehart was always bringing over casseroles?" she asked.

"I do." I had a lifelong aversion to tuna casserole because of it. Dad had never asked Chrissy Rinehart out that I knew of. He hadn't ever dated that I knew about. I'd never really thought about it. We had been a unit.

"So what does all this mean?" Jasmine set the photo down.

I drummed my fingers on the table. "I'm not sure, but I think I've gone from finding out that a lot of people didn't like Violet to finding out that a lot of people might have had reasons to murder her, but I told Donna and Uncle Joey I'd drop it."

"So that's it? You're going to let it go?"

"I told them that before I found the photo of Dad.

There's some connection there. I don't know what, but I feel like I have to find out." I leaned back in my chair, suddenly cold, rubbing my arms. "This isn't just about Violet anymore."

* * *

I had a few hours before I needed to meet Rachel. Orion and I walked back to Turner's. We were barely in the door when the doorbell rang. Orion and I answered it to find Zenia Morrow back. She had on another power suit. It looked like might have missed a button on her blouse, though. It seemed to be unbuttoned a bit lower than the other times I'd seen her. She seemed a little out of breath, too. I guessed even the Zenias of the world had the occasional bad day. "Zenia, I didn't know you were coming back today." I opened the door wider to let her in.

"Who's this?" she asked, looking down at Orion, who did his standard handshake routine. Before she could say anything about how adorable my dog was, Uncle Joey came jogging down the stairs. "Zenia, come in."

There was something funny in his voice. Something I hadn't heard before. He looked okay. In fact, he looked a little better than normal. He'd trimmed his beard and his hair was combed. He was wearing a blue sweater that made his bright blue eyes pop.

"Joseph." She nodded her head and licked her lips. "Thank you for letting me know you were ready for reinspection."

"My pleasure," he said, come this way.

"Would you like a glass of water or some coffee?" I asked as they walked away from me.

"Not necessary, Desiree," Uncle Joey said over his shoulder. "I've got this."

I went upstairs to tell Donna that Zenia was back.

"That's fast," she said. She was on the couch with her feet up and her laptop open.

"I know. She said Uncle Joey had called her to let her know that we were ready for her to come back." I sat down on the floor and Orion snuggled into my lap.

"You haven't run an ad for that dog yet," she said, barely looking up from her keyboard.

"His name is Orion and do I have to?" I asked. He looked up at her, too, head cocked to one side as if he knew now was the time to be the cutest ever.

She glanced around her screen. "I know he's cute, but a dog, Desiree? That's a lot of work."

"I think he could be a real plus here, Donna. I think he has a future as a therapy dog."

She snorted. "Just because you like to sit with him when you're sad doesn't mean he's a therapy dog."

I didn't push any further. I'd figure out how to win her over to my side. "I wonder what's going on downstairs. Do you think I should go peek?"

"Do you think you can without getting caught?"

"Maybe. Maybe not. I could bring her a glass of water. She looked thirsty when she came in." She'd licked her lips several times as if her mouth was dry.

Donna nodded her approval. "Solid plan. Go give her a glass of water and then come up and report back."

I got a glass of ice water and made my way down the two flights of stairs to the main floor and then headed for the last flight down to the office and embalming area. I could hear their voices, soft and murmuring. Then I heard a little gasp. What had gone wrong? I hurried down the last few steps and turned the corner into the office.

Zenia was half on top of Uncle Joey's desk. Her hair had been released from its tight ponytail and her glasses had been flung aside. I was right. She was seriously gorgeous. Uncle Joey held her, half-inclined, their bodies pressed together in a tight embrace and their lips pressed together in what looked like a seriously passionate kiss. I withdrew back around the corner, hoping that they hadn't heard me. I peeked back around. If they had heard me, it certainly wasn't slowing them down one bit.

I retreated back up the stairs, careful to avoid the squeaky step second from the top. Then I scampered as fast as I could back up to the third floor. I was panting as I skidded into the family room.

Donna looked up from her laptop. "What? She didn't want the water?"

I looked down at the glass still in my hand. "I saw . . . I saw . . ." I couldn't seem to come up with the right words to say next.

"Something nasty in the woodshed?" Donna laughed.

I shook my head hard. "No. Not that. Uncle Joey and Zenia."

"Yes. That's pretty much what you went to see. What were they doing? Going through files? Checking behind the cabinets?"

I drained the glass of water. "They were making out."

* * *

I decided to make myself seriously scarce until I heard Zenia leave. I wasn't sure how I felt about what I'd seen, except that I knew it could never ever be unseen. I couldn't remember Uncle Joey ever dating anyone. Just like Dad. Surely he must have. He was a good looking man with a steady job plus he was actually nice. There really should have been ladies lining up out the door. It had never occurred to me that he would have a love life. Maybe he'd had a whole lot more going on than I knew about. Maybe the Turner men were better at keeping secrets than I'd ever known. What I'd thought was an open book was apparently a locked diary with secret compartments inside.

When it was time to meet Rachel, I let Donna know we were leaving and went out the back, got into the Element with Orion and left. Zenia's car was still sitting in front.

Rachel was just pulling into her driveway in a green Toyota Corolla when I got there. Had she been the one cruising around Violet's neighborhood? I told Orion to stay in the car and walked toward her.

"Hi, Desiree," she said. She pointed at a Maple tree that had started turning red and gold. "Should we do the picture there?"

"That's okay," I said, holding up a printout of the photo I'd found on Violet's thumb drive. "I already have one. Should we print this?"

Rachel stared at the photo in my hand and then lunged toward me, trying to grab it from my hand. I stepped back, wishing that I hadn't left Orion in the car. Of course, who knew how he would react? Maybe he'd take the photo from me and deliver it to Rachel with a handshake. "Give it to me!"

I shrugged and handed it to her. "You can have it. It's a copy."

Her fist came back, once again making her sweater ride up and showing the bandage on her arm.

I pulled my phone out of my pocket, unsure if Luke Butler would be any more help than Orion might be. "Should I call the police?"

Rachel froze. "No. Don't do that. I'll . . . I'll explain it all."

"Including how you cut your arm on Violet Daugherty's back window? Greg said you were a fast learner. Clearly you are since you didn't cut yourself when you tried to break in at Turner's."

Her hand went to the bandage. "How did you know?"

"I didn't. At least, not for sure. Now I do, though."

She shoulders slumped like a wilted sunflower. "You might as well come inside. I'll explain everything."

I shook my head. "I don't think so. I don't want to end up like Violet."

"What do you mean?" She set her groceries back down.

"I mean I don't want someone to murder me for whatever this photo means." I waved the printout again.

Rachel staggered back a step. "Murder? Violet died in a car accident."

"A car accident caused by someone injecting her with insulin so she'd pass out behind the wheel." I cocked my head to one side. "You're diabetic, aren't you? You're why the

196

office had sugar-free cake. It takes you a little longer to heal, too. You have access to insulin."

Her hands went to her mouth. "This is crazy. Absolutely totally crazy. I did one little thing wrong. One tiny thing that I was going to make up for right away. But before I can do that, I get blackmailed and now I'm being accused of murder?" Her voice wobbled. She was about to cry.

Clearly, I was getting somewhere. "Why don't you tell me about the tiny thing? The thing that started this all? What did you do, Rachel?"

Rachel smacked her head. "You don't know? You don't actually know anything?"

"Well, I know a little something now. I know Violet was blackmailing you. You might as well tell me the rest of the story." I crossed my arms over my chest.

A single tear leaked out of Rachel's eye and trickled down her cheek. Her mascara didn't run. Aren't pretty criers the worst? No mercy. "I only borrowed the money to get us through a really bad week," she said.

"Where did you borrow the money from?" I asked.

"Petty cash. It was sitting there. No one was going to need it. It was Friday afternoon. Nearly everyone was gone. Jimmy was out of work then and we were barely scraping by. I didn't think anyone would even notice if I took a few twenties so we could buy groceries and gas." She stopped for a second, trying to compose herself.

That would take quite a few twenties, but I decided to keep my mouth shut about that. "So you stole the money from petty cash."

"Borrowed," she said. "Only borrowed. I was going to pay it back as soon as I got my next paycheck. Seriously."

"So you left a note? An IOU?" If she had, why would Violet have anything to hold over her head?

She looked down at her feet. "Not exactly."

"How did Violet find out?" I asked.

She looked back up at me with narrowed eyes. "Violet found out everything. If you made a typo on a letter, she'd find out and tell the whole office about it. If you were five minutes late, she'd notice and make sure everyone else did, too. If you forgot to file a piece of paperwork, she'd somehow know. I thought she'd already gone home like everybody else, but no, she was lurking around somewhere in back and saw the whole thing."

"So she figured out that you had 'borrowed' money from the petty cash." I made air quotes around borrowed. "But she didn't tell everybody else? She only told you?"

Rachel nodded. Her chin trembled a bit. "She said that she'd gotten a kit from the Internet and taken fingerprints off the box, too. She said she'd be able to prove it was me and that I'd get fired and that I'd probably never get a decent job again because no one wants to hire a thief."

Whoa. That seemed a pretty harsh way to deal with a coworker who was down on her luck. Stealing the money was wrong, but a person could have a little empathy. It did explain the fingerprint card in Violet's receptacle of regret. It seemed a little far-fetched, though. "Wouldn't lots of people's fingerprints be on the petty cash box?"

"Maybe. I couldn't take that chance. My paycheck was

the only money coming into the house. We couldn't both be out of work." Another tear leaked down her cheek.

"What did Violet want from you?" It couldn't have been money since Rachel clearly didn't have any. If she had had some, she wouldn't have needed to 'borrow' it from petty cash.

"She wanted my time." She pressed her lips together. "Anytime Violet needed someone to cover the phones so she could go out, I had to say yes. Anytime someone needed to work on a weekend to get a special project done, I had to volunteer. If she wanted to take a vacation day to turn a three-day weekend into a four-day weekend, I had to cover her desk."

"Why didn't you look for a different job?" I asked. It seemed the simplest way to deal with a bad situation with a coworker.

"She said she'd make sure that anyone thinking about hiring me would know about the petty cash, too." She wiped her cheeks with the edge of her sleeve.

Something occurred to me. "You'll be covering her desk permanently now, won't you? You got promoted into her spot."

A small smile played over Rachel's lips. "Yes. I did. Turns out everyone noticed how I was always the first to volunteer to help out and the first to stay late or take over a last-minute project. Greg said I was a team player and that I was the kind of person they wanted to promote."

I shook my head. "So Violet kind of did you a favor." An echo of Not Vodka Mom's comment played in my head. Was Violet the worst blackmailer ever? Or the best?

"Not that she meant to! Stupid cow." Rachel kicked the tire of her car.

Most people stopped short of speaking ill of the dead. I'd seen plenty of funeral services where I knew the deceased was a miserable SOB, but everyone found something nice to say anyway. To actually name call the dead? That showed a pretty high level of hatred. Rachel could totally have done it. She could have administered the insulin somewhere, somehow. We'd definitely established motive and means. Now to nail down opportunity. "Did you see Violet at all on the day she died?"

"Of course. We worked in the same office." There was an implied 'duh' in her tone that I didn't care for.

"What would happen if you'd injected Violet with your insulin before she left work that day?" I asked.

Rachel reared back. "She'd have gone into shock almost right away. I use regular insulin. It works within minutes."

I thought for a moment. Violet hadn't crashed her car until seven-thirty PM. "When did you last see her that day?"

"You really expect me to remember that?" she asked, rolling her eyes.

"Yeah. I do. Especially if you don't want to be accused of murder."

She shook her head. "No. No way. I didn't. I wouldn't. Not ever."

"Really? This woman was blackmailing you. You had to have been angry. Plus, we know you're a thief. You clearly don't have much respect for the law." I pushed.

She gasped. "Stealing a little bit of money from petty cash and killing someone are two very different things, don't you think?"

I did, but there was still at least a little connection. "A felon is a felon is a felon," I said.

She snapped her fingers. "Wait. I worked late that day. I had to deliver some papers to a client. Isaiah Causey. He talked my ear off. I remember because I heard about the car accident on the radio when I was on my way home, but I didn't know it was Violet until the next day."

I made a face. Old Man Causey was a sweet guy, but he was a talker. If you let him get his hooks in you, you were sunk. It could be hours before you could extricate yourself.

"Yeah. Exactly," Rachel said, interpreting my facial expression correctly. "Nobody wanted to deal with him. Violet gave me the side eye and I volunteered. I delivered the papers and then he went into one of his stories about when he was a kid. It was nearly eight when I got home. I couldn't have done it."

"So you say." It was a nice story, but right now it was only a story.

"I'm pretty sure Mr. Causey will back me up on this one. Go ask him." She crossed her arms over her chest, a triumphant look on her face. "Or ask Greg. He'll know."

"Fine," I said. "But don't go anywhere."

She laughed. "You're the one who should go somewhere before that dog eats your entire car."

I whirled around. I couldn't see exactly what Orion was up to, but it didn't look good. I ran to the car. A substantial corner of the back seat of the Element was gone, chewed to within an inch of its life. "What did you do?" I asked Orion.

He glared at me in return.

"Did you chew the seat up? Bad boy!" Apparently, Orion

didn't like to be left in the car when I went some place and wanted to make sure I knew it.

He barked.

"You're talking back to me?"

He barked twice.

Grumbling, I gathered the bits of foam and fabric that he'd shredded all over the back seat to put in the garbage. As I scooped, I saw something out of place, something white and thin. Something paper. It was an envelope, or at least what was left of one after having been chewed within an inch of its life. I could make out parts of the address on it. It must have been wedged down in the seat. I got into the car next to Orion and ran my fingers along the crease of the back seat. He stuck his tongue in my ear. "Usually I expect a guy to buy me dinner before I let him do that," I told him.

He licked my nose.

I wiped my face and went back to the fold of the seat, finally hitting on the rest of the envelope. I teased it out, careful not to tear it anymore. I managed to get it out in two pieces. I took the partially chewed one and the two he hadn't chewed on and laid them out on the part of the seat that hadn't been eaten. The name on the envelope was Quinn. The last name wasn't readable anymore. I could see a few street numbers. A two and a four. The first three letters of the name of the city were still legible, too. Lag. Like Laguna Palma?

Laguna Palma was where Violet lived before she moved to Verbena. Two and four were the two numbers visible on the mailbox in the photo of my father. Laguna Palma wasn't all that near here. It was at least a two-hour drive toward the coast.

I didn't know where the envelope had come from and I'd been pretty much the only one to drive the Element since Dad disappeared. Had the envelope belonged to him? The cops had been over and over this car. Of course, the chief cop who had done that was Luke Butler and I wasn't feeling all that good about his thoroughness right now. I'd been over it, too, but this envelope had been jammed really deep down into the seat. I'm not sure anyone would have ever seen it if Orion hadn't chewed it all up.

I patted him on the head. "Good boy."

He licked my nose again.

I got into the front of the Element, considering my next move. What ifs ping-ponged around in my brain. What if Violet had seen my father in her hometown of Laguna Palma and had also seen him on the news? If she'd done any research on Verbena before moving here, she might well have seen news reports about him. There were also all those missing posters and ads we'd sent far and wide right after he disappeared. Knowing Violet, she wouldn't have told us or the police about it. She would have found something she wanted from Dad. What if her working in Greg's office wasn't a coincidence? What if she'd tried to find a job here in Verbena with a connection to us? We weren't hiring at the funeral home. Maybe that was the only spot she could find where she might be able to keep an eye on what we were up to.

My cell phone rang. It was Donna. "What's up?"

She sighed. "Reita didn't make it. Can you pick her up at the hospital?"

* * *

203

Poor Reita. She looked even smaller inside the body bag. I'd gone home, switched out the Element for the van and gone to the hospital. I didn't bother Uncle Joey. I could handle the pick up on my own and, frankly, I wasn't quite sure I could look him in the eye yet. Once I got her back to Turner's, I called Nate to let him know we'd picked her up.

"I hope you don't mind hosting the autopsy," he said. "She was going to your place eventually no matter what. I figured it would be easier."

Since business was still slow, it didn't seem to matter much. I told him what I'd found out about Rachel, too.

"Now that I think about it, Rachel was right when she said Violet would have reacted within minutes. It doesn't make much sense with slow-acting insulin," he said. "It works slowly enough that it would make her woozy, but I don't think it would make her pass out behind the wheel."

"Whoever injected her had to have done it just a little bit before she crashed?" I asked.

"Yes."

"So what we really need to do is figure out where Violet was right before her accident. Whoever injected her must have done it there." I tapped my pencil against the desk.

"How do you anticipate doing that?"

"I have the calendar on her phone and on her computer. I'll look it up. Call you back in a bit?"

"Sure."

I fired up her computer and her phone. Then wilted. There was nothing on her computer for the Monday she had her accident. Nothing at all. For all I knew, she'd spent that Monday sitting on her couch in her jammies eating popcorn and watching movies. Wait. That wasn't true. I knew she'd gone to work that day. Rachel had mentioned it. Violet had been the one to send her off to see Old Man Causey.

Of course, we all do lots of things that we don't put on our calendars. We grocery shop and do laundry and go to work. None of those things ever get put on a calendar. I chewed my lip.

I opened Violet's Facebook account, looking for a pattern that I might be able to figure out for what she did on Monday nights. I scrolled backward through her timeline. A listicle about tweets your dog would send if he had thumbs. A recipe for eggplant parmesan. An ad for an exercise skirt with ruffles that was perfect for Zumba.

Zumba. Violet was a member of a Zumba Facebook group. That would imply a certain amount of commitment to the class. It would be something a person would do on a regular basis, but wouldn't put on their calendar. I dug Violet's keys out and looked at the tags on them. Sure enough. There was one of those tags that you scan as you walk in and out of a place. It was for Verbena Fitness.

I went to the Verbena Fitness website and clicked on their schedule for group classes. Zumba was on Monday nights at six. Violet crashed her car at around seven-thirty. I clicked open a map of Verbena and found Verbena Fitness. It was on the opposite side of town from Violet's house. It would make sense for her to cut around town on County Road 202 where she'd crashed to avoid going through town. It was a longer route, but would probably cut five minutes or more off the time it took.

I had one more thing to look up on the computer before

I was ready to move on. I typed in Laguna Palma to the map program. First I looked up all the streets that started with "Wh." There were five: Whaler, Whittier, Whistler, White Sands, and Whispering Pines. Then I looked to find houses whose street numbers ended in a two and a four. It took a while. Hours, in fact. But I found it.

The address was 5724 Whittier. I looked at the street view. It was the same house in the photo of Dad that I'd found in Violet's collection.

Someone had killed Violet Daugherty. I was sure of it. Nate was sure of it. They might not have shot her with a gun or stuck a knife in her, but they created a situation where she would almost certainly come to harm. What's worse was that whoever did it, didn't care about how many other people might be hurt in the process. Violet didn't hit anyone, but she could have. She could have triggered an accident that would involve any number of people just trying to get from one place to another on a Monday night.

No one was looking for justice for Violet. All her friends were online. She had no family to speak of. No wonder she was searching for some place to belong with all those Facebook groups and e-mail lists. I'd spent a lot of time trying to get away from the family and the community that laid claim to me. I'd had that luxury, knowing that they'd always be there, no matter what. I could leave for decades, but I'd always be welcomed back in Verbena and back at Turner Family Funeral Home. What would it have felt like not to have that in my life? How lonely and insecure Violet must have been?

Well, I cared. Maybe I didn't care a lot about Violet, but

I cared about Verbena. There was someone out there who did this thing right here under our noses. It was likely that the person lived in Verbena. Walked alongside us. Shopped alongside us. It wasn't the kind of person I wanted in my community. If no one else was going to step up and do something about it, I would.

Chapter Eleven

Nate came the next day to do Reita's autopsy. I waited patiently for him to finish. Okay. Not all that patiently. Orion and I went for a walk. We paced. We played ball. Finally, he came out and sat down in an office chair by the desk I usually sat at when I worked in the Turner office.

"So what happened to Reita?" I asked.

He sunk down the chair. "It sounds crazy, but it's like her heart literally broke." There was a catch in his voice. "There's nothing else wrong with her. She's in great shape, unlike her husband. No underlying problems I could find anywhere. Her heart just stopped working."

I told him about her saying she had felt it when Jordan had died.

He shook his head. "I think that's almost unbearably sweet, but I don't think Reita sensed when her husband died. Who knows what really happened? Maybe a big truck drove by and shook the house a bit and it's a coincidence that it was at the same time her husband fell to the floor."

"That seems like a really tortured way of explaining it all.

Wouldn't it be simpler if we accepted their connection and that she felt it when he died? That we would all feel it if someone really close to us died?" I scooted the chair I was in closer to his.

"You can explain it however you want," he said. "I'm sticking to my version."

"But you think a heart can break?" I asked.

"Of course it can. Grief is stressful. Stress causes things like heart attacks."

"You kill the romance in everything." I pushed my chair back away from his.

He caught the bottom of it with his foot and pulled me back toward him. "Everything?"

Heat blossomed on my face. "Nearly everything."

A few minutes later, I pushed away from him. I wasn't ready to recreate the Uncle Joey and Zenia Morrow scene I'd stumbled on the other day. "I think I figured out where Violet would have been right before her accident on Monday."

"Your idea of sexy talk needs some work." He let his hands drop off my waist.

I laughed. "Solving murders doesn't make you hot?"

"Well, when you put it like that . . ." His hands went back to where they'd been and there was less talking for a minute or so. Then apparently his curiosity got the better of him. "So where was she?"

"Verbena Fitness. For a Zumba class."

"What the heck is Zumba?" Nate asked.

I tried to figure out how to describe it. "It's like aerobics, but more dance-y."

His eyebrows went up. "Dance-y?"

"Yes. Dance-y. Keep up. I'm not sure that matters. What matters is that it was at the gym."

"Why does that matter?"

I thought about those photos of the woman and man on the lat pull. It made sense that it had taken place at the gym. "If I show you, you will never look at a weight bench the same way again." That would be a bit more sexy than I thought either of us was ready for.

*　　*　　*

I was dying to drive to Laguna Palma and cruise past the house in Violet's photo, the house with the address that might be on an envelope that had been jammed deep behind a seat in my father's car. There was no way to do it that weekend, though. With Reita's autopsy and then her service the following day, I didn't have any five-hour blocks of time to make it there and back. Plus, I wasn't sure what I would find there. It might take a lot longer depending on what I saw when I got there.

I'd decided to check out Verbena Fitness closer to the time that Violet would have been there on Monday so I was kind of stalled on that investigation, too. I called Jasmine to see if she wanted to meet me at the Zucchini Carving Competition. She did. Then I texted Rafe to let him know I was going and I'd cover it for the paper. He texted back that he'd be there anyway since he was one of the zucchini bake-off judges, but he'd appreciate the back-up.

The first Zucchini Carving Contest took place in Verbena in 1957. According to town legend, the year before Ella Whitehead found a four-foot zucchini in a neglected corner of her garden and wanted to share it with neighbors and invited people to her home to carve up the monster squash. The event was so enjoyable, she purposely grew a five-footer the next year and a tradition was born. Participants are judged on intricacy, originality, and spookiness. There are also zucchini baking contests, booths about the history of zucchinis, and pretty much anything else zucchini-related you can think of.

We only had one appointment scheduled for the day. Annamarie Oh was scheduled to pick up her husband's ashes. Not everyone actually comes to pick ashes after a cremation. They're not sure what to do with the ashes and as time goes on the actual disposal of them seems to matter less and less. We had an entire area of the house with shelves where urns full of people waited for someone to come get them. We couldn't do anything with them. We just had to hold them. I was pretty certain that some of them had been there before I'd been born. By law, we only had to hold onto them for four years, but Uncle Joey read about a case where a woman showed up to pick up her great-grandfather's ashes seventy years after his death. "Imagine how bad we'd feel if we had to tell the person we had scattered them ourselves," he'd said.

I figured it was about a fifty-fifty chance that Annamarie wouldn't show up. I would have put the odds even lower that she'd show up in her bike gear with twenty-five or so other people all similarly garbed. Shows what I knew.

"We're here for Blaine," she said standing out on the front porch.

"Blaine!" The group yelled in unison.

I looked over them. It was like a human cloud of confetti with all the brightly colored bike jerseys. Each one also had a ribbon pinned over their hearts. It took me a second to make it out, but the ribbons all read: Blaine Oh with a birth and death date. "Right," I said. "Do you want to come in."

She shook her head. "That's okay. There are kind of a lot of us."

It was hard to argue that as they spilled down the front porch steps and out into the yard. Men. Women. All colors. All sizes. All here to honor their friend. "So what exactly are you planning on doing."

"I'm going to ride at the back of the peloton and release his ashes bit by bit as we ride the hills out there." She pointed to where the Vaca Mountains rose up from the flat land of the valley.

"Uh, okay. I'll just go get him then." I turned to go back inside.

"Desiree," she said stopping me.

"Yes?"

"Is Orion here? Could I see him?" She clasped her hands in front of herself like a little girl asking for a special Christmas present.

"Sure." I whistled and in a few seconds he came trotting down the stairs. Annamarie knelt down on the porch and he approached her, tail wagging so hard his whole back end wiggled.

The peloton shouted, "Dog!"

Within seconds, he had disappeared into the crowd of bikers.

I went back inside and got the urn with Blaine's ashes in

them and came back upstairs. It took me a second to get Annamarie's attention, but when I finally did, she stood and moved out of the throng around my dog. I handed the urn to Annamarie. She looked inside and pulled out the plastic bag that contained the ashes. "Perfect," she said. "I can snip a tiny hole to let them slip out as we ride. He loved feeling the wind rush past him. Now he'll be part of the wind." She choked up a bit and lowered her head.

I put a hand on her shoulder. "It's a lovely way to honor his memory. Do be careful of the disc, though."

"Disc?" She lifted her head. Her eyes were wet.

"There's an identification tag in there. You should hang onto it. Otherwise someone might find it and turn it in and then things get complicated. Also, if you end up on anyone's private property, make sure you have permission, okay?" I glanced over her shoulder to make sure Orion wasn't getting overwhelmed. He looked like he was laughing. I couldn't stop the smile on my face.

Annamarie threw her arms around me. "Thank you so much, Desiree. I'm so glad I picked Turner from that list the hospital had. You've helped so much."

I started to protest. I hadn't even given her a ride home on the day her husband died. She stopped me before I could utter a word.

"I mean it. You've let me mourn in my own way, in my own time. It means a lot." She turned to face her friends. "Are we ready to ride?"

A cheer went up and they all clicked down on the steps on their bike cleats out to the bicycles they'd lain down on the lawn. I stood by Orion, holding his collar gently to make sure he didn't chase them. Then they streamed down the driveway, calls of "left!" echoing from the front of the peloton to the back.

In a few minutes, they were gone. Blaine would be carried away on the wind he loved and I hoped Annamarie would find some peace.

* * *

Orion and I met Jasmine and Carlotta in front of the gazebo. A pack of children ran by us squealing, trailed by long green balloons painted to look like zucchinis. Orion strained at his leash to chase after them. I gave him a look and he sat. I pulled a treat from my pocket for him.

"You're good with him," Carlotta said. It was funny to see her out of uniform. Everything about her changed. Her hair was loose instead of pulled back into a bun. She had on makeup. Her whole posture seemed different. Less stiff. Less erect. Her head was still on a swivel, though. I supposed that was instinctual.

"He's easy." I smiled down at him and he smiled back.

We started touring the booths set up around the square. The historical society had a series of posters detailing the history of the zucchini from its start in Mexico and South America, to its development in Italy, and its appearance in North America in the 1920s. The high school science club had a series of zucchini-based science projects including a zucchini-powered clock and a cross-pollinated zuash. There was also an information placard explaining why the zucchini was a fruit and not a vegetable. I snapped a photo of Rose Fiore explaining the clock to a wide-eyed kid. She smiled and waved. Maybe their whole family didn't hate me. That would be nice. The high school band had made horns out of zucchini stems and were performing a spirited rendition of "Werewolf of London" with pumpkin drum accompaniment. I recorded a bit of it on my phone. It would be a nice addition to the *Free Press* website. Rafe was always looking to maximize our digital content.

We toured the actual zucchini carving entries. "That submarine is intense," Carlotta said as we walked through.

"It's good, but a little on the nose, don't you think?" Jasmine said. "I kind of favor the Noah's Arc with all the little zucchini animals stuck to it."

"Do you think it's more of an assemblage than a carving?" I asked. "It could get disqualified on a technicality."

Carlotta shook her head. "It's a vegetable carving contest. Not an Olympic event."

"I think we all learned a little bit ago that it's actually a fruit carving contest," I corrected.

"Still not the Olympics," Carlotta said.

We rounded a corner and made it to the zucchini baking contest booth. Rafe and Nate stood behind the table, face to face and clearly not happy with each other. Nate pointed at a pyramid of zucchini brownies, his long fingers making stabbing motions toward them. Rafe threw his hands in the air and then pointed just as vigorously at a zucchini Bundt cake. Bernadette Kim physically pushed them apart, whispering furiously at them.

"Uh oh," Jasmine said.

Carlotta's posture changed. She still had on makeup and her hair still waved around her face, but she squared her shoulders and planted her feet. She was out of girlfriend mode and back in cop mode. "Excuse me," she said, striding over to the trio.

I snapped a few photos although I doubted Rafe would ever let them be published. At least, not in his paper. Carlotta stood between the two men, speaking quietly. There was a stillness to her that gave her even more of an air of authority. Then she took a bite of a brownie and then a sample of the cake. Her brow furrowed. She reached for something with cream cheese frosting and sampled that. She spoke again to Rafe and Nate. They each sampled that cake, conferred, and then shook hands. Bernadette Kim lifted the blue ribbon and announced it would be going to Vera Figueroa's zucchini-carrot cake.

Carlotta rejoined us. "Those two would fight over a burned out light bulb."

"Not destined to be besties?" Jasmine asked.

"Not in this lifetime." Carlotta shook her head and glanced over at me. "And I think we all know why."

*   *   *

Reita's service was on Sunday. I put on my funeral director clothing and went downstairs to check on Uncle Joey. I hadn't really had a chance to talk to him after seeing him with Zenia macking for all he was worth on his desk.

I didn't remember Uncle Joey ever dating. I didn't remember Dad ever dating. Somehow, in my mind, I never really thought about whether or not they might be lonely, whether or not they might want someone special in their lives. Had not thinking about that, not acknowledging that led my father to need to stage his own death to go be with someone? The thought pained me on so many levels.

Uncle Joey was just finished putting the last touches on Reita as I got downstairs. "Hi, Desiree. Everything ready upstairs?" he asked.

I nodded, trying to come up with a way to say what it was I wanted to say to this man who I'd counted on my whole life. I traced my finger along the wood grain of the desk outside the embalming room.

He looked up, seeming startled that I was still there. "Is there something wrong?"

I shook my head. "No. Maybe."

He set down the makeup brush he had been using and waited, quiet and patient, big and solid. The calm strong pillar whose support I'd taken for granted my whole life.

"Nate said Reita's heart just broke," I said.

Joey nodded. "I know."

"It's like she loved Jordan so much that her heart broke as we buried him." I bit my lip, not quite sure how to take this to the place I needed to go.

Joey waited.

"It's sad, but also beautiful that that kind of love exists."

He still didn't say anything.

"I just wanted you to know that I think love is great and that if a person has a chance at love, they should go for it. They shouldn't worry about what other people think or how they might react. And if they might be wondering how I would react, I would hope they would know that I would be happy for them." I felt something wet on my cheek and brushed a tear away. Damn it. I was turning into a big cry baby.

"Thank you, Desiree," Uncle Joey said. "I will take that under advisement."

I nodded and went back upstairs to finish setting up for Reita's service.

Chapter Twelve

On Monday afternoon, I loaded Orion into the Element and drove over to Verbena Fitness on Meadowlark Lane.

In the gym's entry area, someone had set up a little memorial notice about Violet letting people know she'd passed away. There was a photo of her with Orion and a suggestion to make donations to the SPCA in her name. Violet had been a nice-looking woman. Maybe a little more on the handsome side than the pretty with a strong Roman nose and a cleft chin, dark eyes and dark hair. There had been a place for people to write remembrances, but some had been scribbled over. That seemed rude. I craned my neck to try to see if I could figure out what had been written from another angle.

"Were you a friend of Violet's?" a voice asked next to me.

I turned. A woman wearing a lot of Lycra with her hair pulled back in a ponytail bounced a bit on her sneakered feet behind me. "Oh, hi. No. Not really. I mean, I never met her."

She pointed to Orion and then to the notice. "Isn't that her dog?"

Awkward. "It is. I'm taking care of him for a bit until her cousin decides what to do with him." I was surprised at how easily the lie rolled off my tongue. Orion wasn't going anywhere.

"How'd you get roped into that?" She shifted her gym bag to her other arm and tossed a small towel over her shoulder.

"The cousin lives really far away and I told her I'd help her with some of the details until she could get here." Finally, I got an angle where I thought I could make out what was written under the scribble. I took a step back, shocked. "Did that say what I think it said?" I asked, pointing at the sign.

The woman pressed her lips together. "People have no propriety anymore. I know Violet wasn't the most universally liked person, but writing that on a public expression of sympathy is pretty tacky."

I had to agree. You had to really not care about social niceties to scrawl "Good Riddance" on an In Memoriam poster. "Tacky is one word for it." I could think of a few others. Disrespectful. Mean-spirited.

"Sometimes you reap what you sow," she shook her head making her ponytail bounce again.

Now we were getting somewhere. "Violet wasn't nice?" Orion walked over and nosed at the memorial. He whined. He'd been such a fun companion, it hadn't occurred to me that he might miss Violet. Say what you would about her, she was clearly crazy about her dog. I knelt down to put my arm around him. He'd been there for me these past few days when I was sad. It seemed like the least I could do was return the favor.

The woman gave me a weird look. "Who are you again?"

I stuck out my hand. "Desiree Turner. I work for Turner Family Funeral Home. We're handling her services and I'm trying to give some extra help to Violet's cousin. She seems really stressed out."

She shook my hand. "Laverne Cason. I teach the Zumba class Violet used to take." She looked around as if to see if anyone was listening. "Things always seemed to happen to people who crossed Violet."

I straightened. "Like what things?"

She pressed her lips together. "I feel like I've already said too much, but I know one woman who beat Violet for a parking spot and ended up in divorce court after someone sent compromising photos to her husband."

I was pretty sure I knew who that could be. "Were you teaching on that Monday? The day it happened?"

Laverne nodded and her expression changed. "The day she had her accident was the last time I saw her. So sad."

"Did you notice anything out of the ordinary? Anything that might explain why she might have fallen asleep or passed out in her car?" I asked.

Laverne furrowed her brow. "Come to think of it, she was a little extra sweaty when she was getting in her car in the parking lot. I noticed because she hadn't been sweaty in class." She made a face. "She was almost never sweaty in class."

That was interesting. Hadn't sweatiness been one of the symptoms that Nate had mentioned? On the other hand, it was pretty normal to leave the gym sweaty, although apparently not for Violet.

"Why do you want to know?" Laverne asked.

"Oh, just trying to figure out why she passed out behind the wheel. It seemed weird. You know, perfectly healthy woman passes out and crashes," I said.

"I guess," Laverne said. She glanced at her watch. "I should probably go in. I need to get set up."

I'd called to request a tour a little before Violet's Zumba class was scheduled to meet. I waited until Laverne had already disappeared into the back to walk up to the desk. A young white man with seriously huge biceps looked over the counter at Orion. He had short blond curly hair and a name tag that read Ty. "No pets," Ty said. Apparently he hadn't looked too closely at the memorial sign.

I didn't want to leave Orion in the car. I couldn't afford to buy that many more seats. "He's a therapy dog," I blurted out. "An emotional support animal."

Ty came around the counter and Orion, bless his heart, offered up his paw to be shook. "Aw," said Ty. "So like you have to have him with you or you'll like freak out?"

"Totally," I said.

"Okay, then. I guess I could make an exception. Especially for such a cute support animal." He gestured for me to follow him. He took me through the group exercise room where Zumba class would start in thirty minutes. "We also have yoga, step aerobics, and bootcamp classes."

Then he took me down the hall to show me the room with the treadmills, then the Nautilus machines and then the free weights. As we walked along, I spotted a display of photos. "Our Personal Trainers." I recognized one of them. This photo was an 8 × 10 of his face, which I have to say I preferred to some of the other views I'd had of him on the lat pull. His name was Brice. I scanned the rest of the faces, but couldn't find his lifting partner.

The weight room didn't look quite the same as the one in the photos I'd seen. "Is this the only weight room you have?" I asked. "Are there any that are more . . . private?"

When Ty gave me a funny look, I reached down to pet Orion and said, "I'm shy."

He nodded. "There's a private one where the trainers can work out with their clients. You know, just one on one. Wanna see it?"

I did and when I did, I'd found the spot where Brice had that very private one on one time with whoever his partner was. We walked through a room with bikes and Ty suggested I take a look through the women's locker room on my own and then meet him back at the desk. I did.

"So what do you think?" Ty asked. "Wanna join?"

"I'll have to think about it, Ty. Thanks for the tour, though!" I glanced at my watch. It was the perfect time to go outside and watch who was coming in and out of the gym at the time that Violet would have been going in.

We said good-bye and Orion and I turned to leave. A small group of women stood outside the aerobics room with Laverne. I recognized a few of the people including Iris Fiore. I hadn't known she went here. Laverne then pointed over at me. The group all swiveled around. I waved and ducked out. I had no desire to have any more conversations with Iris. She looked daggers at me every time I ran into her, which seemed to be happening a lot lately. It was kind of like learning a new word and then suddenly seeing it everywhere. It must have been there all along, you just didn't notice it. I could see not noticing Iris. She was one of those women who could kind of fade into the woodwork. It had even happened at her father's funeral. Everyone had flocked around Daisy. Iris had stood on the edge of the circle.

I didn't have much time to think harder on that because as I walked out of the gym, I walked smack dab into the woman who'd been doing extra special aerobics with her personal trainer and had showed up in Violet's Collection of Extortion, the one whose life Violet may have torpedoed.

*   *   *

Orion and I went for a walk—we figured Miss Fitness would be in the gym for at least an hour—and then took a seat on the low retaining wall by the gym watching the bees swarm around the sage and lavender plants in the last rays of fall sunshine. She walked out at about the same time that the women who'd been going into the Zumba class Violet had attended walked out, but she didn't appear to be part of the group. They clustered near the front door and she headed down the street to a parking area out of the lot. I could see not wanting to park in the crowded lot if a fight over a parking space had already ended my marriage.

I followed her. If anything she was even more fit than she'd been in the photos. Whatever had happened, it hadn't made her want to stop working out "Excuse me?"

She stopped and turned. "Yes?" She asked.

"I'm Desiree Turner."

She stuck out her hand. "Rosalyn Compton."

"I wanted to talk to you about Violet Daugherty."

She retracted here hand, took the towel from her shoulder and dabbed at the sweat along her hairline. "Ding dong."

That made me take a step back. "Pardon me?"

"You know. Ding dong. The witch is dead. Like in the movie?" She turned to walk away.

I jogged up next to her, Orion at my heels. "So you're not exactly broken up about her death."

"No. Not exactly." She walked a bit faster.

"Rosalyn, did Violet blackmail you?" I asked. I pulled the photos out of my jacket pocket and held them up.

Rosalyn stopped walking. She turned back to me slowly. "Why do you want to know? She's dead. She has no hold over me anymore." Her eyes narrowed and she took a step toward me. "Unless you think you're going to take over where she left off."

I backed up, hands in front of me. "No. Absolutely not."

She shook her head. "Then drop it, Desiree. Let Violet's secrets be buried with her."

"But she did blackmail you?" I pressed.

Rosalyn blew out a breath. "She tried. She told me she had photos of me with Brice, the trainer here. I told her to go to hell. Two days later, my husband received photos of me with Brice and now I'm getting divorced."

"You hated her for that." It wasn't a question.

"Yeah. I did." She laughed, but it didn't sound like she thought it was funny.

"You wanted her dead." Again, not a question.

Rosalyn snorted. "Why? She'd already done her worst to me. It was over."

"Revenge?" I suggested. I'd had all kinds of fantasies about keying my boss's car or lighting bags of dog doo on his porch after he fired me. I hadn't done any of them, but I'd dreamed about them. Dreaming about them enough could make them seem kind of normal after a while. Would it be that big of a step to then actually acting on what seemed like a normal thought?

She laughed and held out her left hand. It had a ring with a teensy tiny diamond on it. "The best revenge is a life well-lived. Brice and I are getting married. He might not make as much money as my ex-husband did, but he makes up for that in a lot of other ways."

I was pretty sure I'd seen at least a couple of those other ways. I didn't want more details.

Rosalyn stopped at her car. She turned to me, a funny look on her face. "You know, in a lot of ways, Violet did me a favor. I was unhappy, but cheating on my husband wasn't the right way to deal with that. I needed to leave and start over. Because of Violet, that's what I did. I should have probably sent her flowers or something."

It felt like I was hearing an echo of Not Vodka Mom and Rachel. Even the mayor had seemed a little relieved to make a clean break with his mistakes and do better in the future. "I don't suppose you're diabetic?"

She looked confused. "What would that have to do with Violet?"

I shook my head. "Nothing," I said. "Never mind."

I walked back toward the gym and my car. The person at the gym with the clearest motive to want Violet dead didn't really want her dead and I felt like I'd hit yet another dead end.

* * *

It was getting dark. I didn't think I'd find out anymore by hanging out at the gym. As I was driving home, my cell phone rang. I glanced at the Caller ID. Jasmine. I hit the button to put the phone on speaker. "Okay. Talk now."

"So what have you found out?" she asked.

Orion barked at the sound of Jasmine's voice.

"Hello, good boy," she said in that funny baby talk voice that people use with animals.

He barked again.

"Hello," I said. "I'm right here."

"Right. So what did you find out?"

"That pretty much everyone in this town has a secret they don't want anyone to know about and that Violet Daugherty somehow knew about all of them." That seemed as succinct a way to put it as possible.

"Hmm. She must have been a very observant person."

"I'm an observant person. I wouldn't have known to follow any of those people around to get photographs of them doing stuff they shouldn't do." Of course, I also wouldn't blackmail any of them, despite them all seeming to think that was what I was setting out to do. I turned onto Robin Street and drove past the corn maze. There was something extra creepy about it in the twilight.

"There are different levels of observation. She clearly saw something—"

A loud cracking noise cut her off. Glass exploded into the car from the side window. I screamed and swerved.

"Desiree, Desiree. What happened?" Jasmine sounded frantic.

"My side window. It just exploded." I pulled over to the side of the road to try to catch my breath. My hands shook as I brushed glass off of Orion. My hand came away bloody. It took me a minute to realize that the blood was mine and not his. "Jasmine, I'm bleeding."

"A lot?"

The blood started to trickle down my arm. "Enough."

"Can you drive to the emergency room?"

I took off my jacket to wrap it around my arm. "I think so."

"I'll meet you there."

I screeched away from the curb. The hospital was on the other side of the freeway from most of Verbena. I raced over to Sparrow Street and then onto Nightingale. I came up over the rise of the overpass and saw the sign for the emergency room on the right.

Jasmine pulled in seconds after me. "Let's get you inside," she said, taking my unbloody arm.

"No," I said. "You have to stay out here. You have to stay with Orion. I can't leave him out here in a car full of glass."

"Fine," she said. "But I'm calling Nate. Someone needs to be inside with you."

I didn't want to admit how relieved that made me feel.

Verbena Memorial Hospital's Emergency Room was a surprisingly calm place. A little too calm. There was no one there. Seriously no one. I stood for a second, dripping blood from my arm to the tile floor before I noticed a bell to ring by a window. I did. A man in scrubs came into the little room behind the window, calling something to the people behind him. "What seems to be the problem?" he asked, biting back a yawn.

I held up my arm. That made him sit up.

"Nasty cut," he said in a tone that suggested he admired it. "We probably should take a look at that."

There were a surprising number of questions to be answered before that actually happened, though. By the time I was in one of the little curtained-off exam areas, Nurse Bob knew more about me than most of my friends. "Doctor will be in to see you soon," he said, drawing the curtain around me. It rattled on its metal clips.

Nate arrived before the doctor did, though. "Can I see?" he asked. I nodded and he unwrapped my jacket from my arm. "Not too bad," he said. "You'll need some stitches, though. Tell me what happened."

I shook my head. "I don't know. We were driving along by the corn maze. The window just exploded. Maybe a rock hit it or something?"

"It would have to be a big rock." Nate rubbed the back of his neck. "I'm going to go look, okay? Keys?"

"Jasmine has them."

"Great. I saw her outside. Back in a few, okay?"

"Okay," I said, but my voice sounded a bit shaky. He paused, came back around and kissed my forehead. "I'll be back fast. I promise."

This time I just nodded.

The doctor who came in was brisk and businesslike. She took a look at my arm, made me move it a few different ways, then called for a suture kit. "It's a slow night," she said. "We'll have you out of here in a few minutes."

Nate came back in and the two had a spirited conversation about possible infections while I pointedly looked the other way as she stitched. "All done," she said. "You're going to want to follow up with your regular doctor to get those stitches out in a few days. Keep it dry for forty-eight hours. If you have more pain or it gets swollen or there are red streaks, get yourself back over here right away. Okay?"

"Okay," I said. I stood up, feeling a little wobbly.

Nate put his jacket around my shoulders. "It's cold out," he said. "And yours is kind of a lost cause."

He was right. My fleece was a mess. "Can you give me a ride home? Is Jasmine still here?"

"She's waiting for us outside with Orion and of course I'll give you a ride home. There's something you need to see first, though."

"Can it wait? I'm so tired."

"No. It can't wait. You need to come now." His voice was tight.

I looked over at him. Nate didn't panic easily. He never had. He's awesome in crisis situations. Whatever it was, he really needed me to come look at it. Probably some huge shard of glass that had narrowly missed my face or something like that.

We went outside. The Element looked like a sickly color of gray under the street lamps. It reminded me of the one in the photo of my father. Could it have been weird lighting? Was the car in the photo really gray? Jasmine got out of her car with Orion as we walked up.

Jasmine opened the driver's side door and pointed to something on the dashboard. Or perhaps I should say in the dashboard. Something had made a round hole right in the radio. Whatever CD I had in there was toast. That was for sure. I hoped it wasn't my Dad's favorite Beatles' album.

"What is it?" I asked.

She brushed her hair back as it tangled in the wind. "I think it might be a bullet hole."

Chapter Thirteen

Luke Butler sat across from me at the table in the Lilac Room at Turner Family Funeral Home the next morning. He'd relented and let me go home the night before. He'd arrived so hot under the collar I thought he was going to arrest me to get me to go to the station to answer questions. I won't lie. I shed some tears. He agreed to wait until the next day. He also agreed to come to me since my car was currently being processed as a crime scene.

Luke rubbed his hand over his face. He looked tired and a bit older. Or maybe I was starting to see him for who he was now rather than the obnoxious high school boy who had been close to the bane of my existence. "So you were going around town confronting blackmail victims in order to ascertain which one might also be a murderer?" he asked.

It wasn't how I would have described it, but it wasn't factually incorrect so I said, "Pretty much."

He slammed his fist down on the table. "Damn it, Desiree!"

I jumped. Orion jumped and squeaked. The newspaper

on the table shuffled. Uncle Joey stuck his head in the door. "Is everything okay?"

Luke shut his eyes and took several deep breaths before answering. "No. Everything is not okay. Your niece is endangering herself unnecessarily."

Uncle Joey took a step inside the room. "We've tried to dissuade her. She's hurting business."

"Well, she damn near became one of your customers last night and I simply won't have it. I won't." I thought he was going to pound his fist again, but he seemed to think better of it. Luke was a big guy, but Uncle Joey was bigger.

This wasn't actually the response I'd been hoping for. I'd hoped that he would leap into investigative mode. Apparently, Luke didn't leap anywhere at anytime unless there was a beer involved. I shooed Uncle Joey away. He didn't need to hear all this. "I didn't know what else to do," I said.

He threw his hands up in the air. "Talk to the police? There's a crazy idea."

"I tried. You wouldn't listen," I reminded him.

Now it was his turn to look chastened. "So give me the names of the people you spoke to." He pulled out his notepad and pen like he was about to make a grocery list.

I was afraid that was where he was going to go. I shook my head. "Nope." I needed him to dig out the bullet and check ballistics and fingerprints and all that stuff the super smart people do on those TV shows with the labs and stuff. The people thing? Well, that was going to have to stay with me.

He looked up, surprised. "Why?"

"I'm protecting my sources." Violet had asserted power

over these people by threatening to expose them. They'd all made mistakes. They'd all done things they shouldn't have done. They'd all found ways to straighten out their lives and to make amends. That deserved to be protected, not threatened.

Luke shoved back in his chair. "So now you've got journalistic integrity?"

My face grew hot. I narrowed my eyes. "I've always had journalistic integrity. I didn't have discretion, but integrity I had up the wazoo." Discreet people didn't mock their boss on a hot mic. I knew that. It didn't make me a bad reporter, though.

He blew out a breath and tapped his foot for a few seconds. "I could take you before the court."

"Go ahead." I crossed my arms over my chest. "I still have Janet Provost on speed dial. You want to go up against her?" I held up my phone.

He shuddered and for good reason. Janet was a damn good lawyer and a formidable opponent. He'd gone up against her before and it hadn't worked out in his favor. Plus anytime you dealt with her, you'd probably gain five pounds because she also liked to bake. "Can I see what else is in the box? Maybe someone got wind of what you were doing and tried to head you off at the pass? If you haven't talked to them yet, you can't have made any promises to them."

I thought about it. Then I shook my head. I wasn't sure how many more of the things in the folder were illegal, how many people I'd be getting into trouble, how many people had turned their lives around because of Violet's threats. I wasn't sure how my father was involved in the whole mess. "Nope. Definitely not."

He stood and loomed over me. His fists that were clenched tight enough that the knuckles were turning white. "I can probably subpoena you."

I shrugged. "Go for it, big guy. Until then, though, it's time for you to leave."

If I'd thought the wrath of Luke Butler was the only thing I was going to have to face, I had a whole set of other thinks coming. He was barely out the door when Donna came in and sat down across from me, arms crossed over her chest. Uncle Joey followed her in. He sat on her side of the room. "You promised," she said.

I cringed. "I know."

"You pinky swore."

"I know."

"You double pinky swore."

"I know."

"Then you did whatever you wanted anyway." She threw her hands in the air. "What were you thinking?"

"I was thinking that if I could prove Violet had really been murdered then everyone would understand that they wouldn't be randomly accused of killing their loved ones when they brought them to Turner's." I crossed my arms over my chest and uncrossed them right away. It pulled at my stitches.

Uncle Joey tilted his head as if he was considering the validity of my statement. Donna did not look like she would ever consider the validity of anything I ever said again. She put her face in her hands. "Someone shot at you. With actual bullets."

"Bullet, singular. At least, as far as I know." I reached down to pat Orion.

She straightened up fast and glared at me. "Don't make jokes about this. It isn't funny. It's . . . it's . . ." She didn't get farther than that. She cried.

"I'm fine," I said, rushing over to her and kneeling by her chair. "Look. I'm totally fine. It's only a few stitches."

She slapped my shoulder. "But you might not have been fine. You might have been hurt. You might have been . . . dead." Then the sobbing began in earnest. "Stupid pregnancy hormones."

Then Orion was there, nosing into our embrace. He pressed his head against the two of us.

It took us a few minutes to get ourselves back together, but we managed it. I got a doggie treat for Orion and tissues for Donna.

Uncle Joey pointed at Orion. "Does he always do that when you cry?"

"I haven't actually cried that much in front of him, but you should have seen him with Annamarie Oh. He put his chin on her lap and let her cry on him as long as she needed to. She thought he was a therapy dog." I gave Orion another treat. I mean, he was doing an awfully good job.

Donna went a little still. "We don't have a therapy dog."

"I know. It's not like I told her he was one. She assumed he was one because of how he acted."

"I understand." She blew her nose again. "You're not getting rid of this dog, are you?"

It wasn't a question. I shook my head. "No. I don't think I can. I think my heart might break if I did."

"Then why don't you find out what you would have to do to make him into a real therapy dog. Then he could earn his keep around here." She reached down and scratched behind his ears. "Because then you would be a very good dog, a very good dog indeed."

Orion thumped his back leg.

Then Donna turned back to me. "You really have to drop this Violet Daugherty thing, though. It's too dangerous."

I was going to have to come clean and tell her everything so she'd understand why I couldn't do that. "There's something I haven't told you."

Donna rolled her eyes. "Color me not surprised."

I didn't think the situation called for that much sarcasm, but there were too many important issues here. "There was a picture of dad on that thumb drive of Violet's."

She grabbed a tissue and mopped at her eyes. "So?"

"It was a photo of dad in front of a house I didn't know with a car he didn't own talking to a little girl I didn't recognize."

"Show me," she demanded.

I went upstairs and got the laptop and thumb drive and came back down. I pulled up the photo and turned the laptop so both Donna and Uncle Joey could see.

Uncle Joey took a shuddery breath.

I reached over and put my hand on top of his. He covered my hand with his other one. It was like being sandwiched by giant paws.

Uncle Joey is a big man and with his size comes a certain

kind of gravitas. Not all big men have it, but a lot of the good ones do. They're aware of their presence and they use it to calm things, to make things more serene, to defuse situations and emotions. Because of that, sometimes their own emotions got overlooked, or at least Uncle Joey's did.

Except by Zenia. She apparently didn't overlook them at all.

I was pretty wrapped up in how much I missed my dad. I was aware of the ache that Donna felt when she thought of him. Sometimes I forgot how much Uncle Joey must miss him, too. My dad was more than his brother. He was his business partner and his friend. When Grandpa Turner—a blessed memory—died and left the business to the two of them, there'd been an immediate and easy divvying up of the tasks associated with running a funeral home. Uncle Joey was responsible for the behind the scenes work. Dad took over the front office stuff. I didn't remember ever seeing them argue about anything. Not that they didn't disagree. They totally did from time to time. They just didn't fight about it. They discussed.

When Mom died, Dad wanted to be the one to lay her out. Uncle Joey backed away and let him while staying close enough to steady his hand when it was needed. In the photos we had of Dad and Uncle Joey's childhoods, they were almost always in the same photo because they were so rarely apart. I asked Dad about it one time. "We get each other," he'd said. "I never had to explain anything to him and he never had to explain anything to me."

Uncle Joey had lost that person in his life—a person like Greg was to Donna knowing that she needed the salt before she knew it herself—and instead of losing it like I had, he'd done what he'd always done. He'd provided that big strong solid presence for Donna and me. He'd been our rock. I'd forgotten that sometimes rocks can break.

"No," Donna said. "No, no, no. We're not going down this rabbit hole again, Desiree. This photo could have been taken anytime, anywhere."

"Or it could have been taken a few months ago. I don't recognize that house or that child. I'm pretty sure that car is the same one I saw months ago out at Cold Clutch Canyon. Back when someone left that little hiking boot charm on my car." Dad's old car, I added in my head.

"You can't tell one gray Element from another. There's no way."

She was right about that. I also wasn't even one hundred percent certain it was even gray anymore. I told them about the storage space, too. "Don't you think it bears some looking into?"

"You're losing it, Desiree. You have to drop this stuff about Dad. It's making you nuts and it's going to destroy our business, his life's work." Donna pounded the table with her fist. Her face had gone red. "My life's work. Maybe you can decide to waltz out of here whenever you want, but I can't. If you destroy this place chasing a ghost, you destroy me, too."

"Don't you see? This must mean I'm getting somewhere. I'm getting close. Plus, whoever it is that took a shot at me thinks I know more than I do. If I'm right and it's the same person that killed Violet, they're willing to do whatever is necessary to keep their secrets. If I don't push through and find out who it really is, I'll never be safe. We'll never be safe. People will always think I make up crazy stories. It's the only way to stop the destruction of what we've built here." I paused before I brought my next point. "And even Tamara Utley doesn't think Dad's a ghost. She said she hasn't been able to contact him and she's tried."

Donna opened her blue eyes wide. "You're using Tamara Utley as evidence Dad isn't dead? If there were such a thing as ghosts, Dad's ghost wouldn't talk to Tamara. He really didn't like her."

I knew she was right, but I felt a little deflated nonetheless.

Uncle Joey asked, "What do you know so far?"

I gave them the rough outlines. The insulin. The blackmail—without details of who and why and how. The strange fact that Violet's attempts to extort people had actually helped them turn their lives around.

Uncle Joey stroked his beard. "So far everyone you've talked to really wouldn't have any reason to want to kill you, would they?"

I thought about it. "They wouldn't. Although, I'm not sure anyone was trying to kill me. I think maybe they were trying to scare me, to make me back off a bit."

Donna shook her head. "They clearly don't know you well."

I thought about that for a moment. "Well, that's one more hint as to who it might be, I guess. Someone who knows who I am, but doesn't know who I am."

"Don't play word games." Uncle Joey shook his head. "This is serious."

I held up my hands. I hadn't meant to play games. "Fine."

Donna's face went white and her hand fell to her stomach.

"What? Are you having cramps? A contraction? Do I need to call Greg?" I got halfway up out of my chair, but she motioned me to sit back down.

"No. Not a cramp or a contraction. Just a sharp kick in the ribs." She settled back onto the couch.

Donna threw her hands in the air. "Desiree, don't you see how all this highlights why you should be keeping your nose out of this?"

"Which means there's something there."

"Which means you should let someone else handle it. Someone like Luke. It's kind of his job, right?" Donna said.

"This was all sitting there for him to investigate. He didn't see it. Even after Nate and I pointed it out to him. He certainly doesn't seem interested in following up on anything I tell him."

"Don't you think you getting shot at would make him a believer?" Donna asked. "And one more thing. If Dad disappeared, has it occurred to you that he might not want to be found?"

Before I could answer, the doorbell rang. Uncle Joey went to answer it and came back with Rafe Valdez on his heels. He stopped in the doorway, hands on hips, "What the actual hell, Turner?" he said by way of greeting.

"And top of the morning to you, too, Mr. Valdez." I leaned back in my chair and put my feet up on the coffee table. Uncle Joey rolled up a newspaper and whacked my foot with it. I put my feet back down on the floor.

"Are you freaking kidding me? What are you on to that

someone is taking pot shots at you?" He sounded angry, which surprised me. I was onto something. My editor should be happy about that. People don't shoot at reporters when they're not pursuing something interesting.

"I'm not sure. I thought I the thing with the mayor was the big scoop, but apparently there's something even bigger." I sat up straighter, sure that he'd be on my side about digging deeper into whatever it was I was excavating.

"What's the scoop?" he asked.

What was it? What was in that box that had someone worried enough to shoot at me? "The only thing I know for certain is that this town is way more interesting than I remember it being when I was in high school."

"I don't care if it's bona fide *Peyton Place*. There is no story worth you getting hurt. None." He clamped his jaw shut so hard I could almost hear the click.

The front door opened and seconds later, Nate came in. "For once, I agree with Rafe. Are you okay?" he asked, giving me a hug.

"Fine, thanks. You?"

"No one is shooting at me. I'm completely fine. You on the other hand? You I'm not so sure about."

"Well, I'm fine." I tucked my injured arm beneath the other one.

Nate sank down into a chair and leaned his elbows on his knees. "This is because of Violet Daugherty, isn't it?"

"I can't prove that yet, but it seems to make sense."

He put his head in his hands. "This is my fault then. I put you put to this. I encouraged it. I egged you on."

"I didn't do anything I didn't want to do."

"You're responsible for all this?" Donna glared at Nate.

Nate nodded, looking miserable. "But she's going to stop now, right? We drop it now."

"Now? Now we know we're getting somewhere. We can't drop it." Now was the time to push forward. It was like the end of a race. You didn't slow down when you saw the finish line. You turned on the after burners and went for it.

He shook his head. "Desiree, someone shot at you."

"I was there. I saw the glass shatter. I'm pretty well aware of what happened." It wasn't like I didn't comprehend the issue. I had a near constant throbbing in my arm at the moment to remind me.

He lifted his head and stared at me. "Then you should understand why this needs to stop. It's too dangerous. We're dropping this."

Rafe moved to stand next to Nate. "I agree. This is over. Now."

I looked over the people standing ranged around me. Every one of them stared at me, jaws set, eyes hard, arms crossed. Suddenly, I felt very tired. I dropped my head. "Fine," I said. "It's over."

I pled exhaustion and took Orion back upstairs with me. I could hear them all still talking downstairs. I didn't care. I lay down on my bed, but despite feeling like exhaustion was making each one of my legs weigh about eighty pounds, I couldn't sleep. My mind still raced. I might as well get some work done. I grabbed my laptop and sat up, crisscross applesauce.

I had a long list of e-mails. Most of them were junk. I was about to look for the unsubscribe button on an e-mail from the *Fresno Post*, but something in the body of the e-mail caught my eye. I scrolled back up to start at the top.

Dear Ms. Turner,

I caught your article on the corruption scandal in Verbena. Excellent work. Great story and great voice in your write-up, too. We're actually looking to expand our staff here at the *Post*. We specifically need someone who can bring in stories that impact our readers and can't be found anywhere else. I'd love to talk to you about the opportunity if you're interested.

Sincerely,
Loreta Godfrey

I blinked a few times, then reread the e-mail. Then I read it again. A real reporting job. Away from Verbena.

I'd come back because my family needed me and because I had destroyed my career. Now I was destroying their careers and maybe the people of Fresno needed me. It wasn't like I was getting a whole lot of appreciation from the people of Verbena.

I hit reply.

Chapter Fourteen

The next day, Luke called and asked me to meet him at the station. "Can I borrow the Altima?" I found Uncle Joey in the kitchen and asked.

"Where are you going?" He narrowed his eyes to squints as he turned away from the counter where he was pouring coffee.

"To the police station. Luke asked me to come down."

He pulled the keys from his pocket and handed them to me. "Don't get shot at, okay? I'm going out tonight and I'd like to have a vehicle free of bullet holes."

"Out where? With whom?" I asked, suspecting I knew at least part of the answer.

He crossed his ankles. "Why do you need to know?"

"Know what?" Donna asked, coming in and sitting down at the round oak table.

"About Uncle Joey and Zenia," I said. "I think they have a date tonight."

He froze halfway to putting his coffee cup on the counter,

245

then turned to face me with great deliberation. "What do you know about Zenia and me?"

I looked over at Donna. She shrugged. "I came downstairs to see if anyone wanted a glass of water," I said. "You were . . . busy."

He sank down into one of the kitchen chairs. "So you know then."

I sat down across from him. "We do. What I don't know is why you felt you had to keep it a secret?"

"Was that what your little speech about love was about the other day?" he asked.

"Yes. I thought I made it pretty clear." To think I'd moved myself to tears and he'd had no idea what I was talking about.

"Not to me. You should just come out and say what you mean. It would be easier." He rubbed his face. "And as far as keeping it a secret goes, well, I think I might have been keeping it a secret from myself."

"What do you mean?" Donna asked.

"When Zenia sold her business I was so angry with her, I couldn't even talk to her. When she came back here as an inspector, I had to ask myself why. I mean, she was our competitor. I should have been glad she was closing shop. It took me a while to realize that I wasn't angry about her selling her business. I was sad that she wouldn't be around anymore." He smiled a little. "I guess she felt the same way."

"I'm happy for you," I said. "You deserve to have someone nice in your life. She is nice, right?"

"Very," he said with a grin.

"Why didn't you tell us about it?" I sat down at the kitchen table. Luke could wait.

Donna sat down next to me. "I'd like to understand that, too," she said.

He sighed and sat down, too. "One of the things your dad and I were always very clear about was our priorities. Family first. Business second. Everything else a distant third. That everything else included dating."

"But Dad must have dated Mom," Donna said.

"Of course." Uncle Joey nodded. "But our father was still around then. That made it different. Then he died. Then your mother . . ." His words trailed off. He cleared his throat and went on. "Well, after your mother died, our priority was you two."

A wash of guilt flooded over me. Why had I never seen what they were sacrificing before? "You could still find happiness for yourself, though. You deserve that. That and more."

He smiled. "Thank you, Desiree. I appreciate that. I do. I don't think your father and I ever thought about it that way when you were younger. But you're older now. You can understand these things. I thought maybe it was too late for me. Then suddenly Zenia was back here right in front of me and I thought I'd take that chance. I didn't know how to tell you about it, though."

"For the record, next time I'd rather not find out by walking in on you two making out, okay?" I said.

He grinned. "Got it."

I left with the car keys jingling in my pocket. I'd laughed

when Uncle Joey had said not to get shot at, but a few minutes later as I was about to turn out of the shelter of the plum and crape myrtle trees that lined our driveway and onto the open road, the thought of getting shot at again didn't seem so funny. In fact, it didn't seem so funny at all.

I leaned forward, trying to peer up and down the road as best as I could. Was there a place where someone with a gun could be hiding? Was there a vantage point from which someone could take a shot at me? Could someone be hiding in the corn maze, ready to open fire the second I was in range? Or behind the sign for the pumpkin patch?

I couldn't stay out of sight forever, though. Eventually, I was going to have to leave. Besides, whoever shot at me was trying to, at the very least, intimidate me. I would not let them win.

I would also not necessarily sit up all the way in the car though. I sunk as low as I could go in the driver's seat while still seeing over the steering wheel and braced for another window to explode as I inched forward.

Nothing happened.

Well, nearly nothing. Before I could even get onto the road, I saw Nate's Acura coming toward me. I reversed back into the driveway amazed at how much easier it was to get air into my lungs as I got closer to the house.

Nate pulled up so he was across from me and rolled down his window. I did the same. "What are you up to?" he asked.

"Luke called. He says I have to come down to the station for something." I made a face. "I'm hoping he's done with my car so I can pick it up."

"I was just dropping something off for your uncle. Hold

on a minute and I'll give you a ride. Then you won't have to worry about ending up with two cars downtown."

"Thanks," I said, feeling way more relieved than I wanted him to know. I parked the car behind the house and went inside to give the keys back to Uncle Joey.

"Thanks, Nate. I really appreciate it," Uncle Joey was saying.

"It's as much for my peace of mind as yours, Joe." Nate's back was to me as I came around the corner.

Uncle Joey made a funny noise and his eyes bulged. Nate turned. "Oh, hi, Desiree. Ready?"

We left and drove downtown. I pretended to tie my shoe as we passed the corn maze. I wasn't sure Nate bought it, but he let me save face. We parked about a half a block from the entrance to the police station. I got out on the passenger side and stopped. It would only be five steps to get to the side of the building and the linden trees planted every ten feet along the sidewalk. My heart pounded and my mouth went dry. I swallowed hard. Then I did it again. Nope. Still dry. If I crouched down and slithered my way over to the wall, I'd only be exposed for a few seconds. Before I could do it, however, Nate was at my side. "You coming?"

"You're going into the station?" I asked.

He shrugged. "I have some stuff to drop off to Luke about a case."

I looked at his empty hands, my eyebrows arched.

He pulled a thumb drive from his pants pocket and wiggled it. "Miracles of technology, Desiree."

"Well, okay then." We walked into the station with Nate between me and the street.

Luke was in the lobby when we came in. Nate handed him the thumb drive. Luke looked down at it confused.

"That information you wanted," Nate said with very slow and careful diction.

"Oh, yeah." Luke nodded. "Right. The information. Thanks. Got it."

"See you later then," Nate said and left.

I sighed. "You wanted to see me?"

He motioned for me to follow him back into the station. We ended up in one of the interview rooms.

"We're releasing your car to you." He handed me the keys to the Element. "The bullet was from a BB gun and given that it was fired from the corn maze, it might actually have been a prank." He shifted in his seat.

Sounded like a pretty dangerous prank to me. Shooting at someone wasn't much of a joke. "Why do you say that?"

"Like I said, the bullet was from a BB gun. It was a lucky shot that it even shattered the window. It wasn't going to kill you. It would have stung pretty good if it had hit you, but it didn't. And hitting you would have been an even luckier shot."

"Lucky for whom?" Certainly not for me. "So you're writing this off as a trick gone wrong?"

"I think it makes the most sense." He shrugged. "Kids like to go out in the maze at night. You remember what it was like."

I did. There were bets and dares and challenges. Who could get through the maze the fastest in the dark. Who could spend the whole night in the maze. Who was most likely to get caught making out in one of the maze's dead ends. "I don't remember any of us ever taking a gun."

"Really?" he asked. "You don't remember Winfred Hermann and Jack Mena have a target shooting contest?"

I bit my lip. I did remember that. It had been stupid. We were all lucky that no one had gotten hurt. "This wasn't target shooting, Luke. This was someone shooting at my window. Or if it wasn't meant for me in particular, the window of a car out on the road."

"Wrong place. Wrong time." He grinned. "Story of your life, right?"

I'd known he wouldn't investigate any farther than he had to. I took the keys to my car. "Thanks tons, Butler."

He shrugged. "That doesn't mean you should be running around poking your nose into anybody else's business, though. This might have been a prank. It might also have been a warning." He clenched his jaw for a second, then said, "There's been a complaint, by the way. Iris Fiore says that you're stalking her. She's accusing you of harassment."

I rolled my eyes. "Luke, that is ridiculous and you know it."

"We take claims of harassment very seriously in this town. If you'll remember, Jasmine came damn close to getting seriously hurt because of a stalker she didn't take seriously."

I did remember. It had been a terrifying moment. Someone with a knife coming at your best friend. I shuddered thinking about it. "But I'm not a stalker."

"Ms. Fiore claims that you're following her around town. That you've shown up at her gym, at her insurance agency, when she's meeting her realtor. She said you're even harassing her daughter. Taking photos of her at public gatherings."

"I had good reason to be at all those places. Reasons that had nothing to do with Iris Fiore. Why does she think I would be stalking her anyway?" I put my hands on my hips. "She's not really stalk-worthy."

"She says you're obsessed with her father's death, that you're still trying to prove that she murdered him."

"Okay. That's simply not true. I'll admit. I overheard her and Daisy talking and thought she said something kind of suspicious, but Nate said there was nothing fishy about her father's death and I believe him. I've already apologized to her."

"Great. Then leave her alone and this won't go any farther."

"I can't leave her anymore alone than I've left her." I threw my hands in the air. How was I supposed to stop harassing someone I wasn't harassing in the first place?

He just looked at me.

I held my hands up in front of myself. "Fine. I'll be sure to stay out of Iris Fiore's way."

My car was parked behind the station so I could go directly to it without going back on the street. No serpentining or slinking required. There was, however, some slumping as I scrunched down again in the driver's seat. The first stop was to get the window fixed. I took the car over to Baumann's Best Auto Shop. Angela Baumann came out of the back, wiping her hands on a rag that looked greasy enough to possibly be putting dirt back on her hands rather than removing it. She had on a gray coverall that had not been cut for the female form, but did have her name stitched over the pocket. Her blonde hair was swept into a side ponytail and she carried a clipboard.

"I wondered when you'd be bringing her in." She held out her hands for the keys.

I dropped the fob into her outstretched hand. "Oh yeah? How's that?"

She came out and walked around the car. "Heard you got shot at. Knew you'd need a repair done, right?"

"Right." We'd never taken our cars any place but Baumann's as far as I could remember. It was a decent assumption.

"Luke got any idea who did it?" She started making notes on whatever was on that clipboard.

"Luke thinks it was a prank and someone got a lucky shot in."

She looked up from her writing, one eye squinted shut. "Not so lucky for you."

"That's what I said!" I sighed. "He thinks whoever did it fired from the corn maze."

"He find anything in there that would help figure it out? I don't care if it was a prank or on purpose. Folks shouldn't be shooting off firearms inside the town." She ripped off the top page of the form she'd been filling out. My estimate was at the bottom.

Angela had a point. "He didn't say anything about checking it out." Had he? What would there be to be found?

Angela made a shooing gesture. "Then you better go look, right? Before whoever it is knows that Luke knows where they were or before the kids all trample it up. I got the Element. I'll call you when it's fixed up."

I was at the door, ready to walk back home, but then it was time to take that first step into the open. Panic rose inside me again, just as it had when I had to pull out onto the road from the shelter of home. I slid one foot out onto the sidewalk. My heart beat a little faster, though. My mouth went dry.

"You okay out there?" Angela called to me.

"Uh, yeah. Sure. Fine." I was anything but.

I stepped into the square and froze. It seemed bizarrely quiet. Like the birds had stopped chirping. The breeze had stopped rippling the leaves. Or maybe everything was drowned out by the buzzing of an incipient panic attack in my ears.

"Hey, Desiree!" Rafe jogged up to me from down the block.

"Hey, yourself," I said.

"Where are you headed?" he asked.

"Home."

"Want a ride?" He turned to walk back toward the newspaper office, realized I hadn't moved, then stopped and held out his hand. "Come on. I'll take you."

I stared suspiciously at his hand. "Why?"

He put both hands on his hips. "Because if someone had shot at me, I'd feel a little jumpy about walking around in the open by myself."

"Who says I'm jumpy?" A car drove by on the street and I darted into a doorway.

He looked down at his feet, but I could have sworn I saw a smile twitch at the corner of his mouth before he did. When he looked back up, however, his face was blank.

"No one says you're jumpy. I was saying that I might feel that way."

"Well, all right then." I fell into step next to him. He took the spot closer to the sidewalk, just like Nate had done earlier.

"Does Butler have any idea who did it?" Rafe asked.

"He thinks it was a prank."

Rafe looked over at me, his forehead wrinkled. "Seriously? Why?"

"It was a BB gun. A lucky shot." I bit my lip.

"Not so lucky for you," Rafe observed.

True that.

We got to his car. He opened the door and shifted so he was between me and the street as I got in "Thanks, Rafe," I said.

"No problem. Buckle up." He got into the driver's seat and off we went.

The panic started to set back in as we got closer to the corn maze. We had to drive past it. The only other route would be to get on the freeway, go two exits, and then wind around on the back route favored by the bicyclists who jammed the roads on weekends with their skinny-tired bikes and Lycra-covered butts. It would take an extra half an hour.

Plus, it would mean giving in. It would mean that if whoever had shot out my window had wanted to scare me off they would have won. They would have successfully cowed me into slinking off home and staying there. Well, screw that.

I pulled myself up straighter in the seat. We drove past. There was only one car there at the moment—van, actually—parked over by the makeshift office in one of those portable pods. I glanced up at the big sign for the maze that included the names of all the businesses who had donated money or services to help set it up. Turner Family Funeral Home was there. So was Cold Clutch Canyon Café and You're Covered Insurance. So was Canty Construction.

"Hey," I said. "Did you see that? Canty Construction helped sponsor the corn maze."

"So?" Rafe said.

"So maybe someone who works for them knows the corn maze really well from sponsoring it and knew where to hide to shoot at me. Maybe somebody's still angry about exposing their bribery scheme with the mayor."

He signaled and pulled into the Turner Family Funeral Home driveway. "Interesting."

"Interesting and worth following up on," I said. "Turn around. Let's go look."

"No," he said.

"What?"

"No. It's a pretty simple word. One syllable. Easy to read. Easy to say. I suspect it's one you haven't heard a lot though." He made a bit of a face.

"I've heard it plenty. Now is the not the time for it, though. Now is the time to say yes. Let's go take a look." I looked back over my shoulder at the maze.

"No."

"Fine." I got out of the car and slammed the door behind me. A fine mist of anger started to form in my brain. I liked it. I'd way rather be angry than scared. I jammed my hands into my coat pocket and walked out onto the road.

Rafe pulled up next to me in the car. He rolled down the passenger side window. "What are you doing?"

"I'm walking over the corn maze to see what I can find."

"The corn maze from where someone shot at you?" he asked.

"I don't see any other corn mazes here." I kept walking.

He inched his car along next to me. "Is there any way I can talk you into going home and letting the proper authorities investigate this?"

"Maybe if I thought they would." I marched on.

He stopped the car, reached over and opened the door. "Get in. I'll go with you."

We pulled into the lot. I got out. Rafe grabbed his phone and started furiously texting someone.

Taylor Nieves wheeled down the ramp of the portable and out into the driveway. He had a beard that was a tiny bit shaggy and a wool skull cap pulled down almost to his eyebrows. He hit the joystick on his wheelchair and rolled up to me. I heard Rafe get out of the car behind me. "Good morning, Desiree. Rafe. I'm surprised to see you out here. Sure you don't want to take cover?"

I did, but I didn't feel like broadcasting that information. "I take it you heard, too."

"News travels fast in Verbena." He scratched at his beard. "What can I do for you?"

I pointed at the sign. "What did Canty Construction donate to the maze?"

Taylor repositioned himself to look at the sign. "Oh, they were awesome. Came out with some nice machinery to help me really cut sharp corners into the maze. Titus came out himself to do it. Great guy." His brow furrowed. "Except for that whole corruption thing, of course."

I let that go for now. "So he'd know the maze pretty well?"

"Probably nearly as well as I do."

I threw a glance over at Rafe. "Any chance I could go into the maze?" I asked. "Luke is pretty sure the shots were fired from in there. He thinks it was probably kids horsing around. Someone got off a lucky shot and hit my window."

He snorted. "Not so lucky for you."

"I know." I was glad I wasn't the only one who thought that way. A consensus was definitely forming. "I'd like to take a look around. See if I can find anything that might point to who it was."

"You think Canty might be involved?" he asked, frowning.

"I wrote an article exposing their bribery of an elected official and then I got shot at from a place they know well. Seems worth looking into." I was happy my voice didn't shake when I talked about being shot at.

Taylor nodded and scratched at his beard. "That's crazy. I can see it, though. It makes sense to take a look. Want a map?"

"It wouldn't hurt."

He reached into one of the pockets of his wheelchair and pulled out a trifold brochure. "Let me know if you need anything else."

"I will." I turned the map so I was looking at it in the same direction as I was looking at the maze. I looked out at the road. Where exactly had I been when the window had shattered? I'd been talking to Jasmine, but she'd been on the speaker phone and my eyes had still been on the road. What was the last thing I'd seen before that popping noise and the window imploding? I shut my eyes, trying to visualize the whole thing. Jasmine's voice on the phone. Orion sitting in the passenger seat. The moon about a quarter full. The road in front of me.

It all came flooding back. I had just passed the three oak trees by the Thacker's driveway. I looked at where that was and back at the map, then put my finger on where someone must have been if they'd been shooting from inside the maze. "There," I said.

"You're sure?" Rafe asked.

I shrugged. "Reasonably."

We entered the maze.

Things are different inside a corn maze. Sound from the outside is muffled as if the world beyond has somehow faded. Whatever scents might have been in the air before you came in were masked by the scent of green growing things and fecund soil. The breeze might rustle the tall corn tassels, but it didn't make it down to where we walked. The air was close and warm. I slipped off my jacket and consulted the maze map again. It looked like we needed to take three rights and a left for the first part. I set off with Rafe next to me.

Once there, I looked again. If I'd done that correctly, now I needed to make another right and then two lefts. I kept my finger on the map to keep my place. We were nearly there. Two more turns.

We reached the spot I thought was the right one. I turned in a slow circle. There wasn't much there except dirt and some leaves that must have blown in. There were a few bits of trash. The label off a bottle of beer, a wrapper from a cough drop, a shred of worn fabric from a flannel shirt. I reached down to pick them up.

Rafe grabbed my wrist.

"What?" I asked.

"What if that's actually evidence? There could be fingerprints. DNA. Who knew what else? You'd destroy it by picking it up."

I straightened back up. "It's not like I walk around with gloves and evidence bags in my purse."

"Poop bags for picking up after Orion?" he suggested.

Bingo. Why hadn't I thought of that? I pulled a plastic bag out of my purse, turned it inside out, and picked up the items. Rafe took it from me. "I'll drop them off at the police station after I drop you off at home. Okay?"

"Will they do anything with it? Law enforcement has seemed pretty uninterested in people shooting up Verbena." Especially since law enforcement was Luke Butler and the person getting shot at was me. "What will Luke do with a few scraps of trash anyway?"

Rafe heaved a sigh. "Law enforcement will do what it needs to do. You might want to give Butler a chance. You might want to give all of us a chance. That's really all I ask," he said, then he turned and walked back to the parking lot.

*   *   *

Rafe dropped me around back and I trudged up the stairs. Orion greeted me at the kitchen door.

"He's been whining since you left without him," Donna said. She was cutting up an apple at the kitchen sink.

I bent down. "Sorry, boy. I'll try not to do that again."

I'd left my laptop on the kitchen table that morning. I opened it up and let my e-mail load. Right at the top was one from Loreta Godfrey suggesting a time for an interview. My calendar was pretty open these days. I e-mailed her back that next week sounded great. I should probably put together some clippings for her. I looked at my computer. The desktop was cluttered with memorial videos and layouts for funeral programs. It might help find what I was looking for if I cleared those off. "How long should I keep these?" I asked.

Donna looked over my shoulder and offered me a section of apple. "You can get rid of them as soon as you're done with the service. I back them all up every week."

"Great." I started sorting through the hordes of them I had stored as I crunched through the apple. It was good, but it would have been better with peanut butter on it. I had the icons set so each one showed the beginning image of the video. Somehow that was easier for me than searching for them by name. It was when I hit Frank Fiore's video that I froze. That face. His face. His face much younger than it had been when he was laid out in the Magnolia Room. I hadn't really looked at the video before. Donna put them together and I'd been busy running the service when it was playing. The opening image was the face of the man that had looked familiar in the photo on Violet's counter. I ran upstairs to get it to be sure. I dug it out of the box I'd put in the corner of my closet, and ran back downstairs with it. I opened Frank's video and froze it on that image. It was the same man. Why did Violet have a photo of Frank Fiore with her mother?

"What's gotten into you?" Donna asked.

I started to tell her and then remembered the way she'd held her stomach when she'd told me to drop all this. I remembered that I'd promised her that I would drop it. Twice. "Nothing. Just making sure I got it all right." I closed the laptop and carried it back upstairs.

My brain clicked along. There was a connection between Frank Fiore and Violet Daugherty. Or at least between Frank and Violet Daugherty's mother. Olive or Grace had made some remark about him being a flirt. I'd figured he had been kind of like my dad. No harm in it. Maybe he'd gone a little farther than my dad had. Maybe he wasn't just a flirt. Maybe he was a player.

Violet had found out she had relatives she didn't know about and shortly after she had moved here. Iris had said something about Rose doing a science project on genetics. Maybe Rose had used Helix Helper and had shown up as a possible relative. Maybe she was one of those possible relatives that had made their profile private and refused to answer Violet when she messaged them. So how would Violet have known to come here? Violet knew an awful lot of things that no one else seemed to know. Maybe she'd figured it out from something else she'd seen. She'd taken an awful big interest in her background recently. She'd become obsessed with her Italian heritage, putting up corny signs in Italian, investing in an expensive pasta maker, drinking Frangelico. Frank Fiore was of Italian descent. He was also diabetic and had relied on his daughter for everything. Iris could still have had insulin around and she'd know how to give it.

Could Violet have been a relative of Frank Fiore? Could she have been his daughter? Violet. I'd assumed she'd been named for the color. What if she was named after the flower? The way Iris and Daisy were named after flowers? What had Daisy said her father called them? His little flowers? Maybe he had more than two. Maybe he had a whole freaking bouquet. What would that mean, though? Why would that lead to her being murdered? Knowing Violet as I felt I had come to, she'd have found something she wanted from Iris. Not money, though. She'd never seemed to want anything that prosaic. Violet had wanted to belong, more than anything else. It was probably part of why she was so observant. She was always looking for ways she might fit in. Maybe she wanted family. Maybe she'd come here to try to connect with the family she'd discovered. How sad to figure out who and where your father was just to find him at death's door. Then, of course, Violet had died before Frank by a day or two.

But what if she hadn't died before him? What if he'd died and she was somehow entitled to part of his estate? Iris had had a pretty ready rant about what made someone a daughter. Had she already given that speech? To someone who wanted all the rights and privileges and assets that a daughter who had spent years caring for their father was getting? As his daughter, would Violet have stood to inherit some of Frank's dwindling fortune that Iris had been counting on to send her daughter to whatever school she wanted to attend?

I opened Violet's photo program. There were about a bazillion pictures of Orion. Orion sleeping. Orion running.

Orion standing looking noble. Orion sitting looking cute. Orion as a little tiny puppy with giant paws at the ends of his legs. Violet may have been a manipulative blackmailer, but she loved her dog.

There were hardly any pictures of Violet, herself, though. I supposed that made sense she was the person holding the camera all the time. Not everybody liked to take selfies and even if Violet had, I wasn't sure if they would have shown me what I wanted to see.

I called Nate. "I need to see those photos of Violet's hands again."

"No."

I was hearing that word an awful lot that morning. "Please, I think there's something in the photos that will help us figure it all out."

"We're not figuring anything out. We're dropping this."

"Please, Nate. I might have figured out how to make it all end. I'll be a whole lot safer if the person who shot at me is in jail. My family will be better off, too. Everyone will know I'm not some crazy weirdo randomly accusing people of murder."

"Tell me and I'll look and then I'll tell you."

"No." That was not going to fly. I was not going to get cut out of the last few steps of this.

He made a funny noise. "Fine. I'll come over."

"No." I didn't want Donna to see any of this.

"Fine. Meet me at Tappiano's in an hour."

Before I left, I went into the folder that had the photos Donna had used to make the slideshow for Frank Fiore's memorial service. I found a few that showed what I wanted and printed them out.

"Wanna go get a drink?" I asked Orion. He stood up, wagged his tail, and barked. I took it as a yes. I got his leash and a jacket for me, checked in with Donna, and left and got as far as the foot of the driveway when Jasmine pulled in.

"Where are you going?" she asked.

"Tappiano's to meet Nate."

"Get in." She clicked the unlock button. We got in and I sat up straight all the way past the corn maze. Screw fear.

We found Nate, sitting with a folder in front of him, looking uneasy. Orion walked up to him, cocked his head to one side, and did that thing where he rested his head on someone's lap. Nate's hand fell to Orion's ears giving them a thorough scratch and somehow his shoulders relaxed, lowering away from his ears. The dog was a natural. We were going to rock that puppy training. Nate was already more relaxed. Add another glass of wine to the mix and he'd be fine. He'd see that it was better this way. It was better, wasn't it?

"So you just want to see her hands and face?" he asked.

"I have no desire to see her kidneys or her liver or anything else like that," I confirmed.

"Ew," Jasmine said. "Who would?"

"You'd be surprised." Nate opened the folder and sorted through. He pulled out a couple of photos and set them down in front of me. I saw what I'd expected. I pulled the photos of Frank Fiore out and put them side by side with Violet's.

Nate looked at them. "I'm not sure I get it. I mean, there's a slight resemblance, but not enough to really be remarkable."

"Look at their chins." I put my finger on Frank's cleft and then on Violet's.

I watched as understanding dawned on Nate. It was written all over his face. "A cleft chin is passed down genetically."

Then I found the photo of Violet's left hand. It was a little trickier with Frank. Nobody had taken a photo just of his hands. I'd needed to find one that I could magnify so his hands could be seen better, but I had eventually found one. I placed those next to each other.

Nate nodded. "The crooked pinky."

"Daisy has the same crooked pinky and Iris has the cleft chin." I looked up at him.

Then I took the photo I'd found on the counter at Violet's house, the photo of Frank with another woman. I tapped the other woman. "I'm pretty sure that's Violet's mother."

"What would that mean?" Jasmine asked.

"I think Violet was Frank Fiore's daughter and she figured it all out after finding out she had relatives in Verbena from her Helix Helper account." Then she'd moved here and done something in her conniving way that had made someone kill her.

"Whoa, whoa, whoa. You're making my head spin here." He grabbed his head as if it really might go flying off.

"Imagine how much it would have made Violet's head spin! Or worse yet, imagine how it would have made Iris and Daisy's heads spin."

He shook his head. "To suddenly find out you had a half sister. Must have been mind-blowing."

"It may have blown more than that. It may have blown all of Iris's plans for the future. Everyone says they were running through Frank's money pretty quickly and Iris needs that money to send Rose to school." I paused.

I was fairly certain that Iris and Daisy had had no idea at all that they had another sister. Violet's sudden intrusion into their life must have been shocking. What would it feel like to suddenly find out your father had that big of a secret? I had a sick feeling that I might be about to find that out myself. There was that little girl in the photo. There was the way Dad was smiling at her. I sat back in my chair.

"What?" Nate asked.

I shook my head, not quite ready to say what I was thinking out loud. What if that was exactly the kind of secret that my father had? Iris and Daisy had had no idea. What if I didn't have any idea either? Everyone's argument against my father having faked his own death was that he would never leave his daughters. What if there were other daughters? What if the little girl in that photo was my half sister? What if he'd kept a relationship secret from us the same way Uncle Joey had tried to do? They were so much alike. Maybe those instincts would be the same. Donna and I had been in really good places when he disappeared. It had all gone to hell in a handbasket, but there wouldn't have been any way for him to know what was going to happen. Then maybe once it all hit the fan, he felt bad about leaving us and left us those notes and those little gifts.

Maybe there would be some little check marks in the possible relative columns on a Helix Helper report if I did one. Maybe there would be half sisters or brothers that Donna and I knew nothing about.

"So you think Iris or Daisy killed Violet so they wouldn't have to share Frank's estate?" Nate asked.

I snapped back to the present. "That's exactly what I think. Frank was diabetic, right?"

Nate nodded.

"Iris was the one taking care of him. She probably gave him his insulin all the time. She'd know how to do it. But wouldn't Violet notice?" I chewed my lip.

Nate shook his head. "The needle mark was in the middle of her back. Those needles are tiny and thin. She might barely notice if someone who's really experienced gave her the shot. I saw one of the nurses give one to a woman so quickly that the woman didn't even know she'd done it. If Violet did feel it, it would only be for a second or two. Like a little bee sting."

Bee stings. I sat up straight. "The gym! The lavender and sage bushes in front are covered with bees right now. What if Iris told Violet there was a bee on her? Or something like that? Then popped that syringe in there when she patted her on the back or gave her a hug."

Nate nodded slowly. "That was the last place Violet was before she crashed her car."

"What are the early signs of an insulin overdose again?" I asked.

He began counting them off on his fingers. "Shortness of breath, sweating—"

I cut him off right there. "Laverne said that Violet was

sweating way more than usual when she saw her getting into her car in the parking lot. More than she'd been sweating in class."

"So what are you going to do? See if anybody saw Iris with Violet in the parking lot?" he asked.

"I can definitely ask the Zumba instructor. I know she saw Violet around then." I chewed on my lip and then remember something I'd learned when I was figuring out who killed Alan Brewer. "We can also see if the gym has a security camera in their parking lot. You know what this means, though, right?" I couldn't help the smile that quirked at the corner of my lips.

"That Iris might have killed Violet. That's what we've been talking about, right?" Jasmine said.

"Yes, but what does that mean?" I prompted.

She shook her head. "I'm not sure I'm following."

I stood up. "It means I was right. There was something wrong about Iris. Nobody believed me. Everybody said I was making things up, but I was right."

"Oh, for Pete's sake, Desiree. Is that what's really important about all this? You being right?" Nate said.

I kicked at the ground with my toe. "It's not the number one most important thing, but it's up there in the top five. Especially since it almost cost my family their business."

"Go see if you can find that security footage. Then we'll know for sure," Nate said.

"I have a few other things to check out first," I said. I took a few steps away from the table and called Janet Provost, best lawyer and baker in town. "Can somebody see someone else's will?"

"Before that person dies? No."

"How about after?" I asked.

"After the death, they become public documents."

That was good. That could help solidify my thoughts. "So how would I go about seeing somebody's will?"

There was a hesitation on the other end. "Whose will do you want to see, Desiree?"

"Frank Fiore's."

"Frank's? Why?"

"Do I have to tell you?"

There was another pause. Janet owed me. I'd been the one to exonerate her client of murder charges, after all. Plus, she liked me. "Give me an hour."

My next stop was still not the gym, however. "I need to go over to the *Free Press*," I told Jasmine and Nate.

They exchanged a glance. "I'll walk with you," Jasmine said. "It's on the way to my office."

It wasn't really, but it wasn't like I didn't want the company. We said good-bye at the doorway to the *Verbena Free Press* office and I went inside. Vern was behind the counter. I pulled up the calendar on my phone. "Can I see the paper from October fourth?" I asked him.

"Sure." He hit a few buttons on his computer and then motioned for me to come around and look. I saw exactly what I expected to see. Front page news about Violet's death. Practically everyone in town got news alerts and read the *Free Press*. Iris and Daisy wouldn't have had to, though. I'd put a copy of the newspaper on the coffee table in the Lilac Room before they got there. It's what they were probably looking at when I'd gone to get Iris a glass of water. It was what had prompted Daisy to ask Iris what she had done.

"Can you search for an article on Rose Fiore winning the science fair?" I asked.

"Sure." It was a matter of seconds and he had that article up, too. As I thought, it was on genetics. She'd had her personal DNA run and had used that as the basis for her presentation. "Thanks, Vern," I said.

Rafe came in just as I was getting ready to leave. "Desiree, what are you up to?"

"Solving Violet Daugherty's murder," I said, unable to keep the grin off my face.

"Ooh. Can I tag along?" he asked, his grin matching my own.

"Even better than that. You can drive."

* * *

Verbena Fitness did have a security camera. I spotted it the second I got out of my car and started looking around in the parking lot. In fact, they had two. One on each end of the lot.

Ty was at the front desk again. "We put those in about a year ago. We had problems with cars being broken into while people were working out. Mainly those real early birds, you know? Especially in the winter when it's still dark."

"That's great," I said, clapping my hands.

He gave me a funny look.

"Not that cars were being broken into, but that you have the cameras. Could I see the film from October second?" I asked.

He gave me an even funnier look. "No."

I stepped back. That hadn't been the answer I'd expected. I thought we were friends now. "Why not?"

"Why should I?" He crossed his arms making his already big biceps bulge. I wondered if that was supposed to intimidate me.

"Because we're trying to figure out what happened to one of your members." Rafe pointed to the sign over the desk. "Safety is your number one concern."

Ty turned and looked at the sign as if he'd never seen it before. "I only have your word saying that's why you need it. We have to think of our members' privacy, too."

"I'm not going to violate anyone's privacy." Except maybe a very clever murderer's, but he didn't have to know that.

He shook his head. "If you want to see the footage from that day, you better come back with some kind of official paper. A court order or a search warrant or something."

I bit my lip. That could take days, especially with Luke blocking me at every turn. "How long do you keep the footage?"

"Two weeks."

It was already October fifteenth. Iris died on October second. I didn't have much time. Getting a court order or a search warrant could take days. The footage would be gone. I tried to think of some way to get this kid to do what I needed him to do.

"What happened to your arm?" he asked, leaning over the counter to look at my bandage.

Maybe I could impress him with the gravity of the situation. "Someone shot at me when I was in my car. I got hit with the flying glass." I edged closer.

The kid reared back. "Was Orion in the car with you?"

"He was. It's just luck that he didn't get hit, too," I said, trying to gauge his reaction.

"Who would do that? Who would put a cute dog like that at risk?"

Rafe said, "Someone very evil. Someone very bad. Someone who might be on the security footage from your parking lot on October second."

The kid looked at us for a long time. Then he grabbed a microphone on the desk and hit a couple of buttons. The intercom clicked on. "Lakeisha to the front desk. Lakeisha please." He clicked the microphone off then turned to me. "As soon as Lakeisha gets here, we'll go look at that footage. No dog shooters are working out at this club on my watch."

Apparently it was okay to shoot at me, but not my dog. I decided not to get huffy about it since I was getting what I wanted. A few minutes later we were all in the back office of the gym. I leaned over Ty as he brought up the security footage for October second on the computer. We watched as Violet arrived at the gym and went inside. Iris arrived a few minutes later, but she didn't go into the gym. She got out of her car and sat down with her purse by the lavender bushes. She stayed there for over an hour.

Then we watched as Violet came out of the gym and walked toward her car. Iris stood up and approached her.

The two women stood and talked. Then they hugged. Iris's arms went around Violet. Her hands were at Violet's back.

"There!" I said, pointing. "That has to be it. That has to be when she gave her the insulin."

The tape kept rolling. Iris walked away from Violet and got into her own car and drove away. Violet started to walk toward her car, too, but she stumbled as if her knees had suddenly gone weak. She pulled a water bottle from her gym bag and took a sip. Then Laverne Cason came out, spoke for a moment to Violet, and then she left as well. Violet made it to her car, got in, and pulled out of the parking lot, the car weaving a bit as she did.

"Is that the proof you need?" Ty asked.

"I'm not sure." In the video, you couldn't see any needle. All you saw was Iris hugging Violet, then walking away. I knew there was a syringe there. I was sure of it. I wasn't sure a jury would see it, though. I felt fairly certain I knew why it happened and how. Now I just had to prove it.

Think, Desiree. Think. What would prove it? Getting the syringe with Iris's fingerprints and Violet's DNA would be a clincher. What would have happened to that syringe? The one Iris used to inject the insulin into Violet? Iris would have had to have disposed of it someplace. I couldn't imagine her throwing it in any old trash can or into the storm sewer. The hospice nurse had described her as fastidious.

I gave Ty a hug. "Thanks, man. I really appreciate it."

"No problem," he said.

We walked out of the gym. "Where now?" Rafe asked.

"Janet Provost's house."

Twenty minutes later, we were tucked into the kitchen

nook of Janet Provost's house with a plate of cookies in front of us.

"Have one," she pushed the plate at us. "They're oatmeal chocolate chip. I figure the oatmeal makes them healthy."

I bit into one. I could taste the butter. It wouldn't matter how much oatmeal there was. These would never be healthy by anyone's definition. They were, however, delicious. I took another one from the platter and put it on the napkin in front of me. "Did you get the will?" I asked through the crumbs.

She nodded and pulled the papers out of a file. "Here. Do you know what you're looking for?"

"Not exactly, but I'm pretty sure I'll know it when I see it."

It didn't take me long to find it. Frank Fiore's will read to divide his estate equally between his daughters. It didn't list them by name. It just said daughters.

I tapped the phrase with my finger. "What would happen if a daughter showed up that no one knew about?" I asked.

"If she showed up before he died, she'd get one-third of the estate, but Desiree." Janet took a cookie, too. "Frank's estate was not that big. It's not like it was something to kill over. He'd chewed through a lot of it these last years while he was ill. Home health care costs a bundle even if most of it's being supplied by your daughter."

"I think that might be exactly the point." Frank's fortunes were dwindling. One half of something was way more than one third of it. Iris had sacrificed her best earning years to taking care of her father. Now she needed that money for Rose to go to a fancy college. "What would happen if the surprise daughter died before the father died?"

"Then the remaining two daughters would split the estate."

That had been precisely what I thought.

* * *

I was convinced we'd seen Iris administer the dose of insulin that would send Violet into a diabetic coma and into a state that would make it likely that she would have a seizure as she was driving. The problem was how to convince other people of it. Maybe if we could find the murder weapon, we would have enough evidence. "What would Iris have done with that syringe after she'd used it on Violet?" I asked Rafe.

He shrugged. "I'm not sure. Throw it in the trash?"

I shuddered. That sounded nasty. Plus, someone could notice it. It might lead people to start asking questions. I didn't think Iris liked people asking questions. Someone had started rumors about Turner Family Funeral Home and I was pretty certain that someone was Iris. Who else would have known about that conversation I'd had with her and have spread it around? No way was it Nate. Whether she'd done it to punish me for asking questions or to discredit me to keep people from listening to me was immaterial. Maybe it was both. Besides, what had the hospice nurse at Frank's funeral said about Iris? She'd talked about how careful and conscientious she was.

"I wonder how they got rid of the syringes they used on her father," I said. "Maybe she used the same method to get rid of the syringe she used on Violet."

"Makes sense. How are you going to prove that?" he asked.

I slumped back in my seat. "I'm not sure yet."

Rafe drove me to the back door of Turner Family Funeral Home "You'll let me know the next steps, right?" he asked.

"Of course," I said, getting out of the car.

He grabbed my arm. "I know you better than that. You'll let me know, right?"

I turned back around. "Yes. I will let you know. Your newspaper will be the one to get the big scoop."

He pressed his lips together. "That's not what I'm most concerned about."

I went inside and called hospice. "Hi. My name is Desiree Turner and I'm doing an article on health safety for the *Verbena Free Press*. I was hoping you could tell me a bit about how hospice handles disposal of things like syringes."

"Oh, we don't dispose of that. The patient's family takes care of that," the woman who answered said.

"How do they do it? What do people do with all those needles? Can they throw them out in the regular trash?" I asked.

"Of course not! Can you imagine the kind of blood-borne pathogens they could spread around the county?" The woman sounded horrified.

I couldn't, but she clearly could. "So what do they do?"

"Well, for hospice patients, the pharmacy provides them with a sharps container."

"What does that look like?" I scratched a note down.

"Just a plastic bin. It's usually red. It has a slot on the top where you put the sharps."

That was something. "So what do they do once the container's full? Can they throw that in the trash?"

"Nope. They have a couple of options. Sometimes doctors' offices will take them as a consolidation point. Some pharmacies, too. There are some mail back programs. Verbena Home Hazardous Waste has specific hours that people can drop off sharps containers."

I chewed my lip. "What do most people do?"

"The drop off. It's pretty easy."

"So what does Verbena Home Hazardous Waste do with them from there?" Maybe there'd be a chance of finding the syringe.

"They either go into an incinerator or an autoclave."

"How often do they do that?"

The woman hesitated. "Why don't you come right out and ask me what you want to know."

Okay, then. Straight-shooter it was. "Would it be possible to find somebody's sharps container and test the syringes in it for DNA?"

"Why would you want to do that?" she asked.

"I'd rather not say."

She sighed. "It would be like looking for a needle in a needlestack."

"But it could be done." Maybe that was all I needed. Maybe I just needed to create the possibility.

She was quiet for a moment as she thought. "It could be done. It'd be really time consuming, but the containers are generally marked with the patient's name when they're delivered. You'd need some kind of search warrant or court order. Then I have no idea how long it would take to test however many needles might be inside the container. It would be hard, but it could be done."

All that mattered for my purposes was that it could be done, that someone would believe that it could be done. "Where can I get a sharps container?"

"Any pharmacy would sell you one."

"Fantastic."

Chapter Fifteen

I called Luke. "We need to talk."

The sigh that blew down the line sounded like he was in a wind tunnel. "Why?"

"Because I know who caused Violet Daugherty's accident. I also know how and when and where and why." That early journalism training sticks with a person. I had my five W's.

"So tell me."

"I think we should talk in person. Can you come here?" The Element was still in the garage.

"Desiree, I'm working."

"I'm pretty sure arresting murderers is part of your job." I considered mentioning that investigating them was also part of his job and that seemed to be falling to me, but I was about to ask a favor of him.

For a second, it sounded like he was growling. Then he sighed again. "I'll send Carlotta to pick you up."

Fifteen minutes later, I was in Luke's office laying out my

plan for him. He leaned back and put his feet up on his desk. "You want me to do what?"

I looked at his feet on the desk. I knew that knocking them off wasn't the way to get what I wanted, but my fingers itched to do it anyway. I tucked my hands under my thighs. "I want you to ask Iris Fiore to come down to the station to sign a complaint against me."

"Do you want me to lock you up? Because if you wanted to get kinky with the handcuffs, I can think of a lot of better ways to do that." He waggled his eyebrows at me.

"I don't want to get kinky with the handcuffs. I want to catch a murderer."

That had him putting his feet on the floor and looking at me with a very serious expression on his face. "I thought you didn't think Iris killed her father. You said Nate put that all to rest."

"I don't think she killed her father. I think she killed Violet Daugherty."

The laugh that exploded from him died in the air. "Wait. You're serious."

"I am. Dead serious."

"Explain this all to me." He took out a pad of paper and a pen. At least he was taking me seriously enough to take notes.

"Violet Daugherty was Iris and Daisy's half sister. I don't know all the details and we might not ever know them, but I saw a picture of someone who looked an awful lot like a young Frank Fiore with Violet's mother and Violet has the same cleft chin and crooked pinky finger that Frank had. I'm pretty sure a DNA test will prove it. In fact, doing one of those home DNA tests was how Violet found out she had siblings. She saw enough of the profile Rose had on Helix Helpers to figure it out before Rose—or Iris—made the profile private."

"Why did Rose have a profile on Helix Helpers?"

"It was for her science fair project."

"Okay. Go on."

"Violet was a sneaky one. She wouldn't have come right out and announced who she was and why she'd moved to Verbena. She'd have waited and watched. She would have gathered intel. She'd have done something underhanded. She'd have found a way to make contact with Iris to get her to do what she wanted privately. They knew each other. That's why Orion didn't shake Iris's hand when he met her. He only shakes hands with people the first time he meets them." He really was the best dog ever.

"You're using that poor dog as evidence?" Luke shook his head.

"It's just one more thing that added up for me. I mean, let's not forget the cough drops that Daisy always has on hand and I found a wrapper in the corn maze. She must have dropped it when she shot at me."

"Wait. I thought Iris was the murderer. Why do you think Daisy shot at you?" Luke shook his head like a cartoon dog.

"Because Daisy isn't a murderer. You were right. She didn't want to kill me. She wanted to warn me off. She was trying to protect her sister. If Iris had been the one in the maze, I might not be here talking to you." A sudden chill crept up my spine.

"But you weren't even investigating them. Or, at least, you didn't know you were."

"Yeah, but they didn't know that. Every time Iris turned around, there I was. If she hadn't accused me of stalking her, I might not have realized how often I was running across her while I was looking at Violet's life."

"Okay. Now how did Iris murder Violet?"

"She injected Violet in the back with insulin as they left Verbena Fitness on October second. You can call there and talk to Ty. He's saving the tape for you."

"You can see it on the tape? The whole thing?"

I needed to be honest here. "No. You can see Iris hugging Violet and you can see that Violet isn't doing so well afterwards, but you can't see the syringe."

Luke opened a desk drawer and got out a bottle of ibuprofen and took two. "You know, before you moved back, I never needed to keep this stuff around."

"Whatever." I shrugged. "Iris needed Violet to die before Frank did and Frank was hovering at death's door."

"Why did she need that?"

"She needs Frank's money to send Rose to college. Even if Rose gets scholarships, she'll still have to come up with a fair amount of money for some of those places that Rose wants to go. Frank might have been well off when he got sick, but every week that went by, there was less money. By the time Frank died, there must have been a lot less left. Right now, she only has to split the money with Daisy. If she had to split it three ways because Violet suddenly showed up and got in on the inheritance, she'd have a whole lot less. Maybe it wouldn't be enough." I thought for a second or two. "Daisy was willing to shoot at me to protect her sister. Maybe she'd also be willing to let her have part of her inheritance."

He grabbed my hand before I could retract it. His palm was warm and his fingers were slightly rough. "This is all speculation. There's no proof here of any wrongdoing. Judges tend to want more than some citizen's wild speculations."

"That's why I want you to get Iris down here to the station. I want to shake her up a little."

"What do you think will happen then?"

"I think she might do something that will help us prove that she killed Violet Daugherty." I tried to pull my hand loose, but he held onto it. "You think you could take it from there?"

His jaw tightened. "Yes. I could."

This was going wrong. I was starting to piss him off. Somehow that was always how it was between Luke and me. We antagonized each other. Sometimes deliberately, I'll admit. But more often, just as a byproduct of whatever else we were trying to achieve.

I knew what I was trying to achieve here and to achieve it, I needed his help. I took a deep breath and stopped trying to snag my hand back from him. Instead I let my hand relax in his. "Luke, I truly believe that Iris had something to do with Violet's death. Violet wasn't a particularly nice person. She didn't have much empathy for other people's situations and could be pretty ruthless about going after what she wanted, blackmailing people to do everything from running her errands to covering for her at work. It wasn't enough, though. It was never enough. She wanted family. She wanted to belong. She found family and they didn't want her. That must have really stung. She might not have even wanted any of the money. She might have just wanted to have some sisters. We'll never know that, though. I don't think anybody will really miss her. Except maybe her dog a little. It still isn't right, though. Please help me find the truth."

He let go of my hand and rubbed at the crease on his forehead with his thumb. "How do you propose we do that?"

"First, I need you to swear out an official complaint against me for stalking Iris Fiore. Or, at least, I need you to tell her that you have."

* * *

A few hours later, I sat in an interview room at the police station with Luke.

He was shaking his head like he had been for the past twenty minutes. "This doesn't feel right, Desiree."

"Does letting someone get away with murder feel right?" I asked.

He dropped his head. "No. Of course not. Iris seems like a nice lady, though."

"A nice lady who killed someone." I pointed out.

"Fine. You've made your point."

Finally, his walkie-talkie beeped. "Iris Fiore here to see you, Butler."

"Coming right up," he said. Then he turned to me. "It's show time, Death Ray. You ready?"

I shook my head. He'd never let that old nickname go. "I

was born ready." I picked up the red sharps container I'd bought at the pharmacy and put it on the table.

A few minutes later, I heard Iris's voice as Luke walked her toward the interview room next to the one I was in. "I'm glad you're taking my complaint seriously," she said. "That woman is harassing me and at such a tough time. I mean, I just lost my father."

"I know. Desiree has never known when to leave things be," Luke said. If he was acting, he was doing a good job of it. He sounded a little too sincere.

Then they were abreast of the open door to my interview room. "Hi, Iris," I said.

She stopped and glared at me. "What is she doing here?"

Luke stopped and leaned on the door frame. "Funny thing. I brought her down here for you to swear out your complaint and she seemed to have some complaining to do about you."

Iris's hand went to her chest. "Me? What reason could she possibly have to complain about me?"

I rattled the sharps container. "Does this look familiar?"

She sighed. "It looks like one of the containers we used to dispose of the syringes we used while I was taking care of my father." She sounded nonchalant, but I detected a slight clenching of her jaw.

Luke nodded. "That's right."

"And?" she asked.

"This is the last one of these you turned into Verbena Hazardous Waste, according to their records." I rattled it again for emphasis.

She shrugged. "If you say so."

"Maybe we should all sit down." Luke led her into the interview room and pulled out a chair for her across from me. Then he sat down next to me. I could see on Iris's face that she knew the power balance had shifted. "If we take these syringes out and test each one of them what are we going to find?"

She leaned toward him, too. "That I used syringes to inject my father with the medications he needed to keep breathing as long as he did and to ease his pain when he was on his way out."

"Is that all you did?" I asked.

"I did not kill my father. I don't know how you got that crazy notion in your head or what you think you're going to find in there." She pointed at the sharps container.

"What if we're not looking for information about your dad?" I asked.

She crossed her arms over her chest. "Then who would you be looking for information about?"

"Violet Daugherty. Your half sister."

Iris's face went white. "My what?"

"You heard what I said. Your half sister. The one you had to get rid of before your father died so you wouldn't have to share your inheritance."

Iris sat statue still. Then very slowly, she said, "I want a lawyer."

Luke shrugged. "Then go get one. You're not under arrest. Yet."

She pushed her chair back. "You can't prove any of this."

"I think we can. You had to get rid of that syringe somewhere. If I were you, I'd have put it with all the syringes I'd used on my dad. Hiding in plain sight, right?" I said.

She snorted. "So? How are you going to tell if any of them were used on Violet?"

"It might take a lot of DNA testing, but I'm betting one of them will have Violet's DNA on it." Luke smiled at her.

Her face went from white to purple in two seconds. "DNA. DNA. DNA. Everything is all about the DNA. Let me tell you something, mister! DNA doesn't make you a daughter. Getting up at two in the morning when he's in pain makes you a daughter. Slitting his shirts up the back so he doesn't get bedsores makes you a daughter. Clipping his toenails, managing his medications, wiping his chin when he drools. Those things make you a daughter. A piece of paper from some fly-by-night DNA testing center? That's bull."

"So you did know," Luke said.

"So what if I did? She had a lot of nerve showing up on our doorstep when Dad was so ill, saying she didn't want money. She just wanted to know her family. Like hell she did. I could see it in her greedy little eyes. She was going to take what little was left and Rose would be stuck here like I'm stuck here. I wasn't going to let that happen."

Luke stood up. "Iris Fiore, you are under arrest for the murder of Violet Daugherty."

* * *

We were back at Tappiano's. Jasmine, Carlotta, Nate, Rafe, Orion, and me. Nate and Rafe fist-bumped as they sat down. Which was weird. Usually there was a lot of tension between those two. Now they looked like BFFs.

Luke walked out of the bar, beer in hand, and sat down next to me. "Celebrating?"

"What would we be celebrating?" I asked, batting my eyes. I wanted him to say it.

He ducked his head. "You were right."

"Again," I pointed out. "I was right again."

"And you're being as gracious about it as ever." He raised his beer bottle to me in a toast.

I didn't want to be gracious. I wanted some help. "I was right about Alan Brewer. I was right about Violet Daugherty. Do you think, just maybe, I might be right about my dad?"

The whole group went silent. Luke groaned. "Not this again. Please, Desiree. Drop it. Let yourself heal."

It's what I'd thought he would say. I was disappointed, but not surprised.

"Besides, I don't think we can keep up protecting you if you piss somebody else off enough to make them shoot at you," Nate said.

"Keep up what?" I asked.

Rafe rolled his eyes. "You are not good at that this secret thing, my friend."

"What secret?" I asked.

None of them said anything. In fact, none of them would meet my eye or look at each other. Then it all started to piece together. After I was shot at, I was never alone outside. One of them had always been with me. "You guys were working together?"

"What were we supposed to do?" Jasmine demanded. "Let you run around town getting shot at by someone by yourself?"

"You tag teamed me?" I was still processing the information.

"We have lives, you know," Luke said. "Work of our own to do. It seemed easiest to kind of pass you around."

I shook my head. I couldn't decide how to feel. No. No. I knew exactly how to feel. Grateful. Grateful to my friends. Grateful to my family. Grateful to my town.

"Thank you," I said.

"You're welcome, Desiree," Luke said.

I kicked him under the table. There was no point in acting too gracious.

"What are you going to do with the rest of Violet's blackmail material?" Jasmine asked.

I stretched and yawned. "I think I'll burn most of it. If the pattern holds, most of those people will have turned their lives around because of Violet."

"Funny how someone can do so much good while trying to do so much evil." She shook her head.

Later, Orion and I walked home by ourselves. It was nice to be without a bodyguard. The house was quiet when we got there. I could hear the television in the family room and figured Donna and Greg were in there. I peeked in. Donna and Greg were cuddled up on one end of the couch. Uncle Joey and Zenia were cuddled on the other. It looked cozy, but I wasn't quite ready for cozy at the moment. I tiptoed past to my room. I opened my laptop and pulled up the e-mail from Loreta Godfrey at the *Frenso Post*. I hit reply again.

Dear Ms. Godfrey,

I'm afraid I'm going to have to cancel our appointment next week. Thank you so much for considering me for the open position at the *Post*. For the moment, however, I'm planning on staying in Verbena.

Sincerely,
Desiree Turner

*　*　*

It was a week later when I drove past the house where Violet had taken my father's photo. Things had been busy. Business had picked back up at Turner. Solving Violet's murder made everyone realize that I wouldn't be accusing people of crimes willy-nilly.

I can only imagine how Violet would have figured out what she did about my dad. Certainly, his face had been plastered all over missing flyers and papers all over northern California. Maybe she'd seen one of those and then seen him in this new town where he was living.

It was early. The sun was coming up. The light was still amber and golden, the shadows long. My dad's favorite time of day. He loved the dawn.

The house was cute. Nothing special. Just a typical little ranch-style house, barely distinguishable from all the other ranch-style houses in the neighborhood. Not nearly as interesting as Violet Daugherty's Eichler. I parked down the street. I could see if someone came or left, but wouldn't be noticeable to them. At least, not at first.

There were two cars in the driveway: a gray Element and a minivan. I didn't know if it was the same gray Element that I'd seen months ago parked near where my dad and I used to hike or not. It hadn't occurred to me to mark down its license plate until after I'd found something on my car that could have been from my father. By then it was gone. It had a roof rack that definitely could be used to carry a surfboard.

As I watched, the garage door rose. Whoever came out was on the other side of the Element and I couldn't see him clearly, especially since he had a surfboard balanced on his head. He flipped it up onto the roof rack. It was when he came around that I could see his face clearly.

I got out of the car with Orion. We walked down the street. The man's head turned at the noise of our car door closing. A range of emotions flitted by on his face. Surprise. Consternation. Acceptance. "Desiree," he said.

"Hi, Dad," I said back.

"I can explain," he said.

I thought about it for a second. "I'm listening. Everybody deserves a second chance."

* * *

The Verbena Free Press
October 17
By Desiree Turner

City Council Refuses to Accept Mayor's Resignation

Jocelyn Headley of the Verbena City Council refused to accept Mayor Wilburn's resignation saying "everybody makes mistakes." Wilburn had confessed to accepting bribes in exchange for construction contracts over the past several years and had voluntarily tendered his resignation.

"Mayor Wilburn showed great strength of character in coming forward on his own to confess. The kind of person who admits their mistakes and takes action to correct those errors is exactly the kind of person we need running our city," said Headley.

Acknowledgments

It has been a great privilege to meet the people of Verbena, California and to be part of their adventures. I know that might sound weird since Verbena is the product of my imagination (plus eighteen years of living in northern California), but it really feels like that some days. These funny, quirky, good-hearted people seemed to pop up in my brain unbidden. When that happens, there's really nothing for an author to do but write it down.

That said, however, I don't know if I'd have opened the doors for the characters in this book, their town, or their adventures without the vision of Matt Martz and the gentle direction of Jenny Chen. Thanks to both of you for your kindness and advice.

I wouldn't have had much idea of what went on in a funeral home without the very generous Mark Alexander who took time out of his busy day to take me through his establishment and to explain to me what he does and how he does it. Beyond that, however, his quiet dignity and clear compassion impressed on me the qualities it takes to be a funeral director. I went in looking for information. I came out with that plus a whole lot of respect.

Acknowledgments

Very special thanks to my sister Marian who devised the murder method in this book. Any details that are wrong are due to my faulty understanding, not to her knowledge. As always, though, I'm left with the very strong feeling that I need to stay on her good side. Love you, sissy! You can borrow any of my clothes that you want.

I am not actually a dog person. I know that sounds terrible, but it's true. Or it was true until Teddy Rendahl and Jolie Law brought Orion into my life. Apparently having a grand-dog changes everything. I couldn't resist putting him into the book. Thank you for sharing him with me.

I am surrounded on a daily basis by an incredibly supportive family and a group of friends who feel like family. Diane Ullman, Alex Rendahl, Carol Kirshnit, Kris Calvin, Catriona McPherson, Beth McMullen, Ellen Shields, Deb Van Der List, Spring Warren, Tilly Rodrigues. You all buoy me up.

Finally, thank you to Andy Wallace. He bears the brunt of those dark nights of the soul when I fear I've taken on a task I can't rise to and remains patient and supportive through it all.